Witness Protection 5
Outside the Wire

Holly Copella

To Attila Hajnal

ACKNOWLEDGMENTS

Copella Books: First Paperback Edition 2017
Printed by CreateSpace, An Amazon.com Company
Cover Artist: Daniela Owergoor
Dani-owergoor.deviantart.com
Model by Grafvision
Model by Pindyurin Vasily

PUBLISHER'S NOTE

Chapter One

The small village outside Rio de Janeiro, Brazil was one of the less traveled tourist spots. Charming shops lined the streets with vibrantly colored flowers, clothing, and foods from different cultures. Friendly locals exchanged pleasantries with a few dozen tourists passing through. Ross Madrid, a handsome, distinguished gentleman in his early fifties with a full head of moderately graying hair, placed a white fedora hat on his head, tilting the brim for a menacing look. He glanced across the hat table to a dark-haired beauty nearly half his age. Leeann Whitley dressed the part of a world traveler, but she had more of a country girl appeal. Lee's gaze fell upon Ross with the making of a schoolgirl in love. She eyed him across the table, grinned her approval of the hat, then flashed a thong bikini bottom and suggestively raised her brows.

Ross groaned softly then turned to the shopkeeper. They haggled in Portuguese over the price of the hat. One might assume Ross just enjoyed arguing with people in different languages. Lee seemed to enjoy it as well. Ross indicated Lee while handing the man some local currency. The man eyed the beautiful woman then grinned at Ross. He said something that sparked a fire in Ross. Another round of arguing ensued. In the end, both men laughed. Ross motioned to his girlfriend.

"It's yours," he announced.

She approached him with her new purchase and stuffed it into her bag. "What was all the arguing about?" she asked.

"He offered to let you have it for free if you modeled it for him," Ross remarked casually. "I politely told him I'd gouge his eyes out with a spoon."

"Hmm, that's pleasant," she cooed while affectionately clinging to his arm.

"Yes," he replied. "Although I did change the body part and the method in which I'd remove it for your comfort."

Lee groaned softly and rolled her eyes. "You're terrible."

"Here I thought I was initiating foreplay," he announced with a teasing grin.

She playfully smacked his arm then hugged it. "It's like I'm seeing another side of you," Lee informed him. "Maybe a small peek into that former Navy SEAL life."

Ross suddenly laughed and patted her hand on his arm. "Oh, my darling, if no one's suffered a throat punch; you're seeing nothing from my SEAL past."

They casually walked through the market attempting to decide what to have for dinner. Ross glanced at several items on stands they passed while Lee talked endlessly about their romantic beachfront accommodations. Ross no longer seemed to be paying attention to her as his muscles tensed against her hand. Lee eyed him with a curious look.

"Ross? Are you listening to me?"

"No," he replied gently and lowered the brim of his hat. "Would you allow me one small moment of paranoia?"

Her expression dropped as she stared at him.

"Don't look at me and keep smiling," he ordered softly through slightly gritted teeth that almost formed a smile.

Lee looked at the stands and the food that suddenly didn't seem appealing. "What's wrong?" she asked while attempting to keep up a jovial appearance.

"We're being followed," he remarked. "If we keep heading straight for three blocks, there will be taxis. I want you to keep walking and get in the first taxi you see. I'll meet you back at the hotel."

"What are you going to do?" she nervously asked, no longer able to maintain her false smile.

"I'm just going to talk to the men following us," he replied simply.

"I'm not leaving you, Ross."

"We're not debating this," he growled softly. "Three blocks. First taxi you see. You don't look back, and you don't stop no matter what."

"Ross--"

"I'm serious, Lee."

Lee slowly released his arm and looked along the aisle in front of them. She nervously touched his arm. "Ross--?"

Two men approached them from the opposite direction, cutting off Lee's path to the taxis. Neither man bothered hiding that they were staring directly at them. They must have known they had Ross trapped.

"Change of plan," Ross gently announced while stopping her in the middle of the mildly busy market area. "To your right. Through that door. Don't stop. Just run." There was a strange pause. "Now!"

Lee turned to her right and ran for the door between the outdoor shops. Ross bolted after her. As the men pursued him, he toppled a stand in their path, stalling them. He ran into the building after Lee. The men scrambled over the scattered market items and ran after them while removing their automatic weapons. The two men ran through the kitchen and looked around. Any cooks in the kitchen were already gone. The two men walked cautiously with their weapons aimed.

The first man suddenly fell to the floor. Ross slid out from under the counter and jumped on top of him. He grabbed him around the neck and flipped their position. The second man fired at Ross, riddling his own man with a spray of bullets. As he shot his own man, Ross remained behind his human shield, raised the man's weapon, and returned fire. The man took several shots and flew to the floor. Ross jumped to his feet with the assault rifle in his hand and ran after Lee. As he ran through the kitchen, the men who had been following him now entered and pursued him. Ross fired at the men and dove into the doorway as they fired back.

"Lee," he cried out while facing the kitchen then glanced back to check her position.

Lee was already on her knees with a heavily armed man standing behind her. He held a gun to her head. She stared at Ross with fear in her eyes. A second man appeared behind the man holding Lee hostage and fired at Ross. Ross dove to the floor, avoiding the barrage of bullets. He rolled into a sitting position and fired back. The man removed the gun from Lee's head and shot at him as well. Ross fired upon both men, tearing into them with multiple shots each. Before they had a chance to go down, their rifles fired through the opening in the doorway. Ross's expression dropped as he looked back and saw the propane tanks just on the other side of the door. He leaped for Lee and took her to the floor. There was a familiar pop followed by a hiss.

Ross looked into Lee's frightened eyes. "I'm sorry," he whispered.

Outside the building, there was a tremendous explosion that rocked the entire marketplace. Vendors and tourists screamed and ran from the area without looking back. The old, fragile looking building collapsed in a cloud of dust and debris that quickly swept through the market.

✝

On the outskirts of Denver, Colorado, in the early morning hour, Holden returned his cell phone to his inner jacket pocket and received a look from another neatly dressed man leaning against the nearby building. Holden Falcone was a ruggedly handsome man in his mid-thirties. He wasn't built excessively muscular, but he had broad shoulders and a toned chest. His neatly trimmed, nearly black hair gave him a professional appearance. Holden eyed the cable and internet van parked alongside the curb a few feet away then seemed to realize the man by the building was still staring at him. He groaned and looked at the man.

"I know what you're thinking, Parker," Holden remarked. "You don't need to say it."

"I'm not saying anything," Parker announced while grinning. "None of my business that your super-hot, spy wife is conquering the world while you're on the streets of Denver chasing after the dregs of society."

"First off," Holden announced, "she's not a spy." He then frowned. "And she's not conquering the world; she's passing love notes on the playground to Beck's girlfriend. This is one time she absolutely doesn't need my protection."

"Let's see," Parker announced while grinning. "She can kick the entire department's collective ass without breaking a sweat." He held back his laugh. "I think it's safe to say the only protection she needs from you is the kind that keeps your swimmers away from her fertile feminine parts."

"That's so romantic, Parker," Holden announced while raising his brows. "Honestly, you should write greeting cards." He then indicated the van. "Can we get this show on the road?"

"Yeah, anything you say," Parker replied with a chuckle.

They approached the van, looked around, and then climbed inside. Holden and Parker entered the back of the van where six men in FBI SWAT gear sat and waited.

"So how reliable is this tip?" Holden asked the lead man in combat gear.

"Well, his phone number is registered to an apartment across the street, and we're pretty sure he's a guy," the man replied. "Other than that, he's your typical anonymous caller."

"Cute," Holden muttered. "Everyone's a comedian today."

"There was a lot of activity coming and going throughout the night," the man in charge continued. "Our eyes in the building across from the warehouse reported two known arms dealers went into the building early this morning, and they're still there."

"If it's good enough for the judge," Holden announced, "that's good enough for me."

Holden and Parker slipped into their official vests and helped themselves to automatic rifles.

"We're looking at no more than six heavily armed men," the man continued. "Apart from our arms dealers, the identities of the others are unknown."

"We'll ID them after we arrest them," Holden announced with a sigh. "Let's knock on the front door. Tell the second team to move in through the rear."

All eight filed swiftly from the van and headed for the warehouse across the street. The first two men carried a battering ram. The man in charge gave the signal, and they plowed the door inward with one strike. The eight men filed into the warehouse. Two-man teams hurried through the corridor checking vacant areas within the office before heading into the abandoned warehouse. They entered the large holding area and met with their two men, who had entered from the back. Dozens of crates filled the warehouse, which was supposed to be empty.

"Boys, I think we've hit the jackpot," Holden announced. "Two-man teams. Proceed with caution."

They swept through the warehouse, carefully passing stacks of crates while keeping an eye out for the six perpetrators. Several men dressed in black suddenly dropped on cables from the ceiling while firing at the FBI SWAT team. Despite their protective vests, two men went down from headshots. Holden fired back at the men dropping to the floor behind crates surrounding them.

"It's a trap," Holden announced through his ear transmitter. "Fall back!"

Although there were only six men, they came at the ten-man SWAT team from behind, trapping them in the center of the warehouse. They exchanged automatic weapon fire in a catastrophic shootout. Holden fired back while watching his men drop one-by-one. Two shots struck him dead center in the chest, dropping him despite his bulletproof vest. Another shot found his leg. Holden pulled himself along the floor and behind a crate. He sat against the crate and fired back, but most of his team was already down. Parker stood from behind the safety of his crate and unloaded several rounds into a man nearly on top of Holden from behind. Holden took another shot to his vest and one to his shoulder beyond the vest. The force of the shot threw him against the crate, where he struck his head.

The room was spinning as shots were echoing from every corner of the building. Holden attempted to raise his weapon but could do little more than watch Parker take several shots to his body and ultimately one to his head. Holden saw the masked man across the warehouse standing near his fallen friend. He raised his weapon at Holden and squeezed the trigger. A shot rang out.

Chapter Two

Jackie Falcone, an attractive woman in her mid-twenties with her long, dark hair worn in a ponytail, struggled to control the disabled helicopter. The sputtering, smoking helicopter hovered over the cliff on Giovanni's island just off the coast of Columbia. Two men, one in the front and one in the back, fought for control of a gun. Jackie's partner and friend, Zack Kinsley, was shorter than average but had a surprisingly athletic build, which would easily go unnoticed beneath his black combat fatigues. He was easily brushed aside as harmless, which was far from the truth. His brown hair was kept short and neat, although moderately spiky on top, lending a look that was somewhere between intimidating and cuddly. She caught a glimpse of blood soaking through Zack's shirt low and off to the side. She thought he'd taken the earlier shots to his chest while they were on the beach, but she must have been mistaken. He'd been shot once beneath his special bulletproof vest jacket.

Judging by the blood running down his hand, he also took a shot to his upper arm as well, leaving him with less strength than usual. As they struggled for the gun in his assailant's hand, both men punched each other, attempting to win the struggle. Jackie tried to ignore the gun close to her face and circled the area just before the cliff, hovering over it. She needed to set the helicopter down. Zack's attacker pulled him into the front with him. Zack nearly struck Jackie with his booted feet as he landed on top of her passenger.

Jackie again struggled with the controls, his actions causing her to spin the helicopter slightly, bouncing it off the ground. The fuel light continued to flash, and the alarm wailed its dire warning. The gun fired, striking the control panel. Sparks flew and sizzled as the helicopter controls jerked in Jackie's hands. She no longer had control. She fought to keep the craft from leaving the safety of the clearing before the cliff. She saw flashes of the ocean below as the craft spun in a circle. It bucked and jerked in her hands while the two men continued to punch each other while wrestling in the seat alongside her. One or both men kicked her several times while struggling. The helicopter continued to pull against her while spinning nearly out of control. The best she could do was keep it from pulling down to the right. Jackie attempted to set it down, but it pulled sharply, insisting on going down on an angle. The rotors nearly hit the ground. The moment she kept it straight, it again spun in circles.

"I can't land," she cried out. "I can't hold on much longer. I'm losing control of her!"

"Bail!" Zack shouted now pinned between his assailant and the door. He punched the man several times, but he refused to release the gun.

"No," Jackie yelled back above the loud roaring of the smoldering engine. "If I let go, she's going to go down to the right. *Your* right! You'll be killed!"

Zack eyed Jackie from his position beneath his attacker as they struggled for control of the gun. His eyes briefly met hers. "I think that's inevitable now," he informed her.

Jackie saw the grenade in his free hand, causing her to gasp. He punched the man twice in the face with the grenade while keeping the gun from pointing at his face.

"I'm sorry, Jackie," he announced then kicked her with both feet in the shoulder.

Jackie flew against the helicopter door, her hands slipping from the controls. Zack kicked her again, throwing her through the door. Jackie fell several feet to the ground, landed harshly, and rolled several feet. She saw the helicopter rotors striking the ground near the cliff. The rotors tore from the craft and flew across the clearing, slicing trees. Jackie screamed and shielded herself. When she lowered her arms, she watched the helicopter hit the edge of the cliff. Several gunshots fired within the helicopter as blood spattered against the inner windshield. Jackie cried out and scrambled to her hands and knees. The helicopter tumbled over the cliff. Jackie made it to her feet and ran for the cliff while clinging to her aching leg. She stopped at the edge of the cliff just in time to see the helicopter hit the water below. A second later, it exploded.

"No," she cried out and ran from the cliff on the long journey to the beach below.

✝

The remains of the helicopter floated in the surf. Some debris had already found its way to shore on the abandoned beach a good distance from Giovanni's island resort. Jackie arrived on the beach several minutes later and saw a man's moderately burnt hand sticking out of water not far from shore. Jackie ran into the surf and clutched the hand, pulling it from the water. She stared at the severed, burnt hand and immediately released it while screaming. She looked around at the smoldering debris and objects floating in the surf. Jackie grabbed a shirt floating in the water that she immediately recognized as Zack's. She stared at the bloodstains and the bullet hole in the torn shirt then looked into the water.

"Zack!"

There was no response. Jackie began to sob while clinging to the shirt.

"Zack!"

Jackie fell to her knees within the surf and softly sobbed while clutching the shirt to her chest.

"No, don't do this to me," she sobbed softly.

✝

A little over an hour later, the five men from the former Navy SEAL team Whiskey Tango Foxtrot and Jackie stood on the beach with their rifles in their hands. An attractive woman in her mid-twenties with long, copper colored hair, Pinto Romano, and her father, Salvatore Romano, a robust man, in his mid-forties with a youthful appearance, remained behind them and watched. Pinto and Sal had both looked better. Sal was recovering from a bullet wound to his arm, while Pinto had been grazed by a bullet to her shoulder and suffered several bruises and lacerations from an earlier incident at Giovanni's luxury resort leading up to the helicopter crash. Jackie and the five men from her team fired their rifles simultaneously and repeatedly in the air giving Zack his final, twenty-one gun farewell salute.

Sal held Pinto while she sobbed softly for the team's loss. A silver sable German shepherd dog, Darth, lay on the beach with his head on his paws and watched in silence. By the final round of the twenty-one gun salute, Jackie was nearly on her knees while sobbing. Monroe Dallas, a tall, lanky man in his mid-thirties, pulled Jackie into his arms, despite nursing his own shoulder wound, and held her while the others watched the helicopter debris continuing to wash ashore with the surf.

"I thought he'd be back," she whispered to Monroe while clinging to him allowing the tears to streak her face. "He always comes home."

"I know," Monroe softly announced while caressing her almost as much for his own comfort.

𝑓

The yacht sailed from Giovanni's private island toward the port in Columbia where the team would disembark and catch a flight home. Jackie stood along the railing with Monroe, who stiffly flexed his injured shoulder. She tried her cell phone again and finally got a signal. She pressed the number for Holden's cell phone, gave Monroe a strange look, and then disconnected the call.

"That's strange," she informed him. "The voicemail isn't picking up. It just keeps ringing."

"Did you try the office?"

"No, not yet."

Her cell phone rang before she had a chance to try a different number. She looked at Monroe and smiled. "It's the Bureau number." Jackie accepted the call with enthusiasm. "Holden?" She hesitated and eyed Monroe. "Mr. Harris, I'm sorry. I thought you were Holden. I've been out of town." She fell silent then suddenly gasped, alerting Monroe. "What?" she cried out. "What happened? Is he okay?"

Monroe gave her his full attention. He seemed to sense the conversation and immediately listened. Jackie shut her eyes a moment while holding her breath. She briefly choked up.

Her voice crackled as she spoke. "Thanks for calling, Mr. Harris."

She disconnected the call and looked at Monroe. He stared at her with indescribable horror on his face. She exhaled softly. "There was an incident during a raid," she informed him while trembling. "Holden's been shot, but he's going to be okay."

Chapter Three

Jackie suddenly jerked awake and looked around with some disorientation. She realized she was in the back of a taxicab with Monroe, who kept watch over her with a slight look of pity. He attempted a smile but didn't comment. Jackie straightened in her seat, frowned, and looked out the side window.

"How much longer to the hospital?" she asked in a weary tone.

It was Sunday morning, and they'd been traveling by boat, plane, and automobile since late Saturday afternoon, making nearly fifteen hours into their journey from Columbia to Colorado. It had been less than twenty-four hours since Zack's fiery crash into the ocean with the disabled helicopter, yet it seemed like a lifetime ago. If she hadn't felt numb already, receiving word of Holden's brush with death during a raid was enough to push her over the edge. Although she wouldn't admit it, she was glad Monroe insisted on going to the hospital with her, even if they reassured her that Holden would be fine. She wished she had a chance to talk to him, but the hospital staff had an excuse each time she called during the last dozen or more hours.

"We should be there in less than ten minutes," Monroe gently informed her and again offered a sympathetic look she'd already come to hate.

She shifted uncomfortably in her seat. Jackie hated to admit she was beyond exhaustion, but she knew sleep wasn't happening. She'd feel better once Holden held her in his arms and reassured her he was fine.

"He's going to be okay," Monroe insisted without hesitation as if reading her thoughts.

"I know," she replied without looking at him.

There was a long, awkward silence between them. Monroe wasn't exactly the strong, silent type, so his actions were somewhat out of character. Jackie cast a glance at Monroe's profile and saw something almost concerning in the way he didn't look at her.

"Is something bothering you?" she finally asked.

Monroe managed a smile as he finally looked at her. She'd seen that smile before. It was his bullshit smile. The next thing out of his mouth would be a well-constructed lie intended to make her feel better.

"No, of course not," he replied. "It's just been a really bad twenty-four hours, that's all." He flexed his sore shoulder from the gunshot wound he received yesterday on Giovanni's island. Monroe then looked away in an attempt to end the conversation that obviously made him uncomfortable.

"Do you think there was something more to Holden's ambush?" she suddenly asked.

He briefly glanced at her and raised a clever brow. "That's ridiculous," Monroe replied while attempting to keep the conversation light. "The guys we took down barely knew your name. I sincerely doubt they intentionally went after Holden." He then seemed to take offense to the question. "Besides, Holden's botched raid happened long before we accepted the assignment on Giovanni's island. The incidents are definitely *not* connected."

Jackie frowned, unconvinced of anything anymore. She'd been through too much in the last few days. Despite the numb feeling she had inside, her body seemed to twitch with anxiety. She wanted to punch something or even scream aloud. She drew a deep breath and attempted to control her emotions. She just needed to be patient. Everything would be better once she held Holden. It always was.

Once the taxi pulled up to the front of the hospital, Monroe and Jackie were on their way to the ICU. They didn't bother stopping at the front desk since Holden's boss had told them which floor he'd been admitted. They headed for the ICU nurse's station to enquire his room number when Jackie saw Holden's boss standing outside one of the rooms with a uniformed police officer. She immediately headed toward Blake and put on a false, brave front.

"Mr. Harris," Jackie announced while squeezing out something resembling a smile.

Blake Harris, a well-dressed, distinguished looking man in his forties, turned when he heard his name. When he saw Jackie approach, his expression immediately dropped. His look frightened her. She quickened her pace with Monroe on her heels and stopped before Holden's boss.

"Jackie," he practically gasped then hesitantly touched her shoulders, frightening her with his unusually warm sediments and an indescribable look in his eyes.

"Is something wrong?" she immediately gasped, feeling her heart pounding as a thousand horrible thoughts raced through her mind.

They said he was alive. They said he would be fine. Actually, they said he *should* be fine. Fear spread through her as she stared at Holden's boss.

Blake held his breath while staring into her eyes with a look that caused her to shiver. "Holden's gone."

Jackie suddenly gasped, feeling her legs suddenly give out beneath her. How was that possible? They said he'd be fine. Monroe was quick to place his arm around her shoulders and support her.

Blake saw her expression and immediately tensed. "I mean, he's disappeared."

She stared at him with a puzzled look while clutching Monroe's lower arm as he held onto her. She wasn't sure how to respond. Thankfully, she had Monroe, who maintained his ability to think straight.

Monroe's brows suddenly knitted as he stared at Blake while increasing his grip on Jackie. "What do you mean he disappeared?" he demanded. "How does a man with multiple gunshot wounds disappear? Did he go for a walk? What?"

Blake looked from Jackie to Monroe and shook his head with uncertainty. "We don't have any idea," he replied, obviously defeated. "The officer here was posted at his door last night. Holden was sleeping peacefully. When the nurses checked on him this morning, he was gone."

Monroe glared at the officer but didn't say what was on his mind. His look said enough.

The officer seemed to feel bad enough and quickly attempted to explain the situation. "I went for coffee twice throughout the night and once to the bathroom," the police officer informed them. "I wasn't gone more than two minutes on any of the three occasions."

"We're looking into the hospital's security footage now," Blake announced, hoping to reassure them they were doing their best. "The nurses assured me there's no way Holden could have gotten out of bed and walked away on his own."

Jackie and Monroe exchanged looks, revealing the same concerns. Blake's comment didn't exactly ease their minds any. Jackie couldn't even bring herself to respond to the comment as she barely heard the conversation.

"So someone took him?" Monroe blurted out, his hostility rising. "In the middle of a hospital?"

"The wheelchair in his room is gone," Blake replied. "Considering he was on some heavy pain killers, that's the only explanation we can come up with."

Jackie stared blankly at nothing while she attempted to process the information, but she couldn't get past Holden being taken against his will. She feared what became of him and who had him. Normally, she'd be the one exploding and demanding answers, but she couldn't pull her thoughts together. Monroe turned defensive enough for them both.

"You're not instilling a lot of faith, Blake," Monroe demanded as he finally released Jackie. He folded his arms across his chest in an intimidating manner, conveniently hiding the pain his injured shoulder caused him in doing so.

Blake hesitated then turned to the police officer and nodded him away. Once the officer left, he looked back at Monroe. "You know I'm eternally grateful for everything you've done for my family and me in the past," he announced then shot him a warning glare, "but you need to keep your head. We'll find Holden without you and your team destroying half my city."

"Then you'd better work fast," Monroe snapped in a low, commanding tone as his arms dropped to his sides and his fists clenched. "We've already suffered one loss this week. We won't lose anyone else."

"I'll let you know what the security footage reveals, Monroe," Blake announced in a reassuring tone. "I want Holden found as much as you do."

Although not completely convinced by Blake's reassurances, Monroe managed a slight nod then motioned Jackie toward the elevator. She stared at the floor with the same blank expression and wasn't even aware he'd been attempting to get her attention. She was stuck in a strange world where she couldn't process her feelings. He gently put his arm around her shoulder, startling her, and then guided her toward the elevator. She didn't remember entering the elevator or Monroe's comforting words. She heard his voice, but nothing registered. Jackie felt oddly cold and numb.

Chapter Four

The old lodge was nestled in a massive clearing in the middle of nowhere Colorado as far as one could get from civilization. Once an impressive resort, the fifty bedroom hotel showed years of neglect. There were several boarded windows, the paint was peeling, and the wraparound porch appeared to be eroding. A small, two-passenger helicopter rapidly dropped down just several yards from the lodge. Its landing was a little rough, indicating a sense of urgency. As the rotors slowed, a handsome man and the German shepherd dog jumped from the helicopter. Gil Rafferty was on the upper end of thirty if not in his early forties. His short dark hair, peppered with gray, gave him a slightly distinguished look. Both Gil and the dog ran for the lodge in the near distance.

Gil and Darth entered the massive lobby that had been painstakingly renovated, despite the condition of the outside. The old-fashioned front desk was possibly antique and added class to the lobby. A large, walk-in stone fireplace took up the entire back wall, and an open, wooden staircase led to the second-floor rooms, which overlooked the lobby. Pinto stood alongside another man within the lobby. Kirk Mandel was a large, muscular man who stood an imposing 6'4" with broad shoulders and biceps the size of tree trunks barely hidden beneath his form-fitting shirt. His buzz cut and thick facial stubble made him look moderately intimidating.

Kirk and Pinto barely acknowledged Gil as he hurried across the lobby toward them. They seemed to be engrossed in the conversation another team member, Beck, was having on the satellite phone. The satellite phone was the only real communication available in the middle of backwoods nowhere. Beck Larue was a ruggedly handsome man in his mid-thirties. He stood over six feet tall and maintained an impressive athletic build. They watched as Beck paced with the phone to his ear while vigorously running his fingers through his light brown hair.

"You stay with her, Monroe," Beck announced firmly into the phone. "Don't leave her out of your sight. We'll figure it out." There was a pause. Beck suddenly turned angry. "I don't know," he shouted into the phone then attempted to control his emotions. It was obvious the stress of acting as temporary commander was getting to him. "Just keep an eye on her. We don't need Jackie going off half-cocked right now. She's been through enough." He held his breath and considered the comment. "We all have." He listened to Monroe on the other end. "Yeah, I'm working on it. I'll call you back."

Beck disconnected the call and looked at Gil, who appeared unusually tense. For a man who never displayed emotions openly, he was sending some strong emotions now. Beck was so distraught after his call, he didn't even seem to notice Gil's mood.

"That was Monroe," Beck informed Gil and the others while having a difficult time holding his emotions. "Holden's missing from the hospital. The nurses said there's no way he left on his own. Someone either helped him or took him."

Gil shut his eyes and exhaled as if in pain.

Beck eyed him, finally noticing his emotional state, and started putting things together. "Did you come in a helicopter?" he suddenly asked then acknowledged his rather unusual mood. "Is something wrong?"

"I heard it on the news," Gil announced and had a tough time finishing his sentence before groaning. "I went straight to Ross's ranch."

Everyone stared at Gil and his pale expression. They all seemed to tense at once and remained unusually silent.

"Ross's brother-in-law hasn't heard from him in days," Gil remarked then fidgeted. "A building exploded in a small town not far from Rio. Witnesses reported hearing gunshots just before the explosion."

There was a strange silence from the others as they stared at Gil, awaiting the rest of the story.

"A man and woman fitting Ross and Lee's descriptions were seen in the marketplace just before the gunshots," Gil informed them then gently touched his graying temple. "They've located several bodies in the rubble."

Pinto gasped while holding her hand over her mouth, the horror clearly on her face. Kirk and Beck stared at Gil and his pale expression.

"Now we don't know--"

"Lee's passport was in a purse they recovered from the debris," Gil gasped while fighting hard to stop the tears from welling in his eyes.

Beck seemed to stare at nothing then sank into the nearby chair. Kirk abruptly turned and walked away. A moment later, they heard a loud thump, his fist undoubtedly striking the first wall just out of sight. Pinto hurried to Beck's side, fell into the chair alongside him, and clung to his arm. Although she was attempting to comfort him, she sobbed softly into his shoulder. Despite her crying, he could do little more than hold his hand to his temple and stare blankly at the floor. Gil stayed only a moment then turned and headed back out the door with Darth following. Only a moment later, the helicopter was heard taking off. Darth sat in the middle of the yard, whimpering while staring at the helicopter as it swiftly zipped away and out of sight, leaving him behind. He lay down, placed his head upon his paws, and stared at the quickly vanishing helicopter.

✝

The charming ranch house sat nestled on a half-acre lot in the cozy, older neighborhood. The well cared for home was lovingly landscaped with colorful flowers, tidy bushes, and two strategically placed weeping willow trees. It was just after midnight on Monday morning, when a mid-sized car pulled into the driveway and stopped short of the garage. A weary looking woman in her mid to late thirties got out of the car and headed for the house while fumbling with her house key. A motion sensor light came on as she approached the house. She wore a nurse's scrub uniform and a hospital nametag clipped to her smock. Despite not wearing make-up and her hair pulled up in a messy ponytail, Ellie Rafferty was an attractive woman.

She approached the small porch darkened by the weeping willow tree blocking the outside house light. As she wearily climbed the steps, she saw a man move within the shadows, startling her. She gasped and stopped halfway up the short set of steps. Gil showed no emotion where he stood facing the surprised nurse. Ellie groaned softly and placed her hand on her chest.

"Damn it, Gil," she gasped. "You scared the hell out of me." Ellie immediately became defensive while glaring at him. "It's after midnight. I thought we discussed boundaries and unannounced visits."

Gil continued to stare at her as his eyes glossed over. "Zack and Ross are dead," he almost whispered.

She stared at him with surprise clearly on her face. Her expression immediately softened as she hurried up the last few steps and pulled him into her arms. "Oh, Gil," she gasped. "I'm so sorry."

Gil held her against him a moment then broke down sobbing for the first time.

✝

Gil sat hunched over the coffee table in the living room with a drink clutched in his hands. He stared into the glass of whiskey that he hadn't even touched. Ellie sat on the sofa alongside him while gently caressing his shoulder. She had changed into a pair of floppy shorts and a worn, comfortable gray sweatshirt with the Navy logo proudly displayed on the chest.

"Are you sure Ross is dead?" Ellie gently asked while studying his sorrowful expression.

"They're still sorting through the rubble," Gil replied with a slight quiver in his voice. "They found Lee's purse with her passport still in it." He hesitated a moment and drew a deep, shaken breath. "They haven't been able to identify any of the bodies yet, but if Lee was there, so was Ross." He finally took a large swallow of the whiskey and immediately cringed.

"Did you want me to come to Colorado for Zack's funeral?" she gently asked.

He didn't bother looking at her and shook his head. "Nah, it's just going to be the guys for a memorial," he replied. "There's no reason for you to travel all the way to Colorado. We gave him a proper, military send-off on Giovanni's private island."

"Twenty-one gun salute?" she questioned.

Gil nodded. "We're just going to drink all day Tuesday," he informed her. "Kirk will be loud and obnoxious. Beck and Monroe will hurl obscenities at each other, and someone will undoubtedly punch Bogart. No reason to expose you to that."

"Wouldn't be the first time," Ellie remarked.

Gil finally looked at her and managed a smile. He finished the whiskey and set the empty glass on the coffee table. He sighed deeply and stood.

"I shouldn't have come here," he announced with little emotion, now appearing mostly sedate.

Ellie sprang to her feet and faced him, appearing slightly offended. "Of course you should have," she insisted. "You've never been real good at showing your feelings around the guys. Some macho Navy SEAL trait, I suppose. You know you can come to me when something's bothering you. It's something we could always count on each other for."

He studied her a moment then placed his arms around her and held her against him. He drew a deep, shaken breath and released it. "I know," he replied. "That's why I came. I knew you'd make me feel better. You always do."

She pulled back while in his arms and met his gaze with a warm and loving look. Ellie gently touched his face and kissed him quickly but warmly on the lips. "Then I'll get no argument when I insist you have another drink and stay the night," she firmly announced. "I'm not letting you drive or fly in your current condition."

Gil managed a smile and snorted a soft laugh. "You know whiskey and I don't mix well," he reminded her. "Add some raw emotions, and you know how I get."

She stared into his eyes while running her hand along his chest. "And I'm willing to let you work out your frustrations," Ellie replied seductively.

He stared at her a long moment in silence then grabbed her by the back of the neck and kissed her passionately and aggressively. Ellie returned the kiss while holding nothing back. She ran her hands firmly along his body, encouraging his aggression. Although only a short-term cure, intimacy was more beneficial than drinking away his sorrow.

✝

Gil and Ellie writhed within each other's arms beneath the covers within the dimly lit bedroom. Her screams of ecstasy met his groans of pleasure. The bed creaked and thudded against the wall with each aggressive movement as the couple came together in long anticipated passion. Although divorced, Gil and Ellie could always share in fleeting moments of unbridled passion. Finally exhausted from their long, wild lovemaking, the couple collapsed to the bed then cuddled in each other's arms while attempting to slow their heavy breathing and rapid heartbeats. Gil nuzzled his ex-wife and appeared relaxed for the first time.

"You'd make a great therapist, Ellie," he announced while panting softly.

"I consider myself lucky your stress release is something you're very good at," she remarked while hiding her smile as she caressed his bare chest.

Gil cast a look at her where she remained nestled in his arms and hid his pleased grin. "I don't know why, but I never grow tired of hearing that."

She rested her chin on his chest, met his gaze with a loving smile, and affectionately caressed his shoulder. "Your 'take charge' attitude in bed is the only reason we've been married so many times," she teased.

He chuckled while clinging to her and nuzzled her head. "Maybe the next time we get married, we should agree to never get out of bed."

She grinned her approval. "Deal."

Chapter Five

The rural residential development just outside Colorado Springs was peaceful for a Monday morning. Average middle-class homes lined the clean empty streets. Most of the residents were coming to life signaling the beginning of their workweek. An official looking black SUV pulled into the driveway of a quaint, modern two-story home nestled on a corner lot. Jackie invited Blake Harris into her home, immediately taking him to the kitchen where Monroe was making them coffee. Jackie hadn't slept much since the beginning of her nightmare, which officially began Saturday afternoon with Zack's fiery crash. Yesterday's news of Holden's disappearance only made things worse for the weary, young woman. She wore one of Holden's official FBI t-shirts and a pair of floppy shorts that had seen better days. She hadn't showered yet that morning, and her hair was barely tamed in a messy ponytail.

Although Jackie was eager to see Holden's boss, there little light in her eyes, which were red from two days' worth of crying and contained dark circles from lack of sleep. Monroe placed coffee on the table before both Jackie and Blake. He'd been Jackie's only saving grace the last twenty-four hours, making certain she ate and tried to sleep. Her endless pacing exhausted him, although he looked shower fresh and dressed with his usual stylish flare. As Monroe joined them at the table, Jackie wrung her fingers together while staring at Blake.

"You brought the footage from the hospital security cameras?" she eagerly asked.

Blake remained tense while sitting across from her. He placed his laptop on the table and opened it. "I don't want you to read too much into what we've found so far," he announced firmly. "We have footage of an unidentified orderly taking Holden from his room in a wheelchair sometime around one A.M." His look was stern and serious. "We don't have anything to support that this man removed him from the hospital. We're still trying to identify the orderly, so he may not even have anything to do with Holden's disappearance."

Jackie eagerly nodded and trembled while waiting to see the footage.

"Nothing is conclusive," Blake again insisted.

"Can I see the footage?" Jackie demanded, becoming impatient and anxious to see who took her husband.

Blake reluctantly turned the laptop to face Jackie and Monroe and played the security footage. Both watched with anticipation as Holden was pushed from the room while slumped in a wheelchair with a blanket wrapped around him. Jackie stared helplessly at Holden's sedate condition. She almost didn't recognize him in the grainy, black and white footage. They saw the orderly who was pushing the wheelchair as he emerged from the room. The large, heavyset man turned in such a way that his face was barely visible in the grainy footage. Jackie and Monroe's mouths simultaneously fell open as they stared at the heavyset orderly with wild, curly dark hair. Jackie jumped up from her chair, knocking it to the floor while screaming. Monroe sprang to his feet, joining her while crying out. They hugged each other with relief and excitement.

Blake stared at them with surprise. "Did I just miss something?"

Jackie pulled away from Monroe while barely controlling her tears of joy that she wiped from her cheeks. "It's Othello!"

"Son-of-a-bitch," Monroe exclaimed and nearly cried with her. "That bastard! Holden is with Othello!"

Blake continued to stare at them, uncertain how to react. "So he's a friend?"

"He's a sneaky, conniving genius bastard of a conman," Monroe exploded excitedly.

Jackie sobbed and again hugged Monroe. He held her against him while she cried with relief.

"I don't understand," Blake remarked while eyeing both, remaining clueless.

"For whatever reason, Othello must have thought Holden's life was in danger," Monroe informed him. "He's on top of underworld gossip. He must have received some information that sent him to get Holden. As long as Holden is with Othello, he's almost certainly safe."

"Then we need to find this Othello guy," Blake announced while collecting his laptop as he stood.

Jackie pulled away from Monroe and shot a horrified look at Blake.

Monroe shared the same look of concern and waved his hands erratically before him. "No, no, no," he cried out. "Holden's safe wherever he is. If the danger were gone, we'd have heard from Othello by now."

"So we just wait for this guy to contact us?" Blake almost demanded, not seeming keen on the idea.

"Exactly," Monroe announced while already scheming, deep in thought. He then looked at Blake. "He'll get in touch with us when he thinks it's safe. If he doesn't contact us, we don't go looking for him."

Blake glanced at Jackie, who wiped the tears from her face. She was still concerned, but she was smiling for the first time. "Are you in agreement with this?" he asked.

She immediately nodded while sniffing. "Yes, Holden's safe wherever he is," Jackie insisted with conviction. "Othello saved my ass once. I trust him with Holden's life."

Blake sighed deeply and placed his laptop into his bag. "I owe you and your team," he announced, although somewhat distrusting. "If you believe in this guy, I'll stay out of it." He stood proudly. "I was never here. As far as the Bureau is concerned, Holden is still MIA."

"Thank you," Jackie announced in a timid voice.

"As soon as you hear anything, let me know," Blake replied then indicated the hallway. "I'll see myself out."

As Blake left the kitchen, Jackie and Monroe again hugged each other in a long, relieved embrace.

Chapter Six

The panoramic, aerial view of the lodge could be seen below as the Bell 412EPI helicopter passed overhead. The commercial 14-passenger helicopter contained a spacious, 220-foot cabin with aft-sliding side doors and adjustable seating for transporting those attending Zack's memorial that Tuesday afternoon. Jackie set the helicopter down within the spacious, overgrown parking lot not far from the lodge entrance. Once she shut down the helicopter and the rotors slowed, her passengers disembarked. Darth enthusiastically raced to the helicopter and immediately jumped on Gil, excited for the return of his best friend. Besides Gil and Monroe, Sal Romano had made the connecting flight from Chicago to join them at the lodge as well.

They made a quick stop at Ross's ranch to pick up his brother-in-law, Liam, and his niece, Selena, as well. Liam was a moderately attractive man in his early forties with a slightly receding hairline. He had been married to Ross's sister before a car accident claimed her life several years ago. Selena was thirteen years old and had sandy brown hair like her mother. Ross often said she looked like her mother. He was happy to have his niece living with him and mostly got along well with his brother-in-law, who tended to his gentleman's farm while he was away on assignments.

Jackie and Monroe were only at the lodge a few minutes before finding out the horrible news about Ross and his girlfriend, which overshadowed the mildly good news concerning Holden. According to Ross's brother-in-law, the last of their teammates, Bogart, still hadn't shown at Ross's farm with his recently acquired horse and there was no word from him either. Jackie was growing concerned that no one had yet heard from Bogart. She assumed he'd call if he ran into trouble while illegally transporting the horse from Giovanni's island just off the coast of Columbia. She'd tried his cell phone, but she continually received a 'not in service' message. Jackie failed to include anyone in her suspicions that Bogart might be her brother. They had no evidence to support the possibility, and with everything that had happened during their last assignment, they didn't have time to have the proper tests done. It was something that would just have to wait.

†

Zack's memorial was kept small and intimate, mostly due to few people knowing he'd been resurrected from the dead after the last time he supposedly died. Technically, this was the second time Jackie and the team attended Zack's funeral. The first time was when the team staged his death some time before her father died. Jackie had been conveniently left out of their secret and didn't find out he was actually alive until some years later. It was a time when every terrorist organization wanted Zack dead and laying him to rest seemed the best way to keep him from being killed. They considered it a form of retirement.

Jackie remembered the funeral very well. They buried his big toe, which was a horrible memory that stayed with her a long time. She never did find out whose toe they buried that day. They laid the toe to rest in the same cemetery as her father and mother. Today, they placed Zack's new headstone in the old garden behind the lodge. Beck, Kirk, and Pinto cleared a lovely spot beneath a large tree. Jackie knew Zack would approve.

Once the sun went down, Ross's niece nestled into one of the many guestrooms, leaving the grieving adults to mourn the loss of their departed teammates and friends with expensive scotch. By the time midnight rolled around, they were all fairly drunk. Kirk turned into a miserable, drunken bastard. He allowed anger to replace sorrow, so he wouldn't have to deal with what he considered a weaker emotion. Pinto surprisingly held her own while drinking with the boys. Jackie had never seen her drunk or even drink alcohol for that matter, so she never expected her to maintain her dignity while intoxicated. Beck and Monroe started arguing the moment the alcohol hit them. They were always in a pissing match when they drank. If Jackie wasn't mistaken, it was the same argument every time playing out on an endless loop.

Sal and Gil, although clearly intoxicated, held an intelligent conversation from politics to real estate. Jackie was bored just listening to them. It wasn't normal. Drunken men were supposed to babble and argue like idiots. Frick and Frack, otherwise known as Beck and Monroe, were how drunken men were supposed to behave, in her opinion. Ross, Zack, and her father would get into heated debates while drinking. Usually, the debate was over something stupid and trivial, but that was what she found endearing. It then dawned on Jackie. They were gone. The three most important men from her childhood were gone. After her father died, she at least had Ross. He was like a second father to her and her life remained moderately normal knowing he was only a phone call away.

Despite being a permanent fixture in her life, Zack was far from a father figure and he made that very clear with his moderately sexual innuendoes. He helped her father teach her martial arts, he taught her life lessons, and he was one person she knew she could count on when she needed him most. She never had to call. Zack was always just there. They shared a strange closeness, not that she wasn't close to the rest of the team. They all played their parts in her life and defined the woman she became, but Zack was her conscience, her mentor, and set the bar for her achievements. She wanted to *be* Zack. It was then that she realized she'd lost her best friend.

†

The last thing Jackie remembered was hearing the guys arguing about trivial matters and someone asking her where she was going. She didn't remember responding, and she wasn't sure where she was going. She remembered the world going dark and nothing else. As Jackie drifted off, she was once again on Giovanni's island sitting on that godforsaken beach. She stared at the debris floating in the ocean and the remaining helicopter pieces from the explosion that gently washed to shore. She seemed to sit there forever, although she was certain she hadn't been there that long. Zack was out there somewhere in the water. She wanted to recover his body, so she'd have something to bury, but she somehow knew he was where he wanted to be when he died. Something glistening in the surf caught her attention. Jackie stared at the object as the water washed past it a second time. She finally stood and approached the surf before the water could take away the object. Jackie picked up the ruby and diamond tennis bracelet and stared at it a moment with surprise. It was a rare and valuable find, yet its presence seemed almost odd. She placed it in her pocket and stared back into the ocean. Unfortunately, Zack wasn't coming back.

Jackie slowly woke to darkness surrounding her. There was an intense pain circulating through her entire body. She could feel the cool, damp grass beneath her where she lay on her back staring up at the Colorado night sky. For a moment, she was disoriented and the world seemed to be spinning. She groaned as she managed to pull herself into a sitting position not far from Zack's headstone. She stared at his name embossed on the gray marble. Her head was still spinning from the alcohol. She then looked at the nearby tree, stared at it a moment, and groaned. She vaguely remembered climbing the tree, which would explain why she didn't remember falling from it.

"You idiot," she muttered then held her head to keep the world from spinning.

She collapsed near Zack's headstone and again looked at it. Her dream about the island flashback was still fresh and strong in her mind. She uncertainly pulled her sweatshirt sleeve from her wrist revealing the ruby and diamond tennis bracelet she'd found that afternoon among the debris. It seemed odd that its presence in the surf suddenly bothered her. Her drunken mind seemed to be working in overtime. She'd seen the bracelet before she found it in the surf. She tried to think where she'd seen it. Bogart flashed in her mind. It came back to her all at once. Bogart admired the bracelet while they were in the ship's casino on their last assignment. The wife of a notorious mob boss was wearing it! How did the bracelet get on a beach so far from the resort? Had it been in the helicopter prior to the crash? Did Bogart have it on him when he pulled her from the water? Had he stolen it? Her head started to hurt from thinking too much.

She finally gave in to the world spinning around her. It was actually quite pleasant, like a large carousel. While enjoying her spinning world, she allowed her thoughts to stray to her missing husband. Jackie had attempted to keep Holden from her mind. She wanted to believe he was safely tucked away with Othello. She didn't want anything to disrupt that fantasy. Holden couldn't be dead because she couldn't handle losing him too. Was Holden's ambush merely another coincidence? What about the timing of the attack on Ross? Oddly, they both seemed to coincide with the attacks on the rest of the team while on Giovanni's island. Was it a coincidence or a well-coordinated attack? Was it possible what happened to them on the island spread out to Ross and Holden?

Chapter Seven

It was a little after three o'clock in the morning when Jackie stumbled through the lodge lobby. Everything was quiet, signaling that all the drunks had gone to bed. She knew to be careful not to trip over anyone passed out on the floor. That actually only happened once when she was much younger involving Kirk, who was barely dressed at the time. He was a big guy and could pound them down with the best of them. Unfortunately, when the alcohol had finally hit him, he didn't make it to his room and just sort of made himself at home wherever he crashed. She hated to admit Kirk was the first naked man she'd seen, because she was a little young to see such things.

When Jackie was halfway to the stairs, she heard the sound of glasses clinking. She looked across the lobby toward the massive front desk and saw Sal placing the dirty glasses on a tray. She was surprised to see anyone still up let alone cleaning the mess. He saw her and smiled with a little added warmth on his cherub face, which was now slightly red from drinking too much.

"Everyone went to bed," he casually informed her, not sounding the least bit drunk.

"Shouldn't you be there too?" she asked as she approached him while slightly unsteady on her feet.

"Alcohol and I have a strange relationship," he replied cheerfully. "It keeps me awake. I won't crash until sunup. You've been gone a while. Monroe was looking for you. Unfortunately, he passed out in the lounge."

"I guess I wandered off," Jackie announced with a sigh and attempted to sit on the arm of the sofa.

She slipped and collapsed onto the sofa. She turned on her side, propping herself up on her elbow, and made it look intentional. Sal was aware of her condition but didn't comment. He just smiled and continued collecting glasses.

"I keep thinking about what happened last Saturday," she remarked with a frown. "I was right there. I should have been able to save him."

"You know you couldn't have," Sal replied without hesitation. "I know it's of no comfort, but he died on his own terms. He went out the way he wanted to go."

"Do you honestly believe that?"

"He died a hero, Jackie," Sal informed her while leaning against the front desk. "He died saving you." He managed a tiny smile. "Pretty much a blaze of glory. That's the way he'd want to go."

She considered his comment then nodded in agreement. "Yeah, you're probably right," she replied. "I just wish he hadn't followed in my father's footsteps."

"Oh, how's that?"

"My father died saving my life too."

Sal stared at her a moment and tensed slightly. "I didn't know that. I'm sorry."

She drifted off a moment while deep in thought and stared at nothing in particular. "I always knew Zack would die because of me."

"Don't say that," Sal scolded, catching her attention. "It wasn't your fault. I'd give my life for my daughter. It's what you do when you love someone."

Jackie rested her head on her arm and stared at Sal from her horizontal position. "I know you're right, but I can't convince myself to feel any better." She eyed him without lifting her head. "I have this nagging feeling there's a large piece of the puzzle still missing. That entire assignment doesn't sit well. Everything that happened on the island and everything that's happened since we've been back. I wish I understood what I'm feeling."

Sal approached and sat on the arm of the plush chair across from her. He casually leaned against the back. "I understand what you mean," he replied and sank into his own thoughts while flexing his sore, injured arm then looked back at her. "It seemed as if everyone had their own agenda, and we were all just caught in the middle."

"That's an understatement," she muttered.

He adjusted his thin wire glasses and leaned forward with a serious look. "I'm still shocked that Mac showed up when she did," he announced and shook his head. "If she weren't such a devil, I'd swear she was an angel fallen straight from heaven. That's been bugging me since we left the island."

Jackie struggled to prop herself back on her elbow and stared at him with surprise and disbelief. "Mac?" she practically cried out. "You mean *that* Mac. Who used to work for you then vanished without a trace?"

"Yes, that Mac," Sal replied then eyed her with some surprise. "That's right. You had already gone off on your walk when we were discussing that." He shook his head still in disbelief. "She just showed up out of the blue, saved my life, and declared 'we're even'." He snorted a soft laugh and grinned while shaking his head. "I don't even know what that was supposed to mean. Even for what?"

Jackie returned her head to the sofa although remaining deep in thought. "That is strange." She gave him a puzzled look. "You didn't happen to run into a very attractive female Russian spy, did you?"

He stared at her with a puzzled look, not understanding the question. "Excuse me?"

She laughed softly. "Nothing."

Sal stood with a deep sigh and returned to the front desk to claim his tray of dirty glasses. "I think I'll wash these glasses and see about getting some sleep," he announced, now slightly weary. "Gil offered to fly me from the private airfield in Colorado Springs to Chicago tomorrow after you drop us off in the helicopter." He laughed and shook his head. "I hope he can fly hungover." He then considered the comment and appeared curious. "I hope *you* can fly hungover. Anyway, I guess he's taking Monroe home to his beach house off the coast of Florida after he drops me off." He managed a soft laugh and grinned. "He's heading back to Virginia. Don't quote me, but I think he's hooking up with his ex-wife again." He then gave the comment some thought. "I should offer them my beach house in Maui for a few weeks. Love always deserves another chance to bloom." Sal turned to face Jackie while holding his tray of glasses. "Don't you think--?"

Jackie was sound asleep on the sofa. Sal smiled, set his tray down on the desk, and approached the sofa. He gently placed one of the throw pillows under her head then covered her with a quilted blanket.

"Goodnight, Jackie." He was about to turn when he noticed the familiar ruby and diamond tennis bracelet Jackie wore. Sal sank into thought while staring at it. "Mac," he whispered then eyed the sleeping woman. "How did you get the bracelet Mac was wearing?"

Chapter Eight

Late afternoon.   Jackie entered her house just outside Colorado Springs with her flight bag in her hand.   After she had dropped off Liam and Selena at Ross's farm, she flew Gil, Monroe, and Sal to the nearby private airfield where Gil had his plane.   He would then fly them to their respective airports despite the amount of time he'd have to spend in the air.   He didn't seem to mind, and the guys were glad to avoid flying commercial.   Jackie shut the door behind her and looked around the empty house.   It was so quiet; she could hear the gently swaying pendulum of the grandfather clock in the hallway.   Normally, she loved the sound of the grandfather clock, but in the silent, empty house, it sounded like a freight train.

She dropped her flight bag on the foyer floor and leaned against the front door, staring at nothing in particular.   She didn't know how long she remained against the door before straightening.   Her hangover was finally fading and hunger was taking its place, but she didn't feel like eating.   The thought made her nauseous.   She removed her leather flying jacket and hung it in the foyer closet next to Holden's favorite casual jacket.   She gently touched his jacket sleeve and pulled away when she felt tears welling in her eyes.   She collected her emotions and finally headed into the kitchen.

An hour later, Jacket sat at the island counter and stared at the plate of heated leftovers she'd brought with her from last night's memorial service.   Her thoughts strayed to Zack and images of his

37

tombstone beneath the tree. She held her head and sniffed while staring at the plate of grilled chicken. When she closed her eyes, she saw her last image of Zack as he kicked her from the helicopter just before it went over the cliff. Tears streaked her face. She drew a deep breath and straightened, collecting herself and her emotions. She sat there a second then violently cast the plate from the island counter and didn't even flinch as it shattered against the kitchen cupboard.

Sometime later, Jackie stood within the master bathroom shower beneath a stream of hot water. She didn't move as the water ran down her body. She stared off, indulging in a memory of her last shower encounter with Holden. Despite being late for work and jumping in the shower with her to save time, he couldn't control himself when she offered to wash his chest and regions beyond. She could still feel his hands caressing her flesh while pressing against her body from behind. She drew a deep breath and enjoyed the phantom sensation. Her eyes suddenly opened to reveal hostility and rage. She punched the glass shower door, cracking it. A trickle of blood-tinged water ran down the glass. Jackie flexed her hand then shook it, instantly regretting her actions.

An hour later, Jackie paced the living room while making tight fists then releasing them. Resting on the sofa were framed pictures of Ross, Zack, and Holden with each positioned on a separate cushion. She'd glance at the pictures every so often without interrupting her pacing. Throw pillows were scattered on the floor. Every so often, Jackie would approach one and kick it across the room. Her hostility would eventually fade, and she'd start crying again. It was a vicious cycle that she couldn't seem to control. At least the annoying sound of the grandfather clock wasn't bothering her anymore. She could hear the muffled sound of her cell phone ringing from somewhere within the house and realized she'd left it in her flying jacket.

Jackie ran from the living room and into the hallway toward the foyer. Several wooden rungs on the stairs were broken with the jagged posts dangling free. The glass on the grandfather clock was shattered and scattered along the floor surrounding the carelessly discarded pendulum. Jackie ran to the foyer closet, threw the door open, and grabbed her cell phone from her inner jacket pocket. She was quick to answer it without first checking the caller ID. Her cell phone had an unlisted number, so there were only a select number of people who'd possibly be calling her.

"Hello?" she practically gasped into the phone, feeling her heart racing with anticipation.

"Hello," came the computerized woman's voice. "This is an important message from your cable company--"

Jackie struck the disconnect button with added vigor and was about to throw her cell phone when she reconsidered the action. She screamed in anger and karate kicked the closet door several times, cracking the heavy wood. Jackie panted with anger and rage while holding her head. She took several deep breaths and attempted to control her emotions. Once she was relatively calm, she stuffed her cell phone into her pants pocket and stormed through the hallway toward the kitchen. A moment later, she appeared from the kitchen carrying a bottle of wine and headed up the stairs. Maybe after a bottle of wine, she'd feel like sleeping. If not, there were always a few more rungs on the stairs she could kick out.

Chapter Nine

Sal Romano's country mansion just outside the Chicago city limits was nestled on a large parcel of land beyond tall, stone walls. The professionally landscaped estate didn't have a hedge out of place. Weeping willow trees and faux split rail fencing lined the long driveway. The driveway split off to circle a large fountain outside the front door, while the remaining driveway branched off to the left. The driveway led to the kitchen, staff wing, and eventually to the massive, detached, eight-car garage. It was a little after one o'clock in the morning Chicago time yet the inner and outer lights remained on brightening a large portion of the massive estate. Sal's luxury sedan pulled up to the front of the mansion and parked. Given the late hour of his return, Sal didn't bother parking his expensive car in the garage.

It had been a long travel day despite Jackie's helicopter service and Gil's private plane ride. They got a late start, being everyone was moderately hungover from a night of drinking expensive scotch. If Sal hadn't bothered to stop at his office building to check on business details from the days he'd missed, he would have been home nearly four hours earlier. Considering he didn't have anyone to return home to, there seemed little point rushing home. There wouldn't be any staff to greet Sal as he unlocked the front door and entered the mansion.

The mansion once had more than two dozen employees with nearly half living in the staff wing. After a monstrous betrayal by several employees, Sal downsized his live-in staff to three and had several temp workers come in a few times a week to clean and tend to the yard. The only staff remaining was his devoted, longtime maid, Rosa, and two security guards. Once inside, Sal immediately entered the alarm code into the panel, disabling the system before locking and bolting the door for the night. He reset the alarm and headed for the broad staircase.

After a quick shower and a fresh dressing to the wound on his arm, Sal changed into a pair of black, silk pajamas with his initials embossed in red on the left breast pocket. He crawled under the satin covers of his massive, king-sized bed. He was so tired; he didn't even bother removing all the decorative pillows from the bed. Some he shoved to the floor while others were allowed to remain where they were. It didn't matter. By morning, they would all be scattered on the floor. Despite his aching arm. He fell asleep the moment his head hit the pillow. What should have been a deep, heavy sleep was riddled with confusing dreams of his hellish weekend on Giovanni's private island. Within his dreams, he was transported back to last Saturday afternoon.

Sal lay on the ground clutching the bleeding bullet wound to his arm as he stared up at the man holding the gun on him. Sal showed no fear despite his obvious pain.

"They'll find you," Sal informed the man and offered an unsettling smile despite his situation. "And when they do, they'll kill you."

"We'll deal with them when and if that time comes," the man replied and tightened his finger on the trigger while aiming the gun at Sal's head.

Sal closed his eyes and held his head up proudly, waiting for the sound of the shot and the sting of the bullet. The guard suddenly groaned. Sal opened his eyes to see an attractive, dark haired woman in her mid-thirties, kick the guard several times before tossing him to the ground and disarming him. Macbeth aimed the pistol at the guard and, without hesitation, shot him in the head. The elegant ruby and diamond tennis bracelet around her wrist added a touch of warmth to her otherwise callus kill shot. She looked back at Sal and tossed the gun before him.

"We're even," Mac announced then hurried for the dock.

He stared after his former employee, who had gone missing some time ago, with a look of surprise. "Mac?" he gasped in disbelief.

Sal woke abruptly from his dream and stared wide-eyed at the ceiling as if suddenly completely awake. He rubbed his eyes a moment then sank into thought. His eyes narrowed while he shook his head.

"Mac," he muttered softly still in disbelief. Another thought then occurred to him. "The bracelet--?"

He remained in bed only a few minutes longer before climbing out the opposite side, knocking the rest of the pillows to the floor. Without turning on the bedside light, he opened the top drawer and removed an electronic notepad. By the glow of the notepad, he was able to see his reading glasses within the drawer. He pushed the semiautomatic handgun aside and removed his reading glasses. He swiftly slipped into the glasses and typed onto the notepad's attached, soft keyboard. He located the email address for Giovanni listed under the name 'G' and typed a message to his good friend, who was known to most as a notorious mob boss. In the email, he asked his friend to provide information on a woman who may have been employed at his island resort. He finished the email with an attached photo of him standing with the woman from his dream, Mac, and another man, who had died tragically in the line of duty. He hit send then tossed the notepad onto the bed along with his reading glasses.

Sal groaned softly and rubbed his burning, tired eyes. He finally stood, giving up on sleep. As he crossed the large room in his bare feet, his eyes strayed to the security system's master control panel. Sal immediately hesitated at the flashing error message. He stared at the panel only a moment before hurrying back to the nightstand drawer and removing the semiautomatic. He cocked the handgun as he walked past his bed then paused before the nightstand on the side closest to the door. He slipped into his regular glasses then grabbed the landline phone from its cradle. He pressed a single button for security. When there was no dial tone, he immediately dropped the phone and reached for his cell phone sitting on the dresser. He punched in a phone number and waited several rings before the call was answered.

"Paul," Sal announced into the phone. "I need you and Bill to do a security sweep of the grounds. The security system is showing an error message and the landline isn't working." He awaited a response and nodded. "I'm heading downstairs now. I'll be the bald man in black pajamas. Try not to shoot me."

He disconnected his cell phone and placed it into the small breast pocket of his silk pajamas. Sal crossed the bedroom with the gun looking oddly comfortable in his hand. He showed no fear as he left the safety of his room.

†

$\mathcal{S}$al appeared on the backstairs in the dimly lit kitchen and paused at the bottom. He held his gun relaxed at his side, possibly a little too relaxed as he scanned the area for any sign of intruders. There was something almost menacing about the seemingly docile man. The kitchen light came on, surprising him as it brightened the massive area. Sal looked across the room and saw Rosa standing in the doorway to the staff wing with her finger on the light switch. She appeared relieved to see him and managed a weary smile while removing her hand from the switch.

"Oh, Mr. Romano," she gasped and chuckled softly while holding her chest. "I heard someone thumping around. I got worried. I didn't hear you come in."

Sal stared at her a moment with a strange look. "It wasn't me you heard," he informed her.

Her eyes strayed to the gun by his side. She gasped softly and quickly darted looks around the kitchen.

"It's okay, Rosa," Sal gently informed her while holding up a reassuring hand. "Security is sweeping the grounds. I want you to return to your room and lock the door. I'll let you know when it's safe."

She uncertainly nodded and was about to turn around when her eyes suddenly widened at something she saw. She let out a startled cry and pointed toward the island counter. Sal looked toward the large island counter and saw blood pooling on the floor from behind. Sal motioned for her to remain where she was then hurried for the counter. His security guard, Bill, was sprawled across the floor with blood spilling out from a head wound, which was clearly a bullet hole. Sal backed away from the counter and toward Rosa while keeping watch on the multiple entrances into the kitchen. He stopped near his maid without taking his eyes off the surrounding area. He handed Rosa his cell phone.

"Call the police and report an intruder," he announced in a calm but firm tone.

Her hands trembled as she pressed a single button on the phone. She awaited a response while darting looks around the kitchen in unison with her boss. The lights suddenly went out, leaving them in near darkness. Rosa screamed. Sal turned toward her and placed his hand over her mouth to silence her. He slowly removed his hand and stared at her through the dim lighting from outside lights, which remained on.

"The fuse box is in the hallway closet," he whispered while attempting to keep her calm as she clung to the cell phone. The 911 operator was already talking on the other end. "That means the intruder is in the hallway. Very quietly, I want you to go back into the staff wing, enter the first bedroom you come to, and lock the door. Tell the police to come right away."

Rosa clung to the cell phone while staring into his eyes and slowly nodded. "What are you going to do?" she gasped with concern.

Sal indicated the gun he held and cleverly raised his brows, signifying his intentions. Rosa held her breath then disappeared into the staff wing corridor. Sal closed the connecting door behind her and glanced across the dimly lit kitchen. He raised the gun to eye level, holding it in both hands, and silently crept in his bare feet toward the main hallway door. He heard movement on the back kitchen stairs. Sal spun toward the backstairs while casting his back toward the closest wall. A man carrying a gun appeared at the bottom of the stairs. Despite the dim lighting, Sal recognized Paul's outline and relaxed his finger on the trigger. He was about to alert his man to his presence when nearly silent shots were fired from the stairs behind him.

Paul took several shots and fell to the floor. Sal plastered himself against the wall behind him and stood immobile while staring at the shadow of his dead guard on the floor at the bottom of the stairs. Sal immediately aimed his gun at the stairwell and listened to the feet softly moving down the steps. He flexed his hand on the grip and pressed his finger against the trigger. The man on the stairs was almost at the bottom. The kitchen door from the main hallway suddenly opened, causing Sal to twitch and ease his finger on the trigger. He remained in the darkness of the interior wall and watched the armed intruder pass through the hallway entrance as the second intruder appeared on the backstairs.

"Did you get him?" the first man asked in a loud whisper while approaching the man by the stairs.

"He wasn't in his room," the second intruder replied and looked around the kitchen as they met by the island counter. "You take care of the maid. I'll locate Romano."

"What the hell?" the first man demanded in a soft voice. "He came back tonight. I saw him come inside. Where the hell is Romano?"

"He's right here," Sal announced and squeezed the trigger before either man could locate the source of the voice.

The first man took a bullet to his chest and immediately dropped while the second man took a shot in the leg, causing him to drop to his knee. He raised his gun to fire blindly in the direction of Sal's unmuffled gunshot. Sal again squeezed the trigger, shooting the man in the arm. He cried out while dropping his gun and clutched his bleeding arm. Sal casually crossed the dimly lit kitchen toward the man partially on the floor, clutching his wounds in agony. He stared up at Sal, who remained unusually calm. Sal drew a deep breath and casually adjusted his glasses.

"Son," Sal announced with a sigh then shook his head. "You fucked with the wrong family." He casually raised the gun and shot the man in the head. Sal didn't even flinch as the man collapsed to the floor.

Chapter Ten

It was a little before one o'clock in the morning Colorado time. Jackie lay in bed and stared at the gently turning ceiling fan for nearly an hour. She groaned then turned onto her right side and stared at Holden's empty spot on the bed. She could almost see him there. She believed he was safe, but she had a hard time convincing herself it wasn't just an illusion. Jackie groaned with disgust, threw the covers off her, and climbed out of bed. She wore an old tank top and a pair of floppy shorts as her sleepwear of choice. As she headed into the bathroom, her cell phone lit up and vibrated on the nightstand alongside the empty wine bottle. The name on the caller ID revealed 'Sal'.

Nearly half past one, the master bedroom was dimly lit by a faint glow coming from the walk-in closet. Jackie sat on the floor within the large closet and polished Holden's dress shoes. She had her combat boots and stalking boots lined up to be polished next. As she set his neatly polished shoes aside, she bumped a shoebox, dislodging the lid. She could see some papers within the box. She pulled it toward her where she sat on the floor and removed the lid. Jackie stared at the newspaper articles within the box, which she happily dubbed 'the little shoebox of horrors'. She sorted through the newspaper articles, staring at faces she hadn't seen in some time. Although it seemed a lifetime ago, it actually hadn't been all that long.

She didn't know what was wrong with her for keeping such macabre reminders of her past. There were numerous articles on her unfortunate encounter with Governor Lyle Kempton. It was the meeting that changed her life forever. Her brush with death at the hands on the Governor's hired goons brought about her first meeting with Holden. Although she found her FBI protector attractive, he was the biggest pain in her ass. She had to laugh at the memory. That domino effect eventually brought her back into the inner circle of her father's former Navy SEAL team. She'd proven herself to them, and they no longer saw her as a defenseless little girl. She became one of them from that moment on. Naturally, Holden opposed her joining them on moderately dangerous missions, but he conceded all on his own. In hindsight, maybe she should have listened to him in the first place. It made her almost nauseous thinking that what happened to him may have had something to do with the company she kept.

Jackie rested her head against the gun safe within the closet and allowed her eyes to close. Images of Zack's last moments continued to plague her mind. She should have done something differently, but she had no idea what that would have been. The crunching of broken glass from the first floor brought her out of her self-pity. As she listened a moment, she swore she heard someone on the stairs. Then she heard the familiar creak of one of the steps. Jackie sprang up and turned off the closet light, leaving her in near darkness. She turned toward the gun safe and pressed in the familiar code. She didn't need to see the buttons since they were arranged in the same order as a phone pad. The electronic lock hummed then clicked as the lock sprang open. She grimaced at the seemingly loud sound, but whoever was in the house hadn't made it to the second-floor hallway yet.

She felt inside the safe and grabbed the Uzi, the smallest of her fully automatic weapons. The magazine was already in place, although there wasn't a bullet in the chamber. While attempting to make as little noise as possible, she gently cocked it. It made a distinctive sound, but it wasn't nearly as loud as usual. Just because someone was inside her house unannounced, that didn't necessarily mean he was an enemy. Most of the guys frequently let themselves in with her hidden spare key, found an empty bed, and greeted her in the morning. The last few days, she'd been on edge, allowing paranoia to take control. She stood by the partially open closet door and peered into the nearly dark bedroom. Her heart pounded as the bedroom door was slowly pushed the rest of the way open. She could see the silhouette of an unfamiliar man now entering her bedroom. She wanted to believe it was Holden, but she knew his outline in the dark, and it definitely wasn't him. She was positive it wasn't any of the men from her father's team.

Jackie watched the man approach her bed then stop a few feet from it. He aimed a semiautomatic with an extended barrel, indicating the weapon contained a silencer, and fired three nearly silent shots into her bed. Jackie had to admit it startled her. He wasn't there to rob her house. It was a hit! She had a clear shot at the man and could take him out with a single round, but something occurred to her. If this was a professional hit, he may not be alone in her house. If she shot the man, anyone else within the house would hear it and be alerted. She needed the element of surprise on her side, especially if she didn't know how many intruders were in the house.

The killer must've realized something wasn't right. He hesitated, lowered his gun, and reached for the rumpled covers. He pulled the covers back to reveal the empty bed. As he turned to scan the room, Jackie was already standing in front of him. She snap kicked him in the groin, immediately dropping him to his knees. Before he fell, she kicked him in the head and sent him against the bed, softening the noise he made as he hit the floor. Unfortunately, his gun thumped as it struck the floor, making a distinctive sound, which would attract any friends he may have brought with him. She snatched the semiautomatic containing the silencer and immediately darted for the open bedroom door. She hid alongside the door and listened for any more unwelcomed visitors. Jackie could hear the thundering footfalls of at least two men running along the second-floor hallway.

She heard them approaching her bedroom door. The man on the floor alongside her bed groaned and moved to his knees. Jackie glanced at the man who could potentially shout a warning. She casually raised the weapon and shot him in the chest. He collapsed to the floor with a soft thump. Another man ran into the bedroom with his gun aimed and ready to fire. Jackie grabbed his wrist, twisted his arm, and kicked him in the abdomen. The second man entered the room, now knowing something was wrong and aimed his gun at her. Jackie spun the first man around, placing him between her and the second intruder, and allowed him to take the three nearly silent shots fired from his partner. She released the dead man, now holding his gun along with the other man's gun and fired several shots into the intruder in the doorway. His body jerked and jolted in a macabre dance of sorts before he struck the doorframe and sank down it, collapsing to the floor.

Jackie sneered as she watched the man hit the floor. She could feel anger and rage coursing through her body. The feeling was overpowering, unlike anything she'd ever felt before. She wanted to revive each man just so she could kill him again. The stress and strain of the last few days had finally taken its toll on her. She was no longer sad; she was pissed. She discarded the intruders' guns and recovered her Uzi from the closet. It was time to clean house. She had to make sure they didn't bring any more friends with them. Jackie approached the bedroom door then hesitated. There was only one staircase leading downstairs. A smart killer would wait for her to trap herself on the stairs, where he could easily pick her off. She needed a Zack move just to be safe. She returned to the closet for one more item.

✝

Two men dressed entirely in black crept across the front yard. One headed for the front door while the second headed around back. As the first man slipped in through the front door, Jackie silently dropped from the porch roof, landing between the bushes and the house. She wore a menacing looking holster strapped to her thigh containing the Uzi. Jackie watched the man enter her house. The intruder crossed the foyer and stood near the bottom of the stairs. He looked up them then touched his ear and the hidden transmitter it contained.

"Do you copy?" he asked in a loud whisper. There was no response. "Confirm. Is the mark down?"

"Yeah, she's down," Jackie snarled while standing directly behind him.

The man whirled around with his gun aimed. Jackie kicked the gun from his hand then spun for the return kick striking him in the face. The intruder was thrown against the hall table, making more noise than she would have liked. He sprang to his feet while pulling a switchblade and lunged for her. Jackie blocked the swing and caught his wrist, twisting his arm enough to cause him to cry out. She glared at the man with a psychotic look through the dim lighting.

"You haven't got the balls to beat me," she snarled through gritted teeth.

The second intruder, having gone around back to the kitchen door, appeared in the hallway and aimed his gun at her. Jackie saw him but running wasn't part of her plan. As the second man fired at her, she flipped her body through the air, using the first man's arm and body as leverage, wrapped her legs around his neck, and flipped him off his feet, riding him to the floor. The gunshot missed her, although he nearly clipped his own man and no longer had a clear shot. The second man ran down the hall toward them as Jackie grabbed the first man around the neck and easily snapped it. The second man stopped when he heard the frightening crunch. Jackie was already on her knees while removing her weapon. She had the Uzi in her hand and fired a barrage of bullets at the second man. He cried out with surprise and ran back into the kitchen.

The unwelcomed guest silently hid alongside the kitchen doorway while clutching his gun. He attempted to control his breathing and collected his emotions as his hardened, determined look returned. He spun into the doorway with his weapon aimed. The dimly lit hallway was empty and silent. His partner remained sprawled on the floor not far from the stairs. The intruder scanned the hallway with some apprehension. The front door stood open, indicating Jackie may have fled the house. He slowly crept along the hallway while darting looks all around him. Jackie was nowhere to be found. As he passed the stairs, he looked up them. There was still no sign of his hit.

The faint creak on the stairs alerted him to someone's presence, causing him to spin toward the stairs with his gun aimed. Jackie leaped through the broken railing and kicked the man in the chest with both feet, sending him across the hall and into the opposing wall with a crash. Jackie landed gracefully on the floor then straightened as the man slowly recovered from the hard kick and even more painful stop. He attempted to raise his gun, but Jackie was already kicking it from his hand, startling him. She straightened and stared the man in the eyes through the dim lighting.

"Who ordered the hit?" she growled with no emotion in her tone.

The man sneered his response and swung his fist for her face. Jackie blocked his fist, kicked him in the side, and then smashed his face on her knee. She released him, allowing him to clutch his nose while attempting to regain his balance.

"Who ordered the hit?" she again asked.

"Fuck you," the man cried out and lunged for her, thinking he could overtake her with his size.

Jackie spun into a roundhouse kick, nailing him in the chest, and sending him back into the wall. "I'm through asking nicely," she snarled.

The man straightened, preparing for another attempt to subdue her. Jackie punched him repeatedly in the face, knocking him back, and then kicked him several times in the side. He attempted to defend her blows, but she was too fast. She took a step back, spun into a high, roundhouse kick, and struck him in the face. He struck the wall and no longer defended himself. Jackie repeatedly punched him in the face while pinning him to the wall, keeping him from sliding down to the floor. When his body was finally determined to fall from her grasp, Jackie grabbed his head and swiftly broke his neck before releasing him. The killer fell lifelessly to the floor. Jackie stood over the dead man while panting heavily, the uncontrollable rage coursing through her. She could do little more than stare at what she was capable of doing. Once she collected her emotions, she casually turned and headed up the stairs.

Jackie came down the steps a few minutes later with a hastily thrown together duffel bag. She dropped the bag at the bottom of the stairs and approached the man she'd beaten to death. She searched his pockets, removed his cell phone, and fiddled with it. She took a picture of the man then reclaimed her bag while heading for the door. She paused to take a picture of the second dead man, grabbed her leather, flying jacket, and then left the house. In less than a minute, Jackie backed her father's black Mustang out of the garage and onto the once quiet, residential street. She drove away as police sirens wailed in the distance heading toward her house. Undoubtedly, her neighbors heard the gunshots from her Uzi and called the police. Unfortunately, she didn't have time to stick around and answer questions.

✝

The black Mustang pulled up to the private airfield not far from her house and parked alongside one of the hangars. Jackie carried her bag and the killer's borrowed cell phone toward the familiar helicopter. She tossed her gear into the back and prepped her helicopter for departure. She took a moment while sitting in the pilot's seat to fiddle with the cell phone. She easily accessed the killer's phone contacts and typed a text message. It simply read, 'I'm coming for you.' She attached the pictures of the two dead men then pressed send. Jackie tossed the cell phone out the helicopter door, strapped herself in, and lifted off. She fiddled with her cell phone while the helicopter whisked across the countryside. She saw a missed call over an hour ago from Sal, which piqued her curiosity. She listened to the call and immediately frowned.

"Son-of-a-bitch," she cursed under her breath, only now realizing the importance of the missed call.

Jackie ended the voice message and pressed a single, speed dial button for the lodge satellite phone. She wasn't surprised when there was no answer. It was late, and she doubted anyone would be up at that hour. The satellite phone was possibly even turned off to conserve the battery. Jackie cast her phone onto the empty seat alongside her and gave the helicopter additional throttle, racing across the dark countryside.

Chapter Eleven

Monroe's luxurious, two-story beach house was nestled on a long stretch of private beach, isolated from others also living in seclusion on the small island. The newer home contained a wall of windows facing the ocean for a spectacular view. The detached two-car garage set further back from the home. One bay door was open, revealing an expensive, red Ferrari parked within the darkness. It was a little after three o'clock in the morning Florida time. The private beach was peaceful, as it always was in Monroe's little corner of the world. His house was almost completely dark inside and out, although the moon provided enough light to add a romantic glow to the beach surrounding the home.

In the distance, the sound of a helicopter could be heard, interrupting the once peaceful night. The sound grew louder as the helicopter came into view from the beach side of the house. The aft-side door slid open to reveal a man dressed in black seated behind a mounted machine gun. As the man placed his finger on the trigger, Monroe stepped out of the shadows of the house and raised a rocket launcher. His grin was nearly psychotic while positioning the menacing weapon.

"Not this time, motherfucker!"

Monroe pulled the massive trigger, expelling the rocket from the large tube. The man seated in the side opening of the helicopter saw the projectile hurling toward him and screamed. The helicopter attempted to veer to avoid a collision, but it was too late. The rocket struck the helicopter and exploded it over the once peaceful ocean, raining down flaming helicopter parts. Monroe lowered the rocket launcher and grinned deviously. He tossed the massive weapon over his shoulder while patting it affectionately then removed his cell phone. He pressed a single button and only waited a moment for the call to be answered.

"Monroe?" came Sal's concerned voice.

"Yeah, Sal," Monroe replied as he walked past his unscathed house. "Thanks for the heads up."

"You were a target too?" he was heard gasping over the phone.

"Yeah, they came after me too," Monroe replied while cautiously looking around the again quiet area. "Any luck getting ahold of the others?"

"No, none," Sal replied over the phone. "I left messages on Jackie and Gil's cell phones, but I couldn't reach the guys at the lodge."

"If there's no one awake to answer the satellite phone, they won't leave it turned on," Monroe replied as he hurried toward the garage.

"For a bunch of scheming men, that's a stupid system," Sal scoffed from the other end. "They could be in danger. My *daughter* could be in danger."

"I'm heading to the private airfield now," Monroe announced as he entered the garage and deposited the rocket launcher on top of his duffel bag. The action hurt his injured shoulder more than he was willing to admit. He gingerly flexed his sore shoulder then jumped into his red Ferrari and shut the door, the cell phone still to his ear. "I'll have to wake a friend and call in a favor. Do you have reliable contacts?"

"Yeah, I have a few friends I still trust living nearby," Sal replied.

"We'll rendezvous at the private airfield where Jackie keeps her fleet," Monroe informed him. "I'll collect Jackie at her place and meet you there. She'll take us to the lodge."

There was a moment of silence. "You know the reality of what's happening, Monroe."

"I know," he replied with a deep sigh and placed his forehead against the steering wheel as if in pain. "They could have already gotten to her." He immediately straightened. "You keep calling the lodge and I'll keep trying Jackie and Gil's cell phones. Just get your ass to Colorado ASAP."

The Ferrari burned out of the garage in reverse and spun in a semi-circle. Once it cleared the garage, the Ferrari jetted onto the road and sped away from the beach house.

†

It was two o'clock in the morning Colorado time. The lodge was moderately dark in the peaceful countryside of vast nothingness. All the drunken commotion of the previous night was now a faded memory and only Beck, Pinto, and Kirk remained on the premises. Pinto stirred beneath the covers in her bed, being careful of her injured arm, and looked at the empty spot alongside her. She rolled onto her back and glanced at the bedside clock. She groaned while flipping onto her right side facing the window and nuzzled the pillow. Her eyes immediately opened. It seemed sleep wasn't on the night's agenda. She stared at the open window as a gentle breeze blew into the room.

It was cool that night, as were most Colorado Mountain nights. She listened to the sounds of wildlife rustling around, hoping it would lull her to sleep. The secluded countryside was blissfully quiet except for the sounds of nature. The bedroom door opened and Pinto instinctively turned in bed, cringing when she turned onto her injured shoulder with too much vigor. Beck quietly crossed the bedroom, saw she was awake, and frowned.

"I didn't mean to wake you," he remarked gently.

"You didn't," she replied. "I think we both have insomnia tonight."

Beck slipped out of his shirt and pants and joined her under the covers. He immediately turned on his side facing her, leaned on his elbow, and propped his head on his fist.

"It's been a rough week for all of us," he announced while staring into her eyes through the dim lighting from the open window. Her moderately bruised and scratched face was a grim reminder of the hell they'd been through just a few days earlier. "I think we should drive to town tomorrow."

She sighed with little enthusiasm. "I think I'd rather just stay here in bed with you."

Beck smiled more naturally for the first time and gently took her hand in his. He affectionately kissed her hand then caressed it warmly. "You never have to talk me into that," he teased then turned serious. "I'd like to get you a ring and make our engagement official."

"You're sweet, Beck," she cooed softly, "but that can wait. A ring isn't important."

"Maybe not," he replied, "but I'd like to get you one anyway. After all we've been through; it'd be nice to do something for us."

Pinto took up the space between them on the bed and slipped into his arms. He eagerly held her and groaned while rubbing his cheek to the top of her head.

"What I want," she announced in a timid voice, "is to crawl inside you and never come out."

She shivered slightly. Beck felt her tremble and immediately rubbed her shoulders and back in an attempt to warm her.

"I should probably close that window," he announced. "You're going to freeze to death."

"I'm not cold," she replied and held back her tears. "I just can't stop thinking about Jackie and Holden. I mean, we're them. I don't even know what to say to her about it. If I lost you, I'd go completely insane. I can't imagine what she's going through, and then I think about losing you--"

Pinto was nearly down to tears. Beck held her against him and nuzzled her head to his chest.

"Jackie's going to be fine because Holden's going to be fine," Beck insisted. "He's with Othello. He's safe. We're safe."

She pulled back just enough to meet his gaze and sniffed while fighting her tears. Without warning, she kissed him passionately allowing her hands to travel his body. Beck returned the kiss and gently rolled her onto her back, positioning himself on top of her.

†

Kirk entered the kitchen from the backstairs and without turning on the lights headed for the refrigerator. He had little reservation regarding parading around in his black boxer briefs, which clung to his excessively muscular body. Pinto's part-time residence at the lodge didn't sway his dress code regarding his late night strolls to the kitchen. He was proud of his body and didn't care who saw it or how much of it they saw. He removed a plate of leftover grilled chicken and devoured a leg while carrying the plate to the island counter. He cast himself upon one of the stools while tossing the cleaned leg bone onto the plate. He reached for another piece of chicken when the satellite phone on the counter chirped at him. He wiped his greasy fingers on a napkin and snatched the phone with little hesitation.

"Yeah," he gruffly remarked into the phone.

The faint sound of a helicopter in the distance caught his attention. He almost ignored the caller until he heard Sal's frantic plea.

"Kirk?" Sal gasped. "Thank God! Listen closely--"

"Sal?"

"Monroe and I were both attacked in our homes tonight," Sal nearly shouted into the phone. "They could be coming for you. Grab my daughter and Beck and head for the panic room!"

Kirk listened to the sound of the helicopter getting closer and became alert to the sound. "Christ, they're already here!"

He slammed the phone on the counter and ran from the kitchen. Kirk ran down the hall, across the dimly lit lobby, and approached the main stairs. He moved the ball at the end of the railing, revealing a large button. Kirk slammed his palm on the button. Steel panels fell over the windows and in front of the main entrance. Metal doors were heard slamming shut toward the back of the main lodge as well. The sound of crashing metal coming from every corner of the lodge was almost deafening.

Chapter Twelve

Beck held Pinto in his arms while both panted heavily after their passionate lovemaking. They heard the sound of a helicopter in the distance, disturbing the blissful sounds of nature. Before Beck could zero in on the echo, the sound of steel panels crashing down over the windows within the bedroom caused both to jump. They could hear the thunderous crash of panels closing within the entire lodge, nearly rattling the entire building. Pinto cried out with surprise and flew up in bed while clutching the sheets to her naked body.

"What the hell is that?" she cried out.

Beck leaped from the bed and immediately pulled on a pair of pants. "The lodge's primary security system," he cried out. "I heard a helicopter. It must be an emergency. Get dressed. You need to get into the panic room now!"

Pinto sprang from the bed and threw on her clothes from the day before. She barely had time to slip into her shoes before Beck tossed her a leather shoulder holster containing a semiautomatic. She caught the holster while letting out a surprised gasp. Beck slipped into his shoulder holster and removed an assault rifle from the cabinet in the closet. Both could now hear the helicopter not far from the lodge and getting closer. Beck ran to the door and motioned her out.

"Go, go, go!"

Pinto ran out the door while attempting to slip the shoulder holster over her injured shoulder. Beck flung the holster into place as she passed, causing her some discomfort, but they were in a hurry. They ran down the main stairs and looked around. Kirk was nowhere to be found, but they saw several weapons and ammunition setting on top of the front desk. Kirk thundered down the stairs behind them now wearing a pair of jeans and his combat boots with the shoelaces dangling free. He didn't take the time to put on a shirt, but he did take the time to stop by Zack's room. He leaped down the last four steps. Pinto stared at the strange, thick rifle he cradled in his arms while Beck attempted to hurry her to the panic room just beyond the stairs.

"What's that?" she gasped.

Kirk cocked the heavy piece of weaponry with conviction. It sounded like a shotgun's angry father. "Zack's grenade launcher," he announced.

Beck yanked Pinto toward a six-foot by three-foot mirror on the wall. He pulled it away from the wall to reveal a steel door. He struck a button alongside it and the door opened to expose a large, concrete bunker.

"Get inside," he ordered.

Pinto looked from Kirk to Beck with disorientation. "What's going on?"

"We'll sort out the details later," Beck informed her. "Get inside."

"We're being attacked," Kirk lashed out. "I intend to blow the motherfucker out of the sky."

Beck turned to Kirk as he approached the front door now encased with a large steel panel. He slid open a small panel, fondly referred to as a kill slot, and broke the glass just on the other side. The opening was large enough to poke the weapon through yet protect him from enemy fire.

"Before you go all Rambo on that helicopter," Beck called out, "make sure it's not Jackie or Gil first." He then looked at Pinto and seemed surprised to see her still standing there. "What are you doing? Get in the panic room."

"I'm afraid to leave you," she gasped.

"Don't worry about me," he insisted then indicated Kirk. "You heard Rambo. He's going to blow the motherfucker out of the sky. We've got this." He indicated the panic room while shooing her inside with his hands. "You get that." Beck shoved her inside the panic room and hit the button before she could protest. The door slammed shut. Beck closed the mirror and joined Kirk near the front door. He opened another kill slot and looked outside as well. The helicopter came into sight. Kirk looked through the scope on the rocket launcher. The helicopter dropped down allowing several men with assault rifles to jump out the sliding side door and onto the ground.

"Well, it's not Jackie," Kirk snarled and immediately pulled the trigger.

A grenade fired from the launcher and fell short of the helicopter. The grenade exploded and took a few men on the ground with it. The blast was enough to send the helicopter off course, leaving the pilot struggling to control the craft. The remaining men ran for the lodge.

"Six hostiles heading our way," Beck cried out and fired at the approaching men.

Two men went down while the others sought shelter near the porch. Automatic gunfire came from the side of the helicopter, striking the lodge. Neither man flinched, feeling secure behind their steel wall. Kirk tossed the grenade launcher aside, exchanging it for his assault rifle. They fired at the helicopter, but it was out of range for their weapons. Unfortunately, the machine gun bolted to the helicopter floor was bigger and had better range. The large caliber bullets couldn't pierce the steel plates over the doors and windows, but they easily went through the outside walls, striking furniture within the lobby.

"Holy fuck!" Kirk cried out and gave Beck a demanding look. "Who the hell did we piss off this time?"

Beck fired at a man running along the porch, but the tightness of the kill slot didn't allow much maneuverability.

"They're outside the lobby," Beck announced while closing his kill slot.

He ran across the lobby for another kill slot, hoping to get a better shot. A loud explosion rocked the lodge, throwing Beck across the room. Kirk took cover near the floor as part of the wall exploded inward. It was almost as if they knew how to penetrate the building. Beck rolled across the floor and took cover behind the stairs. Both fired at men attempting to enter through the large opening in the wall. The invaders fired back. Kirk flattened himself against the steel plate across the front door and exchanged his assault rifle for the grenade launcher.

Beck saw Kirk cock the massive weapon. He groaned softly with defeat, frowned, and gave Kirk the 'all clear' signal. Kirk stepped away from the door, aimed the grenade launcher at the massive opening in the wall, and waited for the men to spill into the lobby. He pulled the trigger. The grenade flew into the opening and exploded, rocking the entire lodge. As the debris cloud cleared, Kirk and Beck slowly poked their heads out and looked at the somewhat larger opening in the wall. The lobby was covered in dirt, debris, and body parts.

"Beck," they heard Pinto's shout over an intercom.

Beck hurried to the nearest intercom and pressed the talk button. "It's okay, babe," he insisted in a pleasant, calm tone. "Just stay put for now. We're fine. Okay? Just let us make sure it's clear."

Kirk and Beck carefully walked through the piles of debris and body parts on their way to the opening in the wall. They kept to the side and peered out the opening. The helicopter hovered just outside range of the grenade launcher. The gunner in the side door fired at them. The bullets tore through the wall nearly clipping both men. Beck and Kirk took cover behind steel plates covering the windows and exchanged looks.

"We need to take out that helicopter," Beck informed Kirk and immediately cocked his head. "Please tell me Zack has a rocket launcher hidden under his pillow."

"I'm sure he has one," Kirk announced, "but it's not here at the lodge."

"We have to get closer to the helicopter in order for that pussy grenade launcher to be effective," Beck remarked. "I need options."

"You sound like Ross," Kirk scoffed with annoyance. "I'm not the options guy. That's your job, remember?"

"Give me a minute," Beck muttered.

The gunner continued to fire at the lodge, causing both men to curse. They could hear the helicopter getting louder, but something sounded odd about it. From opposite steel plated windows, both opened kill slots and looked outside to where the helicopter still hovered. It sounded as if it were going faster, although it was still just hovering. Jackie's helicopter suddenly appeared and buzzed the tail end of the sniper helicopter. The enemy helicopter veered sharply and almost out of control causing the gunner to fall out the opening. He dangled by a cable attached to his harness. Just as the helicopter stabilized and the gunner started climbing his cable, Jackie's helicopter made another wild pass across their tail section. The crosswind was enough to send the enemy helicopter spiraling. Beck and Kirk now stood in the massive hole in the wall and stared at the cockfight happening in the sky. Beck looked at Kirk and slapped his shoulder.

"Go, go, go!"

Kirk bolted from the lobby, leaped off the porch, and ran into the front yard with the grenade launcher. Beck was only a few feet behind him and fired at the man dangling from the cable, striking him several times like a piñata. Jackie was about to take another pass when she saw Kirk with the grenade launcher aimed at the enemy helicopter. She suddenly veered away. Kirk pulled the trigger, launching a grenade directly into the aft-side opening. The helicopter exploded, raining flaming metal to the ground. Jackie's helicopter whizzed past. They gave her a thumbs-up, indicating it was safe for her to land.

Chapter Thirteen

It was a little after three o'clock in the morning Colorado time. A stock trailer pulled up to the moderately large, two-story barn on Ross's ranch. Bogart climbed out of the passenger seat of the pick-up truck and joined an elderly farmer, who had been driving. Bogart was a well-built man in his late twenties. He was 'hunky actor' handsome with flowing golden-brown hair and sideburns nearly a shade darker. Bogart and the elderly farmer approached the back of the stock trailer and unloaded Bogart's ill-gotten black horse. It wasn't as if he'd exactly stolen the horse. Actually, Bogart had stolen the horse from Giovanni's island resort. He didn't think anyone would miss one horse, and the horse, he happily named Othello, seemed miserable on the island anyway. The country was where a horse like Othello belonged. As they unloaded the horse, Ross's brother-in-law wearily appeared from the house and joined them. Othello let out a loud whinny. Other horses responded from within the barn.

"Keep it quiet, big fella," Bogart informed the horse. "You'll wake the entire house."

Liam approached and stopped before him. "Too late. We're already awake. Don't get many vehicles back here. Heard you coming a mile away."

"Sorry," Bogart replied.

"Everyone was worried about you," Liam announced while attempted a smile, but it was difficult after being awoken at three o'clock in the morning. "I heard you'd be stopping by after your heist."

Bogart groaned and shook his head. "I didn't steal the horse," he insisted. "I just sort of borrowed him. You know, like a foreign exchange program."

Liam folded his arms across his chest and chuckled softly. "Anything you say, Bogart. You can put him in the last stall for tonight. The other horses are in the barn for the night anyway. They're calling for a chance of thunderstorms."

"Might need one of those stalls for myself," Bogart remarked. He handed the older farmer some money and shook his hand. "Thanks, Dale."

The old man returned to his truck and drove away. Bogart led the horse into the barn with Liam tagging along. He secured the horse into the stall after they all had a chance to sing their greetings to one another.

"Naturally, you're welcome to crash here for a few nights," Liam remarked.

"Wouldn't be the first time I crashed on Ross's sofa," Bogart teased while grinning.

"Well, you may as well take his bed," Liam replied. "I don't suppose he'll mind."

"Ah," Bogart fumbled while making a face. "Ross and I aren't exactly tight, you know? I don't think he'd appreciate me sleeping in his bed while he's gone."

Liam stared at Bogart a moment with a strange look. Realization then crossed his face. "You hadn't talked to any of the guys since Columbia, have you?"

"No," Bogart replied. "My cell phone died before we reached Miami. I could've charged it on the train, but I seemed to have misplaced the charger." He then noted the strange look on Liam's face. "Something I should know?"

"Bogart," Liam announced gently. "Ross and Lee were killed in Rio."

Bogart's face lost all expression. He shifted several times but couldn't seem to get any words out. "What?" he finally gasped. "How?"

"They claim it was a gas leak at a restaurant in some little town, but the guys seem to think it was a hit," Liam replied now a little uncomfortable himself. "I'm letting Selena think it was an accident, so don't say anything in front of her."

"Uh, yeah, sure," Bogart replied while staring at the ground as he attempted to process the information. He then looked back at Liam while fighting to hold back his emotions. "How's Jackie? Is she okay?"

Liam drew a deep breath and gently ran his fingers through his hair. "I'm not going to lie," he announced. "That girl's been through hell and back. She seems to be holding it together, but I think it's only a matter of time before she explodes. I mean, can you blame her? First Zack and Ross then Holden--"

Bogart suddenly held his hand up in the air. "Whoa, wait," he nearly cried out. "What happened to Holden?"

"Oh, you did miss a lot," Liam responded. "Holden was ambushed during a raid. He was recovering in ICU and then he up and disappeared without a trace. They think he may be with a friend, but they haven't heard anything."

Bogart fidgeted and alternated running his fingers through his hair and pacing a small area of the barn aisle. "I need to call her," he gasped. "She's got to be devastated." He then looked at Liam. "You got a phone charger I can borrow?"

"You can use the house phone while yours charges," Liam offered and motioned him toward the house.

"I should probably check my messages," he remarked then frowned. "Jesus, she probably left a thousand messages. I should have been there."

"I don't think there was anything you could have done," Liam replied as they headed out of the barn. "Monroe stayed with her for a few days."

"No, you don't understand," Bogart remarked then waved him off. "It's complicated."

Once they entered the charming, refurbished country home, Bogart plugged his cell phone into the kitchen outlet to charge while Liam brought him some sheets and pillows for the sofa. Bogart immediately checked his missed messages and stared at what flashed across the screen with surprise.

"Son-of-a-bitch," he suddenly gasped, catching Liam's attention.

Liam looked over his shoulder. "What is it?"

"I have nearly one hundred missed calls since Saturday," he announced but the more recent ones caught his attention. "This is today! There has to be twenty missed calls from Sal and another ten from Beck."

"I told you they were worried about you," Liam reported with little reaction.

"No, you don't understand," Bogart gasped. "They're from the past three hours!"

"All of them?" Liam suddenly asked. "Why would they be calling you dozens of times in the middle of the night?"

Bogart pressed a button to listen to one of the messages while staring at Liam with a concerned look. "Wake Selena. We may have to get out of here."

Liam stared at him only a moment before running from the room. Bogart's phone indicated an incoming call from Sal. He immediately accepted the call.

"Sal," Bogart cried out into the phone while fidgeting. "What's happening?"

"Bogart, thank God," Sal announced from the other end. "Where are you? Never mind. Stay away from any of the safe houses. They came after us all."

"Who?"

"We don't know," Sal replied sounding distressed. "It's not safe. You need to go into hiding right now. The lodge has been compromised. My house. Monroe's place. Jackie's house. They've hit them all."

"Is everyone okay?"

"I'm told they are," Sal blurted out over the phone. "Our phones may not be secure. I can't say any more. We're still trying to contact Gil, but he's not answering his phone. He may still be in the air."

"Sal," Bogart announced with concern in his tone. "I've reached my destination. Are *they* safe here?"

There was a long pause. "Christ, Bogart," Sal muttered under his breath. "I never even considered--" There was another pause. "Get them out! Beck will have the satellite phone. It's the only secure line. Call when you get your hands on an untraceable phone. Go. Leave now!"

"We're leaving now," Bogart replied and disconnected the call. He unplugged his phone, tossed it to the floor, and stomped on it several times as Liam and Selena entered the kitchen. Both stared at him with horror. Bogart looked up and met their gazes. "We have to go now!"

"The horses," Selena cried out.

"We'll take the trailer," Bogart replied then looked at Liam. "You hook up the trailer and load the horses. Where are Ross's weapons?"

"The rifles are in the gun cabinet in the living room."

"No, I mean, where are Ross's *weapons*," Bogart demanded while cocking his head.

Liam shook his head not understanding the question.

"They're in his closet behind a secret panel," Selena quickly announced.

Liam stared at his daughter with surprise that she knew the answer to the strange question.

"Show me," Bogart announced to the teenager then looked at Liam. "The trailer. Go!"

Chapter Fourteen

Selena pushed Ross's dress shirts aside in his closet to reveal a secret panel that manually slid open. Behind the panel was a large, standing gun safe similar to the one in Jackie's house. Bogart stared at the digital keypad lock then looked at Selena with his mouth partway open and question in his eyes. The conman was good at a lot of things, but safe cracking wasn't one of them.

"I don't know the combination," she announced defensively, answering his silent question. "I'm not even supposed to know that's there."

Bogart crouched before the safe and stared at the keypad a long moment while gently scratching his brow as if it helped him think.

"I've got this," Bogart muttered more to himself as he studied the lock. "There's an emergency override key." He looked back at Selena. "Look for a key. Try his dresser. The nightstand drawer. A jewelry box."

Selena nodded and hurried back into the bedroom leaving Bogart to stare at the keypad lock. He hesitated then punched in six numbers. The safe beeped at him. Bogart sank into thought then shook his head.

"We don't have time for this," he muttered and was about to stand when Selena returned to the closet holding a framed photo. He eyed her with a curious look.

"I didn't find the key, but I found this," she announced and showed him the framed picture.

The picture was of the entire team posing on and around an old WWII military bomb roughly the size of a full-grown man. Although not part of the picture, there were six numbers written across the bomb. Bogart suddenly grinned and laughed.

"Ross, you sly bastard," he remarked then punched the numbers onto the keypad.

The safe buzzed and opened. Bogart indicated an empty duffel bag, which Selena immediately grabbed. He loaded several assault rifles and semiautomatic handguns with pre-loaded magazines then tossed them into the bag. He placed a handgun down the back of his pants while straightening then tossed an assault rifle over his shoulder. He looked at the young teenage girl.

"Anyone ever teach you to shoot?"

"Of course," she replied. "You've met my Uncle Ross, haven't you?"

Bogart handed her a semiautomatic pistol while giving her a serious look. "Only in an emergency. Safety's on. There isn't a bullet in the chamber, so you need to cock it first." He simulated the cocking action.

Selena stared at him a moment then nodded while accepting the gun. She placed it down the back of her pants then covered it with her shirt. Bogart grabbed the duffel bag.

"Let's see if your father has the horses loaded," Bogart announced.

✝

Bogart and Selena hurried across the area between the house and barn, which was well lit by the barn's vapor light. The horse trailer was hooked up but the horses weren't loaded inside. They didn't see Liam, but the inside barn light was on. Bogart dropped the bag of weapons into the back of the pick-up truck then hurried Selena toward the barn. Bogart suddenly stopped and pulled her alongside the outer door.

"Seem a little quiet to you?" Bogart whispered.

Selena eyed him and nodded. Bogart clutched the rifle and cast himself across the doorway while aiming the weapon into the barn. There was still no sign of Liam. The four horses snickered at him from their stalls. Bogart pressed his back against the doorframe and looked outside the barn. He motioned Selena inside. She hurried into the barn. Bogart quietly closed the large door and braced it shut. He kept his weapon leveled and again scanned the interior of the large barn.

"Bogart, where's my father?" she gasped softly.

"I don't know," he replied while looking around. "We can't exactly call for him." He cast a look at the frightened girl. "How well can you ride?"

"Pretty good," she replied then appeared curious. "Why?"

"Saddle three of the horses," he informed her. "Fast and quiet. I'll find your dad."

"I'm scared," she whispered.

"Me too," he replied. "Just concentrate on your assignment. Get those horses saddled and position them in the aisle in front of the door. Anyone comes through that door; you take off and don't stop. You ride for town."

She uncertainly nodded. Bogart hurried for the door, removed the brace, and looked outside. He slipped out of the barn, shutting the door behind him. Bogart kept close to the horse trailer, keeping his back against it, and watched for any intruders. The night was quiet and nothing seemed to move. The only sounds he heard were those of wildlife. He continued alongside the truck and paused before the passenger side door. He looked into the cab. Liam was nowhere to be found. Bogart cursed softly and headed toward the front of the truck. Liam suddenly sprang up in front of the truck. Bogart jumped with surprise and aimed the assault rifle at him. Liam held his hands in the air and stared at Bogart.

"Hey, whoa, it's just me," Liam cried out.

As Bogart relaxed, Liam lowered his arms. "What the hell?" Bogart demanded. "Where were you?"

"The radiator was leaking again," he replied and revealed some duct tape. "I needed to do a quick repair. We should hurry and get the horses loaded."

Bogart groaned softly then hurried him toward the barn. He opened the barn door and looked inside. He didn't see any horses in the aisle, and there was no sign of Selena. Liam and Bogart uncertainly looked around.

"Selena?" Liam called out in a loud whisper.

Selena peered over the top of one of the stalls and looked relieved. "Oh, Dad, it's you," she announced. "I thought you were the bad guys."

"I thought you were saddling the horses?" Bogart demanded with some hostility.

She opened the stall door and led the saddled horse from the stall. "One to go," Selena replied.

"Let's get them in the trailer," he father informed her, "while it's still quiet out there."

Liam took two horses, while Selena took her saddled horse. Bogart followed behind with his horse proudly wearing an old western saddle.

"You clean up nicely, Othello," Bogart informed the horse as they headed for the door.

Bogart watched as they easily loaded the first three horses. A jeep was seen at the top of the long driveway with its headlights off. Bogart motioned to Liam and Selena. Liam shut the trailer door and both ducked alongside the trailer closer to the barn. Bogart led Othello back into the barn and closed the door just enough to conceal himself. He turned off the lights before the people in the jeep would notice the barn lights. As the jeep continued its approach, Bogart signaled to Liam. He indicated he should start the truck and take off once Bogart got their attention. Liam hoisted Selena through the open truck window to avoid opening the door, which would reveal the interior light. The jeep was almost to the barn. Liam climbed in after her. She curled into a ball on the floor while Liam slouched in the seat. The jeep, still without its headlights, passed the truck with the horse trailer and stopped several feet from the house.

The large barn door quietly opened. Bogart suddenly raced across the yard on the large black horse and headed for the woods. The lights on the jeep popped on as the jeep raced after him. Liam waited until they were just out of sight before sitting up and started the truck. He put the truck in gear and raced down the driveway with the horse trailer in tow.

"What about Bogart?" Selena cried out.

"Have faith in him, honey," Liam proudly informed his daughter. "He's one of your uncle's men. He's a highly trained, skilled fighter. He'll be fine." Unfortunately, that description didn't technically apply to Bogart.

Bogart rode the horse at a full gallop in the moonlight toward the woods with the jeep racing behind him. Men fired at him with automatic weapons, exploding the ground not far from the horse's hooves.

"This is nuts!" Bogart looked back at the pursuing jeep, revealing panic on his face. "This is insane, Othello," he cried out in terror. "We're going to die! Faster! We're going to die!"

The jeep was gaining on them as the tree line rapidly approached. Bogart cried out while keeping low on the horse as they headed for the barely visible path in the dark woods. They raced onto the trail with the jeep's headlights upon them. The jeep suddenly skidded to a stop. Several rounds were fired then eventually ceased as Bogart vanished on the trail. The men couldn't follow him into the woods with the jeep and were unable to keep up with a running horse on foot. When Bogart was sure they weren't following him, he slowed the horse and patted his thick neck.

"Othello, I owe you one."

Chapter Fifteen

A little after five o'clock in the morning Virginia time, Gil and Darth departed the private plane at the remote airfield. Gil carried his duffel bag and headed for his rental car parked not far from the first hangar. He opened the door for Darth then collapsed into the driver's seat. It had been a long, exhausting day, despite having slept to nearly noon after their drunken night. He'd landed in three separate time zones and spent more hours in the air than he cared to count. He took a moment to sit in the driver's seat and reflect upon the last few days. He finally turned on his cell phone then looked at Darth.

"Should we stop for breakfast before heading home?" he asked the dog.

Darth licked his muzzle as if understanding the words and agreeing with them. Gil chuckled softly and scratched Darth's ears. His phone repeatedly dinged with missed messages, sounding like a choir. The strange amount of missed calls caught his attention. He looked at the times of the more recent calls along with their frequency and immediately became alarmed. There were calls from Beck, Monroe, Sal, and Jackie all in the last few hours while he was in the air after having dropped off Sal then Monroe. He didn't bother listening to any of the messages and immediately pressed 'call back' to Beck's last message. The phone was answered on the first ring.

"Beck?" he announced into the phone with concern in his voice.

"Whiskey Tango Foxtrot has gone dark," came Beck's urgent response. "We've been compromised. Meet at the rendezvous. Do you copy?"

"Yeah, I copy," Gil announced without further question.

"Beck out."

The phone went dead immediately following Beck's last words. Gil pulled the phone away from his ear and stared at it a moment with horror clearly on his face. He took the cell phone and smashed it on the shifter. He started the car and burned out in the private airfield parking lot. Darth immediately dropped to the seat as if anticipating some high-speed driving.

✝

The once charming ranch house nestled in the cozy, older neighborhood was engulfed in flames as it burned swiftly, lighting up the entire neighborhood. Gil's black rental car pulled up behind several fire trucks. A crowd of neighbors collected on the sidewalk and watched the firemen attempt to put out the blaze that was once Ellie's house. Gil slowly got out of the car and stared at the raging fire, which engulfed the tidy bushes and singed the weeping willow trees he and his wife planted when they first bought the house. Gil's body trembled as he stared blankly almost a minute. He finally snapped out of his daze and looked at the nearby ambulances. He didn't see Ellie anywhere. He approached one of the neighbors he'd never seen before and grabbed his arm with a little more vigor than he'd intended. The man in his bathrobe jumped with surprise and looked at Gil.

"What happened to the woman who lives there?" he announced to the man while almost choking on his words. "Is she okay?"

"We've been waiting," the man replied, "but they haven't pulled anyone out."

Gil stared at Ellie's partially burned car in the driveway not far from the garage, indicating she'd been home at the time of the blaze. Her shift at the hospital ended at midnight, and she was expecting him in the early morning, so it was only natural that she was home when the fire happened. Gil continued to stare at the blaze with his mouth hanging open while his heart ached heavily in his chest. He knew they wouldn't be pulling anyone out of the house alive. It was too late. He allowed his grief to consume him a moment and fought his tears. Beck's warning echoed in his mind. This was no accident. Whoever came after the team went after his ex-wife, possibly thinking he was with her. If not, they were sending him a message. The message was received. Gil's look hardened and his body stiffened. Sorrow was quickly replaced with rage and hatred. Gil jumped back into the car and drove away.

The rental car drove a little faster on the way back to the airfield. Gil attempted to mind his speed since being pulled over by the police wasn't advisable under the circumstances. He kept his eyes glued to the rearview mirror and noticed a dark colored, newer model car following from a distance with its headlights off. His jaw clenched at the sight of the car following him. They'd been waiting for him to show up at Ellie's house, even if he didn't know who *they* were. The people following him weren't in a hurry to catch him, which meant they intended to ambush him at the airfield. That suited Gil just fine. He had a few things he'd like to discuss with them as well. Gil reached into the back seat and unzipped his duffel bag. He removed a rather nasty looking double-barrel, pump action shotgun, which held thirteen shells. One of the assault rifles would be more efficient, but Gil wasn't looking for efficiency; he was looking to make a mess.

†

The dark car followed Gil's rental car through the gates into the private airfield while maintaining its distance. Gil passed an unfamiliar parked car that wasn't there when he left just half an hour ago. Instead of parking the car alongside the hangar, he drove through the open hangar doors into the darkened building. His headlights immediately went out. The dark sedan that had been following him stopped momentarily then crept closer to the hangar while two men from the second car got out. They hurried toward the hangar with assault rifles in their hands and joined the other two men from the first car.

The first two men flattened themselves against the door near the opening then motioned for the second pair of men. The second team moved in with their assault rifles ready for action and slipped inside the dark hangar, immediately switching on lights affixed to their weapons. As they disappeared into the dark opening, there was a brief moment of silence. The sound of shotgun blasts and assault rifle fire echoed from the hangar, resembling a shooting gallery. The first team charged in after the others. More rifle fire and shotgun blasts echoed through the metal building.

A few minutes passed in complete silence and without signs of life. Gil left the hangar with his shotgun slung over his shoulder and his bag in his hand while showing no emotion. Darth trotted alongside him as they headed for the plane. As Gil's private plane taxied away from the hangar and headed for the runway, the hangar suddenly exploded into a fiery inferno.

Chapter Sixteen

The abandoned airfield in Virginia was home to a large aircraft boneyard. Considered an eyesore, the boneyard was located in a secluded area of mostly junk land far from anywhere. Barely considered an airfield and its seclusion made it the perfect rendezvous for the team. They could land their planes or helicopters undetected by locals, and even if a neighboring community saw a plane going overhead, they knew it was possibly being retired to the boneyard. Gil arrived an hour after Sal and Monroe, who had been there since six o'clock that Thursday morning. Both men had secured private transport to a predetermined meeting point in Virginia and then drove together to the rendezvous. They were lightly arguing over the flat tire on their borrowed car, which conveniently came without a spare, when Gil arrived in his private plane.

Even though Gil got a later start than the others did, he was closer to the rendezvous since he was already in Virginia. Sal and Monroe greeted him, but he wasn't in the mood to talk. It seemed best to let him go until he was ready to open up. Neither had a clue what had happened at his wife's house, and he was unwilling to share the painful event. Gil sat on an old plane bench in the middle of the mess and stared at nothing in particular. Darth lay on the bench with him while resting his head on his lap. Gil subconsciously petted the dog but didn't say a word.

The three remained waiting at the aircraft boneyard for several hours before receiving word on the rest of the team. Monroe leaned against an old, rotting twisted piece of metal that was formally a plane and watched Gil in silence. Sal approached Monroe and held up his newly acquired burner phone.

"The guys from the lodge will be here in an hour," Sal informed him. "Bogart dropped Ross's family off at some ranch outside of Colorado Springs. He didn't elaborate, but I think he might mean those girls with the horses."

"The wild horse girls," Monroe remarked. "That's Holden's boss's daughter."

"Oh, I remember them now," Sal replied with a spark of interest. "That's the mission where you nearly destroyed my hotel and casino."

"Don't exaggerate," Monroe remarked with a dreary sigh. "We tore that place down to the ground."

"I was being polite," Sal added. "Anyway, he hopped a train and won't be here until late afternoon Saturday."

"The day after tomorrow? That's over two days away. We'll need to pull out the emergency rations," Monroe informed Sal. "We have MREs, bottled water, weapons, and additional provisions stockpiled for such an occasion."

"I'm glad you've come prepared," Sal replied and even managed a smile.

"Don't get too excited," Monroe remarked with limited enthusiasm. "They've been here a few years."

"Anyone know who they were?" Gil finally asked without looking up.

They hadn't realized he'd even been paying attention to their conversation.

"I'm afraid I shot first and skipped the Q and A portion of the evening," Sal replied.

"Same here," Monroe muttered then eyed Gil. "I'm guessing you didn't have a long conversation with them either."

Gil didn't bother looking up. "They torched Ellie's house," he muttered somewhat sedate. "The neighbors said they didn't pull anyone from the house."

Monroe's expression shattered by the news of Gil's ex-wife. "Ellie?" he gasped then fought his tears as he looked away. "Jesus, Gil. I'm so sorry."

"Ellie?" Sal asked only loud enough for Monroe to hear. "You mean his--?"

Monroe nodded then looked at Gil. "We'll find out who's behind this, Gil," he announced firmly. "We'll find them and make them pay one drop of blood at a time."

Gil didn't respond or bother looking up. Monroe and Sal exchanged looks of shared concern.

"That's not good," Monroe muttered to Sal. "Gil's one of our most level-headed guys. The thought of him losing control is a little scary."

"Behind every level-headed man is a good woman," Sal remarked then raised his brows. "Take away that good woman, and you've got a man with nothing to lose."

Monroe considered the comment.

"Honestly, Monroe," Sal announced and stared at him with a concerned look. "If I were you, I'd keep a close eye on Jackie. She may look like she's holding it together, but that's a woman on the edge."

"I'm not worried about Jackie," Monroe responded without hesitation. "Jackie's always held her shit together."

Sal slowly shook his head in disagreement. "You think you know that woman?" he asked with a curious look. "She's a volcano waiting to erupt. Trust me, Monroe. When she goes, she's taking out everything in her path."

"Be realistic," Monroe scoffed. "You make her out to sound like Zack."

"Exactly my point."

Monroe stared at Sal and seemed to consider the comment a brief moment then shook it off. Sal shrugged conceding for the sake of ending the conversation.

✝

A little after eleven o'clock that morning, an unfamiliar plane circled the aircraft boneyard. All three looked up. They knew it had to be Jackie, but none could figure out where she'd gotten that sort of plane on short notice. The plane landed with a little less grace than they'd come to expect from Jackie's piloting skills. The landing was almost aggressive and came close to clipping Gil's plane parked off to the side. The plane door opened, lowering into steps. Monroe, Gil, and Sal approached cautiously with their weapons securely in their hands just in case they were mistaken about Jackie

79

piloting the plane. Beck and Pinto hurried off the plane while looking back and shaking their heads.

"I've had better crash landings," Beck scoffed while hurrying Pinto away from the plane.

Kirk followed them down the steps while showing little emotion. "I don't know what you're complaining about," he scoffed. "The girl's just blowing off steam."

Jackie was last to disembark the plane. Her look hadn't softened any, and there was something oddly unsettling about her demeanor.

"I'm going on twenty-four hours without sleep," she snapped while glaring at Beck. "If you've got a problem with the way I fly, choose another airline."

Monroe stared at Jackie with surprise. Sal eyed Monroe and gave him a knowing look. Sal then joined his daughter and gave her a long, loving embrace. Pinto eagerly returned the hug, happy to see her father alive and well.

Kirk walked past Monroe and noted his odd expression. "Jackie's in a bad mood," Kirk casually informed him.

Monroe drew a deep breath then approached Jackie and lent a sympathetic smile. "Are you okay?"

She suddenly glared at him as if she were about to take off his head for even asking. "Of course I'm okay," she lashed out with a venomous look in her eyes. "Five men tried to kill me in my own home last night. I'm fucking fantastic!"

Monroe took a step back and watched Jackie storm away.

Chapter Seventeen

Later that afternoon, Beck and Monroe unsealed a vault hidden underground beneath an old plane wing. The vault contained their stored emergency provisions. They left the ammo and weapons, being they'd brought enough with them after the attack. Jackie had several weapons in her duffel bag, and the guys from the lodge brought another duffel bag loaded with weapons and ammo, including the grenade launcher. Beck attempted to talk Kirk out of bringing it, but Kirk was tired of being told not to bring things then always wishing he'd brought them. Jackie passed on MREs. She wasn't hungry to begin with, and the thought of pre-packaged, flavorless military rations turned her stomach. Gil wasn't hungry either and refused to socialize with the team. Darth turned his nose up to the MREs as well. Although the water was still good, the bottle of wine was more of a hit than the preserved water.

Jackie made use of the large, stocked first aid kit to clean the massive scrapes on her knuckles. It was a grim reminder of the brutal assault she'd put on the man who tried to kill her. She didn't like the images flashing through her head. She didn't like her uncontrolled rage. Unfortunately, if she had to do it again, she knew the assault would be one hundred times more brutal. She'd overheard the guys discussing what happened to Gil's ex-wife and some part of her compassion returned. She approached Gil where he now leaned against an old airplane several yards away from the rest of the team. He didn't bother making eye contact with her. She didn't speak to him. Instead, she leaned against the plane a few feet from him and stared where he stared in silence.

Gil finally drew a deep breath and spoke in a moderately sedate tone without looking at her. "I tore apart four men with a shotgun," he remarked, matter-of-fact. "Then I torched their bodies and the hangar."

"I beat a man to death with my bare hands," she countered with little emotion. "Then I sent pictures of his dead body to everyone on the contact list in his cell phone."

Gil uncertainly turned his head and looked at her, a little surprised by her confession. She cast a quick glance at him then resumed staring straight ahead. He looked away as well. They were operating on the same level of hostility, which was moderately frightening.

"They killed Ellie," he scoffed with some emotion finally surfacing. "Why would they do that? We've been divorced a while now. It's as if they knew."

"There are too many coincidences," she replied and fidgeted slightly. "Everything that happened on Giovanni's island? Holden? Ross? And now us?" She straightened and inhaled deeply while drifting into her own world. She quickly snapped back into reality. "Beck thinks it could be related. What happened to us on the island may have just been the beginning."

"We never took out the man behind the hit on us," Gil remarked while glancing at her. "We foolishly assumed it was over when we ended that mess on the island."

She cast a look at him. "Do you remember what Wade said to me?"

Gil studied her a moment and appeared to be reliving that moment in his mind. "Not his exact words. I know he assumed you had more to live for than me. That's why if it's related, going after Ellie makes no sense."

"He said something like, 'she thinks she has more to live for than you'," Jackie announced and eyed Gil while raising a brow. "She *thinks*." She turned to face him while resting her elbow on the plane wing. "Holden was already ambushed by that time. 'She *thinks* she has more to live for'." They exchanged stares. "What if Wade knew about the ambush? What if he knew Holden had been attacked?"

"Then what happened to Ross and Holden was related to what happened to us on the island," Gil remarked. "And what happened to us tonight is just the concluding chapter. That means we were all on the same hit list from the beginning."

"I think so."

"In those final moments, Beck asked them who ordered the hit on us while on the island," Gil reminded her. "Do you remember the response?"

"You'd be surprised," she quoted the response.

"If it was someone from our past, I get why they went after you on the island," Gil informed her. "You were in their way along with the rest of us. You're the Commander's daughter. I get that. What I don't get is Holden."

"Why's that?"

"If they intended to kill you on the island, why worry about Holden? You wouldn't suffer from his death because you'd be dead already," Gil informed her then raised a brow. "It feels personal. I don't think you were an afterthought or merely in the way. You were marked the same as we were."

"Which would mean it's someone from the team's recent past," Jackie remarked and appeared curious. "Someone you've run into since I've been a part of the team."

"Exactly."

"That narrows it down," Jackie muttered.

"Unfortunately, anyone we've come across with that long of a reach is no longer alive."

"Relatives seeking revenge?" Jackie suggested.

Gil shook his head while remaining deep in thought. "No, Beck runs checks on our prominent foes after our assignments. We keep close tabs on that sort of thing."

"Might be worth another look," she remarked and eyed Gil. "Don't you think?"

"We've got time to kill," he replied with a sigh. "Once we reach civilization, he can hack into the secured server and run some checks."

"Maybe he can find some news stories about our recent attacks," Jackie suggested. "If the police have identified some of the bodies we left behind, that might give us some leads. We can follow their known associate's list and trace them back to a common denominator."

"Unfortunately, we can't do anything from here," Gil replied with a defeated sigh. "We need some form of internet."

Jackie stared off into the distance with a strange look. "Or maybe just something like that--"

Gil glanced in the direction she stared. In the distance, they could see a tall tower with a satellite dish. It was several miles away but within walking distance. He patted Jackie on the shoulder and grinned.

"Yes, exactly like that."

✝

Beck defiantly shook his head while glaring at Gil. "No, that's not a good idea," he informed him. "That tower is at least three miles away. Monroe's stolen car has a flat tire, which means I'd have to walk. If something happens, I won't make it back in time."

"We're safe here," Gil insisted with renewed enthusiasm. "We've got nothing but time for two days until Bogart reaches us. In forty-eight hours, we can narrow down our suspect list and maybe figure out who put the hit on us." His eyes then narrowed. "And who killed Ellie."

Beck appeared uncomfortable by the comment about Gil's murdered ex-wife and ran his fingers through his hair while considering their options.

"We already know it's someone who came into contact with the guys from Giovanni's island," Jackie added. "If we can just get a few names of the guys who attacked us last night, we can start comparing their known associates."

"And that takes time," Beck insisted while meeting her gaze. "Even with my fancy software, that could take hours."

"At least we'd know," Kirk remarked from behind them while folding his muscular arms across his broad chest. His look was menacing. "Once we figure out who's behind the hit on us, we can take the fucker out once and for all."

Beck drew a deep breath and glanced at the eyes staring at him demanding action. "Fine, I'll hike up to the tower and patch in, but we need to have a backup plan in the event something happens while I'm gone."

"We've got two pilots and two planes," Gil announced. "If something happens, Jackie takes the others to safety. I'm with you. I'll be your EVAC."

"I'm going with you to the tower," Kirk insisted, allowing no room for argument. "You need someone to watch your ass while you play with your toys. Gil can stay here in the event of an evacuation."

"There," Gil boldly announced while staring at Beck. "We have our backup plan."

Beck eyed Jackie with a stern look and immediately raised his brows. "You'll take the others to safety?" he demanded. "No arguments; no excuses? We don't deviate from the plan."

"I'll agree to that," Jackie replied without hesitation. "If something happens, I promise to evacuate the others and let Gil handle things here."

Beck stared at her a moment and seemed a little reluctant then sighed. "Fine," he replied, giving in. "Let's do this."

Unfortunately, Beck was so concerned with Jackie's ability to follow his orders for once; he'd forgotten about the wild card still in play.

"You expect me to leave without you?" Pinto suddenly blurted out with a look of horror on her face, surprising them with her outburst.

Beck was caught off guard. He looked at Pinto and the expression on her face. Sal immediately cringed and attempted to silence her. She brushed off her father as her hostility increased. Her look was now demanding.

"It's just a contingency plan, babe," he informed her and fumbled for something to say that would reassure her. "Nothing's going to happen." He then hesitated, drew a deep breath, and stood firm. "But if something does happen, you leave with Jackie and the others."

"I'm not good with that," she suddenly snapped back.

Although it wasn't exactly mature, Monroe and Kirk were a little humored by Pinto's crushing take-down of Beck's authority. It was one thing being in charge of a team. It was different when it came down to one's girlfriend. Beck knew all eyes were on him, and he had to say something.

"It doesn't matter whether you like it or not," Beck insisted in a firm tone. "That's the contingency plan. We don't deviate from that plan. Everyone does what they're supposed to do so no one gets killed."

Sal placed his arm around Pinto and gently led her away from the group. She wasn't happy with Beck's comment, but she was willing to let it go.

Beck groaned softly and fidgeted, feeling bad having been curt with his girlfriend, especially when she was only concerned about his safety, but they needed to play by their rulebook in order to survive. Pinto would eventually get over it.

"I need to get my laptop and a few things," Beck informed Kirk. "You get what you need, and I'll meet you back here in ten minutes."

Kirk nodded, and both men went their separate ways. Jackie glanced at Monroe, who seemed to have a permanent frown on his face.

"You don't like the plan?" Jackie asked.

"No, it makes sense," Monroe replied then sighed. "I'm sure we're safe here, but I just have this nagging feeling we've overlooked something. The guy who put the hit on us seems to know us pretty well, and that bothers me."

"That's why we have to find out who it is and stop him," Jackie replied.

Monroe studied her a moment then gently placed his hand on her shoulder. "We're all pretty stressed out, Jackie," he announced while staring into her eyes. "Just promise me you'll keep your head. If you let your emotions get the better of you--"

"I'm fine, Monroe," she replied a little too quickly. "I'll admit; I went a little insane back at my house, but I'm better now. You don't need to worry."

He nodded then pulled her against him, hugging her. Jackie half-heartedly returned the embrace, which almost confirmed she wasn't fine and there *was* reason to be concerned.

Chapter Eighteen

As the sun set over the aircraft boneyard, the weary refugees attempted to amuse themselves with a deck of cards they'd found in the emergency vault. Beck and Kirk were still at the tower attempting to gain intel on the person behind the hit on them. The walk alone would take nearly an hour, and there was no telling how long it'd take to find information if any. That they still hadn't returned wasn't too surprising. No one expected them back before morning. Monroe and Gil happily taught Pinto how to play poker, so they could all enjoy the game since there was little else to do. Jackie was mysterious absent longer than a mere bathroom break, but no one seemed to notice.

Sal suddenly seemed concerned as he looked around the clearing and past the planes. "Where's Jackie?" he finally asked the guys.

Neither seemed too concerned. "Visiting an old friend," Monroe remarked.

Sal stared at him with a bewildered look while cocking his head to the side. "Excuse me?"

Gil tossed his cards down, disgusted with his hand, then eyed Sal and offered a tiny smile. "Old Marge."

"I'm afraid I'm still lost," Sal informed them. "Can you speak English?"

"Old Marge was the first plane Jackie had ever flown," Monroe casually informed Sal. "She crashed the old girl the day her father died. What was left of 'Old Marge' was laid to rest here." He nodded across the boneyard. "Somewhere on the other side of this mess. She hadn't been here since we had the plane's remains transported here. I wouldn't doubt she's sitting outside the old girl reminiscing."

"That must be where Darth went." He then eyed Monroe with a slightly concerned look on his face. "You don't think she'd go inside, do you?" Gil suddenly asked.

"No, absolutely not," Monroe replied.

Pinto followed the conversation and appeared curious. "Why not?"

There was a strange silence as both men fidgeted. Gil drew a deep breath and straightened. "Her father died in the crash," he replied. "There was, uh, quite a bit of blood."

"She wouldn't want to be reminded of that. It's not something she'd care to see again," Monroe added. "She'd never go inside."

✝

Jackie sat on the ground several feet before the old, four-passenger, prop plane. The elegant name painted on the side read, 'Old Marge'. The wheels and one wing had been torn off in the crash. The underbelly was severely scraped, and burn marks were visible beyond the seams of the engine compartment. The side door was missing, as rescuers tore it off to get her out. She could still see some blood resembling a handprint on the inside windshield on the passenger side of the craft. She relived the day her father died over and over while she sat staring at the destroyed plane. She wanted to remember the good times she had flying 'Old Marge', but she couldn't get past the single bad memory.

The boneyard was becoming dark as the sun set in the distance. The rows of crashed and retired planes cast creepy shadows throughout the area. She knew she should join the others, but she couldn't convince herself to leave. She somehow felt closer to her father while sitting in front of 'Old Marge'. She considered going inside the plane but thought better of it. While she sat there, she suddenly had a strange feeling, and a chill swept over her. She glanced around, carefully inspecting the nearby shadows. Jackie didn't

88

understand it, but she felt as if she were being watched. Was it just a spiritual thing? Somehow, her father was watching over her at that moment? No, she didn't buy that.

She moved onto her knees while casing the area. Every nerve in her body suddenly went into defensive mode. She was almost certain there was someone out there. Jackie was about to move to her feet when she felt a sudden and painful sting against her neck. She gasped and slapped her neck. When she pulled her hand away, she saw a small dart between her fingers. Her eyes suddenly widened. She attempted to scream a warning to the others, but her head was already spinning. Before she could even contemplate the dizzy feeling, everything went dark.

Jackie felt warmth against her otherwise cold body. She was almost certain someone was carrying her, but she couldn't open her eyes or force herself to wake. She heard an annoying ringing in her ears. Despite her senses betraying her, she could smell the person carrying her. It was a musty smell with a trace of gunpowder. She was transported back to a time when her father would return home from missions with his team. She could smell her father. The scent was a strange mix of sweat, traces of gunpowder, and ocean mist that seemed to attach itself to all his clothes. For a brief moment, she imagined her father holding her. She slipped back into reality as her senses started returning. She suddenly felt cold yet smelled stale, musty air.

She opened her eyes to total darkness and the feeling of something covering her. Jackie then realized she couldn't open her mouth or move her hands and feet. She felt the stickiness of the duct tape over her mouth. She panicked with the realization that she was tied and confined to some sort of burlap sack. Jackie irrationally fought her bindings a moment then collected her emotions and drew a deep breath. With her bound hands, she managed to remove the duct tape from her mouth then bit at the tape around her wrists with her teeth. It took a certain skill set to pull apart duct tape successfully with one's teeth, but her father and his team often played the 'escape game' with her. She'd willingly allow them to tie her or lock her in places, and they'd give her fifteen minutes to free herself. If unsuccessful, they'd tell her what to do and give her another fifteen minutes.

Once her wrists were free, she slipped her hand to her ankles and freed them. She wasn't sure where she was or what to expect once she escaped the sack she was contained within, but she knew she wanted her feet free to defend herself. She didn't hear anything around her and finally managed to open the zipper of the bag from the inside. Once it was started, it easily opened. Jackie aggressively tossed herself out of the bag, rolling into a crouched position, and looked around. She was still within the aircraft boneyard but far from 'Old Marge' and the guys. There was no one around to surprise attack her, which was interesting. She slipped away from the exceedingly large duffel bag, where she had been placed, and took another moment to assess the area. She then hurried back to where she had left the team with the planes.

Monroe, Gil, Sal, and Pinto were exactly where she'd left them in the clearing by the planes, although Darth was nowhere to be found. They continued to play cards, completely unaware of what had happened to her. Jackie heard movement, however faint, from nearby. She ran from the shadows screaming her warning before whoever attacked her could take her down and silence her.

"Everyone down," she screamed while running for them in the clearing.

Sal tackled his daughter to the ground while Monroe and Gil grabbed their weapons as they threw themselves down. Gil rolled several times with his assault rifle then sprang into a crouched position behind a strategically placed plane door. Jackie grabbed her assault rifle and dived behind a large, rusted engine. Sal hurried Pinto toward Jackie while keeping low to the ground. Monroe crawled on his belly behind the old plane bench seat. They waited a moment in silence, but nothing happened. They then heard a clunk from one of their planes. It sounded as if someone had been startled by Jackie's sudden appearance.

"The planes," Jackie cried out a warning. "Someone's after the planes!"

Monroe and Gil kept low to the ground and ran for both planes. Jackie motioned for Sal and Pinto to stay down and joined Gil near the first plane, where she was almost certain she heard the sound. They saw someone move within the shadows. Just that quickly, they'd lost sight of him. Darth seemed to appear out of nowhere and ran across the clearing, disappearing into the shadows, possibly catching the intruder's scent. Monroe closed in, prepared to fire at the first person he saw. The familiar pop of a gun containing a silencer was heard as it parted the air while firing. Monroe took two shots to the chest and flew to the ground. Gil fired randomly in the general direction of the nearly silent gunfire. He listened for Darth to alert them of the intruder's position, but the dog was unusually silent and nowhere to be found. When he looked alongside him, Jackie was gone as well.

The shooter slipped unnoticed past the plane and through the darkness. Jackie leaped off the plane wing and rode the man down to the ground. Both rolled several times as they flew apart. Jackie sprang back to her feet like a cat and immediately kicked the standing man. He stumbled back a step. She went for the return kick. He ducked and threw a punch she barely saw in the darkness. She immediately blocked his punch and kicked him in the side. He blocked the next kick that followed, knocking them both to the ground. The plane lights suddenly came on, lighting the entire area. Jackie rolled into a crouching position facing her attacker, who was now crouched a few feet away from her. To her surprise and horror, she stared at Zack. He showed no expression as both slowly straightened, facing each other.

"Zack," she gasped as her heart pounded and her head felt light.

She only let her guard down a moment when Zack kicked her in the thigh, startling her. He grabbed her arm and twisted it behind her back while spinning behind her. She felt the barrel of a silencer pressed against her temple as Gil stepped into the light with his assault rifle aimed. Judging by the harsh look on Gil's face, he had no idea who stood behind her.

"Drop it," Gil cried out.

Zack remained positioned behind Jackie, keeping every inch of his vulnerable body concealed behind hers.

"Gil," Jackie gasped but was uncertain how to finish the outburst.

Don't shoot; it's Zack? He just shot Monroe! He attacked her and stuffed her in a bag. He was tampering with their planes! She was suddenly torn. Had she really seen correctly? Was it really Zack or was she just hallucinating from whatever drugs she'd been injected with?

"Gil, wait!"

Gil couldn't take the shot anyway, but he didn't ease his finger on the trigger. She could hear someone thumping around within the plane. It had to be Sal who turned on the plane lights.

"Listen very carefully, princess," Zack whispered in her ear in a low, threatening tone. "Cross my path again, and you'll go down like 'Old Marge'."

The sound of a gun cocking caused Jackie to twitch. Zack's grip on her arm behind her back tightened to the sound. Jackie, Gil, and Zack darted looks just beneath the plane. Jackie held back her startled gasp when she saw Mac crouched beneath the plane, partially hidden behind the wheel with something resembling a shotgun aimed at them.

"Zack," Mac warned in a low, threatening tone. "Put the gun down!"

He repositioned Jackie to keep Mac from getting a shot at him. "We're going to take a little walk," Zack announced softly into Jackie's ear. "No sudden movements."

He took a step back forcing her to back up with him. A small part of Jackie wanted to go along. She wanted answers. She had questions. Another part of her wanted to break her best friend in two after seeing him gun down Monroe.

"Zack, I'm warning you," Mac cried out. "Not another step!"

Zack suddenly released Jackie and dropped something to the ground. A small round disk expelled thick smoke. Jackie immediately coughed and considered which direction to run. Before she could make the call, Zack cast her forward, keeping her between him and Gil then turned and fired at Mac. Mac pulled the trigger of the PHaSR rifle. A laser light flashed brightening the entire area. Jackie was already on the ground when she saw the flash. It was worse than light from a thousand cameras going off in her face. She could only imagine what the effects were to someone standing directly in its path. As Mac lowered the weapon, all three realized Zack was already gone.

"Son-of-a-bitch," Mac cried out and ran in the direction Zack had most likely gone.

Gil ran for Jackie and pulled her to her feet. He hurried her away from the general area while keeping watch for any signs of Zack.

"Did I hear her correctly?" he suddenly demanded while staring at her.

"Yeah, Gil," Jackie gasped while holding her pounding chest. "It was Zack." Concern swept over her as reality returned. "Monroe!"

She pushed past Gil and ran toward the front of the plane. As they approached the clearing, Pinto was kneeling on the ground alongside Monroe who gingerly rubbed his chest. Jackie then saw he had his shirt open to reveal the bulletproof vest. She sighed with relief and helped him to his feet.

"You were wearing?" she suddenly demanded.

"Of course I was," Monroe muttered with some irritation from the sting of the shots to the vest. "I always wear a vest after someone tries to bump me off. Don't you?"

Gil helped Pinto to her feet as Sal ran toward them from the lit plane with Darth on his heels.

"I don't know," Jackie huffed in response. "Every time someone tries to bump me off, I always seem to be running for my life."

"Did you kill the bastard?" Monroe demanded.

"No," Jackie replied while frowning and almost choked on her words. "It was Zack."

Monroe stared at her with a look of disbelief. "Zack?" he suddenly gasped. "Zack's alive?" He then reconsidered the question and turned hostile. "Zack shot me?"

"It's not how it seems," Jackie insisted and shook her head with disbelief. "It can't be. He's either lost his mind or someone's forcing him to hunt us."

"Oh boy," Sal moaned softly while looking away.

He received several looks.

"What?" Gil suddenly demanded.

"You said it had to be someone close; someone who knew you intimately in order to come after you like that," Sal remarked while exchanging looks with the team. "Who knows your team better than Zack?"

"No, it can't be," Jackie remarked with concern. "He wouldn't. Besides, Holden and Ross were attacked while Zack was on the island with us."

"The two may not be related," Sal warned her.

"We need to warn Beck and Kirk," Gil announced. "You guys need to take off. It's not safe here."

"What about Bogart?" Jackie asked with surprise. "We can't just leave without him."

"We won't," Gil informed her. "I'll pick up the guys at the tower and then we'll arrange to meet Bogart at the train station Saturday afternoon."

"We need a rendezvous where we can land planes," Monroe informed them. "Someplace no one will ever think to look for us, even if it's just for a few days."

"A friend of a friend has a ton of land about thirty minutes from here by plane," Sal informed them. "I don't know the guy that well, but if we can land on the back hundred acres, I doubt anyone will know we're there. We'd be completely roughing it without any food or water, but there is a cabin near a stream."

"Perfect," Monroe reported. "We can pack the provisions from the vault and stay there a few days. Hopefully, by then we'll have some answers."

"Or until we come up with a better plan," Gil remarked. "Give me the coordinates, and I'll meet you there after we nab Bogart at the train station Saturday afternoon."

"You can't hike to that tower in the dark," Jackie insisted. "You don't know if Zack is still out there. Obviously, Darth isn't of any use against him. That's why he never barked a warning. He knew it was Zack."

"I wasn't planning on hiking," Gil replied matter-of-fact while raising a brow. "I intended to taxi most of the way." He indicated the plane. "I'm sure Beck and Kirk will hear me coming and meet me halfway."

Jackie frowned at the idea.

He noticed the look he received. "I'll be fine," Gil informed her then eyed his plane. "We'd better do a quick engine inspection on both planes. No telling what trouble Zack was getting into before we caught him."

"Sal and I will stand guard," Monroe informed them.

"Me too," Pinto announced and removed the semiautomatic from her shoulder holster.

Chapter Nineteen

The satellite tower was almost three miles from the aircraft boneyard. It was a little after sunset. There was still some light, but the area would soon be only visible by moonlight. Beck sat on a large rock at the base of the tower with assorted cables plugged into his laptop computer. He accessed files and downloaded anything of interest, so he'd be able to look at it later at his leisure. Kirk paced the area only a few feet away from where Beck worked. He had his assault rifle slung over his shoulder but kept his semiautomatic in his hand. The sounds of the night were nearly deafening. Every cricket in a three-mile radius was putting on a concert for the men by the tower.

"How much longer?" Kirk finally asked.

"Someplace you need to be?" Beck asked without looking up from his laptop.

"I know where I'd like to be," Kirk scoffed. "Anywhere but here and with anyone but you. I'd prefer a redhead, but at this point, any woman with a pulse will do."

"I'm sure," Beck remarked.

"I hate this radio silence bullshit," Kirk informed him while pacing and watching the surrounding area, paying particular attention to the distant boneyard. "I thought I saw a flash of light from the boneyard, and I'd like to know what it was."

"Probably Monroe trying to light a fire," Beck remarked then grinned at Monroe's expense. "Wouldn't doubt he used gasoline as an accelerant. The grill master will probably be missing both eyebrows when we return."

Kirk groaned and threw his head back with annoyance. "Why'd you have to say that?" he demanded. "Now I'm thinking about steak."

"Must be quite the battle royale," Beck teased. "Kirk's stomach versus his dick."

"Just because you finally have a sex life, that doesn't mean you get to make fun of my little dry spell," Kirk remarked. "Your dry spell lasted longer than our last tour of duty."

"No need to get personal," Beck casually replied. "Just passing the time."

"Are you finding anything useful?" Kirk demanded, unable to mask his edginess.

"Coming up with a lot of interesting things in the news. Holden's boss reported a break-in at Jackie's house," Beck informed him and snorted a soft laugh. "Apparently, five burglars were apprehended."

"Apprehended? Is that the new term for mutilated beyond recognition?" Kirk remarked with a curious look. He then sighed. "Always nice having the feds on our side."

"And Chicago police have not yet identified two men who broke into the home of Salvatore Romano last night," Beck continued to read from the news feed he'd found. "According to Romano's housekeeper, two unidentified intruders broke into the mansion of millionaire businessman Salvatore Romano. The two intruders got into a shootout with Romano's security guards. The intruders were killed on the premises. The millionaire businessman was not home during the attack." Beck raised his brows. "Nice of Sal's maid to lie for him."

"So the police scraped up six bodies, but we still don't know who they are?"

"If they know, they're not saying," Beck replied without looking up from his computer.

"Well, that was a waste of time."

"Not exactly," Beck informed him while typing into the keyboard. "I'm using Holden's credentials to login to the FBI's computer network. Blake Harris is an efficient man. I'm sure he has some sort of report on the guys they found at Jackie's house. He'd make that a priority."

"Holden gave you his security clearances?" Kirk asked with surprise.

Beck made a face and casually shrugged. "*Gave* is a strong word."

Kirk snorted a laugh.

Beck watched the screen with great interest then tapped it. "Got it," he announced with enthusiasm. "Two of the five men at Jackie's house have been identified. Blake is just withholding their identities from the press." Beck frantically typed into his computer then pressed enter and sat back. "Now I just need to see if we get any matches in the FBI database when I cross-reference the two men at Jackie's house with the men who attacked us on Giovanni's island."

"Will that take long?"

"Thirty minutes or longer," Beck replied with a bored sigh. "Another few hours if I cross-reference those names with those in my personal database from our missions."

"I suppose you need the internet for that too," Kirk muttered.

Beck eyed him and grinned. "Now you're catching on," he teased and returned his attention to his computer. "And Ross said you couldn't learn new tricks."

"I don't need to learn new tricks," Kirk snapped in a gruff tone. "I'm just here to break things and shoot people." He groaned softly. "I'm going to patrol the perimeter before I fall asleep standing up."

"Happy trails."

Kirk walked along the small path in the slightly overgrown field. It was a beautiful countryside despite the massive, ugly aircraft boneyard just a few miles away. Kirk avoided the shaded areas near sporadic trees but kept close watch for anything that moved. Apart from the crickets, there was little sound. A peaceful, quiet countryside made Kirk suspicious. He kept within view of the tower, making certain Beck remained within shouting distance. Kirk stopped and stared at a small cluster of trees not far to his left. Nothing moved, and he didn't see anything, but something made him stare all the same. All at once, the crickets suddenly silenced. Kirk continued to stare at the trees. He returned the semiautomatic to his holster and removed the assault rifle from over his shoulder. He took a few steps closer to the trees while raising the rifle. One tree, in particular, caught his attention. As he moved closer, he saw an ATV parked in the shadows. He stopped and scanned the area down the barrel of his rifle.

He slowly approached the ATV while keeping an eye on the area. There was a large duffel bag strapped across the back of the four-wheeler. Kirk poked the bag with the barrel of his rifle. Nothing moved. He again scanned the area and felt the vehicle's engine. It was still warm! Kirk spun his back to the ATV, crouched before it, and scanned the area with his assault rifle. Whoever owned it wasn't far away. He remained there for several minutes watching the field, trees, and underbrush. When nothing moved, he again straightened and unzipped the bag strapped to the back of the vehicle. As he peered inside the bag, horror crossed his face. He heard the crunch of a twig behind him. Kirk spun with his assault rifle raised. Zack stood behind him with a sinister grin on his face. Kirk stared at him with a dumbfounded look and lowered the rifle.

"Zack?" he gasped.

Zack knocked the assault rifle from his hand then spun into a high, roundhouse kick, striking him across the face. Kirk was thrown to the ground. He immediately moved to his hands and knees while removing the semiautomatic in his shoulder holster. Zack kicked him, throwing him onto his back, allowing the gun to fly into the grass. Kirk immediately rolled onto his knees, prepared to fight. He saw the barrel of a gun aimed at him.

"You should probably stay down," Zack casually announced.

†

Beck sat before his laptop and peered at what was on the screen with great interest. He heard movement in the distance and realized it was getting louder. Beck shut his laptop, shoved it into his bag, and darted behind the tower pillar. He removed his assault rifle and looked around the area. He didn't see anyone. Everything seemed peaceful.

"Kirk?" he called out although not too loud.

There was no response. Beck cursed softly under his breath, tossed his pack over his back, and then hurried for a nearby tree, darting behind it. He again searched the area then heard an assault rifle blast.

"Kirk," Beck gasped and ran to another tree for a better look.

In the near distance, Beck saw something lying in the field. He scanned the area, knowing it could be a trap, and then hurried across the open field, keeping his rifle close to him and his finger near the trigger. As he approached, he saw Kirk lying face down in the field. His white shirt was speckled with blood, and his shoulder holster was empty. Beck immediately noticed the large caliber bullet hole through the back of his skull, indicating he'd been shot in the back of the head while possibly running from the shooter.

"Kirk," Beck gasped with horror.

He again looked around while crouching alongside his dead friend. He attempted to turn Kirk over, but when he saw the degree of damage to his face from the exit wound, he reconsidered. Beck groaned softly and looked away, allowing Kirk to roll back onto his stomach. The sound of an assault rifle blast brought him back to reality. The shot was so close it tore his shirt and struck Kirk's back. Beck leaped over Kirk's dead body and rolled across the tall grass. He remained immobile on his belly just on the other side of his friend while keeping his assault rifle aimed in the direction of the fired shots. He then saw a man dart between two trees. Beck momentarily froze when he saw it was Zack. He was about to call out when Zack fired his weapon, hitting the ground near him. Despite his surprise, Beck flattened his body into the tall grass.

The sound he had heard a few minutes earlier was now getting louder and the area was beginning to brighten. Beck looked behind him and saw Gil's turbo prop plane gliding along the field toward him. Beck sprang up from the field and randomly fired into the nearby trees while running for the approaching plane. The return assault rifle fire was so close, the ground exploded behind Beck's feet. Gil slowed the plane and stopped by the time Beck reached it. The side door opened, which lowered into stairs. Beck continued to fire at the trees as he scaled the plane steps. Gil fired into the woods as well, giving Beck additional cover. Beck closed the door while Gil returned to the pilot's seat. Several shots were fired at the plane, but it was out of range. No sooner had the door sealed when the plane started its journey across the field back for the aircraft boneyard and a secure runway.

Chapter Twenty

The small, two-room cabin was nestled just inside the woods not far from a babbling brook. As promised, the area was peaceful and far from any sign of civilization. Beyond a large clearing of land they used for a runway, Jackie's plane was partially hidden close to the woods to conceal it from prying eyes flying overhead. It was a little after five o'clock in the morning and just before sunrise. Jackie sat on the slightly rotted porch step of the old cabin that had seen better days. The cabin windows didn't contain glass and wooden shutters were all that kept wildlife out. Remaining on the plane was almost the better option, but they decided to give the tiny cabin a chance.

Jackie clutched her knees to her chest in an attempt to keep warm in the chilly morning. If she got two hours' sleep, she was lucky. Whether she wanted to or not, she was forced to have a lengthy talk with Monroe after they'd arrived at the cabin. Their tragic run in with their teammate back from the dead and the feeling of betrayal was hard on both of them. Monroe wanted to make sure she was okay. She insisted she was okay even though she actually wasn't. Zack shot Monroe. He put a gun to her head and threatened to kill her. She was almost one hundred percent convinced he was the one who shot her with a tranquilizer dart and attempted to kidnap her. She could excuse almost everything else away except that Zack had shot Monroe. Technically, he would have killed Monroe if it hadn't been for the bulletproof vest he was wearing. None of it made any sense.

The cabin door opened bringing Jackie out of her mild trance. She glanced at the sturdy, thick door and saw Pinto walk onto the porch while wrapping an old blanket around her shoulders. She closed the door behind her and subconsciously shivered.

"It's freezing out here," Pinto announced and tightened the blanket around her. She glanced at Jackie and immediately fidgeted, uncertain what to say to her. Pinto attempted to make light of their current situation. "Is the outhouse vacant? No snakes, spiders, or raccoons?"

Jackie managed a tiny smile while wearily placing her cheek on her knees. "I make no promises."

An outhouse would actually be an improvement. They were sharing a co-ed tree behind the cabin. Pinto joined her on the steps, unraveled the blanket from around her, and placed the excess over Jackie's shoulders.

"Couldn't sleep?"

"I don't think I'm ever going to sleep again," Jackie replied with a sigh.

Pinto fidgeted while staring out at the large field. There was an odd silence before Pinto finally spoke. "I can't even imagine what you're going through right now," she announced gently. "I just wish there was something I could say or do to make it all better."

"After everything that's happened--" she started then fell silent.

"It's okay, Jackie," Pinto announced and cast a quick look at her. "Let it out. Say what you're feeling."

Jackie laughed softly and looked away to keep from crying. "You don't want to hear what I'm feeling," she replied. "It would be laced with profanity, and then it'd escalate to destroying things." She groaned and held her head. "It's times like these I need Zack most. We'd spar for an hour sometimes more and wear each other out until we were completely exhausted. Now he's the source of my anger." She groaned and ran her fingers through her hair. "I've been trying to understand what happened, but it doesn't make any sense."

"How did he go from being dead to trying to kill you?" Pinto interjected.

"Exactly."

"I can't believe he's alive," Pinto remarked while shaking her head. "I didn't see any of it, but I'm sure I still would find it hard to believe even if I had." She looked at Jackie and appeared curious while tilting her head. "Did he say anything?"

Jackie sank into thought, although the incident had already played out a million times in her mind. "It was almost gibberish," she replied. "He called me princess. He knows how much I hate being called princess. Then he said something like if I didn't stay out of his way, I'd go down like 'Old Marge'."

"But you said he tried to kidnap you," Pinto reiterated. "That doesn't make any sense. He was the one crossing your path. Why was he telling you to stay out of his way?"

"Weird, huh?" Jackie sank back into thought. "Actually, he said, 'listen carefully, princess'."

"Is that important?"

Jackie was no longer listening to Pinto and remained deep in thought. "Cross my path, and you'll go down like 'Old Marge'," she remarked gently more to herself.

Pinto stared at her. "Jackie?"

She removed the blanket from her shoulder and turned on her hip to face Pinto. "Listen carefully," she quoted Zack with a strange enthusiasm. "Old Marge."

Pinto stared at her and shook her head. "I'm afraid I don't understand."

"It was code!"

"Code? Code for what?" Pinto suddenly asked. "Jackie, he tried to abduct you. He shot Monroe. I'm not sensing some encrypted message here. I'm seeing a man who went over the edge and tried to kill his friends."

"You said you wished you could help," Jackie announced as if she hadn't heard a word Pinto said and sprang to her feet. "You can help. When the guys get up, tell them I had to check on something. I'll be back in an hour or so."

Pinto appeared horrified while staring at her as she jumped to her feet as well. "Jackie, no," she gasped.

"This is important."

"People are trying to kill you," Pinto suddenly proclaimed. "I can't let you go."

Jackie gave her a knowing smile. "Do you honestly think you can stop me?"

"Well, I," Pinto began then straightened proudly. "I'll tell Monroe."

Jackie folded her arms across her chest and smiled almost sweetly while her eyes told a more devious tale. "You do realize I can fold you in that blanket like a burrito."

Pinto groaned softly with defeat. "Please, Jackie, don't go. If something happens to you, I'll feel responsible."

"I need answers," she informed her. "And I think I know where to get them. I can handle myself. I'll be fine."

Jackie took off across the field toward the plane, leaving Pinto standing on the porch steps dumbfounded.

She shook her head while watching Jackie disappear across the field. "Beck's going to kill me," Pinto moaned, "if Monroe doesn't do it first."

✝

Jackie's private plane touched down in the boneyard a little after sunrise that morning, being only a thirty-minute flight from the remote cabin. Although there were still a few shadows remaining surrounding the wrecked and retired planes, she'd at least be able to see anyone lurking around. Jackie carried her assault rifle and wore her double thigh holsters each containing a semiautomatic as well as her back holster containing her tactical batons for added measure. Jackie wasn't taking any chances. Despite having spent the entire day at the boneyard, she couldn't deny she was a little less confident strolling through it by herself. She didn't have any backup; not even Darth, but she needed to know if she was crazy or not. Had Zack sent her an encrypted message? Was he just talking nonsense? Or was it a trap?

She approached 'Old Marge' and stared at the familiar plane longer than she'd realized. She hadn't been inside the plane since the day she crashed it. Anything she wanted from inside was recovered for her. As she approached the missing door, she stared into the darkness beyond the opening. She could still see images of rescue crew removing her father's body in a black body bag from the wreckage. She refused any medical treatment until he was removed from the plane. Her body shivered at the memory of the worst day in her life. Returning to the plane wreck suddenly seemed like a bad idea.

A moment passed. Jackie drew a deep breath and approached the opening in the side of the plane. She was doing this for Zack. If there was some message in there from him, she needed to find it. She needed an explanation, although she wasn't entirely sure what she expected to find. How could Zack possibly explain his actions last night? He tried to kill Monroe. He couldn't possibly have known Monroe was wearing a vest when he shot him. His intent was to kill his friend and former Navy SEAL teammate. Despite her reservations, she entered the wreckage.

'Old Marge' was a four-seater, so quarters within the plane were moderately tight. It was amazing how much the plane still looked as it had that day. It seemed like a lifetime ago, but it really hadn't been all that long. Jackie held her breath then forced herself into the pilot's seat. As she sat in the seat, every childhood memory of her father teaching her to fly came back to her in a tidal wave. There were so many amazing memories with her father. She gently touched the wheel and could almost feel 'Old Marge' beneath her hands. She was a cranky old girl. Jackie glanced at the passenger seat alongside her and immediately saw the bloodstains where her father died.

A chill ran down her spine. The entire horrifying scene played out in her mind like a bad movie. Jackie fought her tears, but it was no use. She sat in the pilot's seat and sobbed for several minutes. 'Old Marge' seemed to groan beneath her, bringing Jackie out of her self-pity. She looked around but realized it was just the plane settling or technically rotting. Jackie drew a deep, shaken breath and attempted to pull her emotions into check. She again looked back at the bloodstained seat and saw something sticking out from the crack. She reached for the piece of paper and pulled it free. Jackie stared at the old photo of the entire team standing around an old bomb from WWII.

She'd seen the photo before in a frame at her father's house within his office. Zack was sitting on top of the bomb with a devious smirk on his face. There was writing on the bomb that wasn't actually part of the picture. Something seemed off as she stared at the familiar yet unfamiliar picture. She remembered the writing being numbers, actually, the code for her father's 'special' rifle safe hidden in his study closet. It was the same code she used for her rifle safe. All the guys used the same code so that they could access weapons in case of an emergency at any location. She continued to stare at the picture. The bomb had writing across it along with an old sketched image of Kilroy from WWII. The phrase typically went 'Kilroy was here' and included the sketch of a man's face peeking over a wall. But instead, across the bomb was written 'Zack was here'.

She stared at the words scribbled across the bomb for a long time, pondering them. She then ran her finger over the writing. Someone had actually written on the photo itself. She knew she wasn't seeing things. It was Zack's handwriting! She looked at the back of the photo, but there wasn't anything on the back. Was it a message? Had it always been there and she just hadn't noticed it? Did it mean something? No, it wasn't a coincidence. Zack was in the boneyard last night. He referenced 'Old Marge' to her. That meant Zack placed the photo inside her father's plane. Now she needed to figure out why. Why was he inside 'Old Marge'? Was he actually telling her to go inside the wreckage last night? She placed the photo in her pocket then searched the plane but couldn't find anything unusual or newly added. It seemed hopeless.

Jackie realized she'd been gone long enough. Monroe was going to read her the riot act as it was. She needed to get back to the cabin and wait for the rest of the team. For some reason, she suddenly didn't feel safe anymore. She briefly glanced outside the open doorway of the plane before leaving. As she rounded the torn wing, she was startled to see Mac just a few feet before her. Jackie flung the assault rifle from her shoulder and into her hand with precision and speed. Mac grabbed the barrel of the rifle and kicked Jackie in the side forcing her to drop it. Jackie immediately launched into a series of kicks, keeping Mac from reaching the weapon. Mac blocked several kicks and punches while Jackie escalated her assault on the woman. Mac easily defended herself but didn't seem interested in a counterattack.

"Enough," Mac suddenly cried out.

Jackie stopped her assault while remaining in attack position and stared at the woman.

Mac stared back at her while shaking her head. "I just want to talk--"

Jackie punched Mac in the mouth, surprising her. Mac dabbed the blood on the corner of her mouth then eyed Jackie, who didn't come back for another shot. She easily could have gone for either semiautomatic in her thigh holsters or her tactical batons, but she did neither. She made her point.

"Okay, maybe I deserved that," Mac remarked.

"Considering the mood I'm in," Jackie announced while raising an angry brow. "You're lucky I didn't shoot you on sight."

"Hey, I saved your ass last night," Mac launched back. "I think I earned a little trust. At least enough to hear me out." Her eyes narrowed. "I didn't start this, and I've certainly gotten more than I signed up for."

"What's that supposed to mean?" Jackie demanded.

"That means I shouldn't have gotten involved, and I'm feeling a little guilty over what's happened with Zack," Mac informed her and again dabbed the blood on her mouth.

"What happened with Zack?" Jackie suddenly asked. "Were you on Giovanni's island?"

"Yes, I was there," she reluctantly replied. "Maybe Sal mentioned he'd seen me."

"He said you saved his life."

"More like repaying a debt," Mac informed her. "I got caught up in the final act. It was my intention to leave before the place went to hell, but I couldn't leave. Something compelled me to stay."

"Do you know what happened to Zack when the helicopter crashed?" Jackie suddenly asked, allowing her interest overshadow her distrust of the woman.

Mac slowly nodded and sat on a large, discarded piece of wing. "Yeah, I was there."

Chapter Twenty-one

Giovanni's island. Saturday afternoon. One week earlier.
Mac maneuvered the speedboat away from the dock and headed past
the beach. The sound of a helicopter caught her attention. She
looked toward the cliffs in the distance. An old helicopter spun
erratically in a circle through the air, buzzing the cliff and flying over
the edge several times. Smoke was pouring from the engine,
indicating the craft didn't have long. Mac slowed the boat and
watched with surprise then horror. The helicopter disappeared from
view, possibly landing safely. Within seconds, a loud banging
followed. Had the helicopter crashed? The helicopter again came
into view but was now missing its rotors. It hit the edge of the cliff,
dislodging large boulders.

Mac could hear the faint sound of gunshots coming from the
sputtering craft. The helicopter suddenly tumbled over the cliff and
plummeted toward the water below. A man jumped from the falling
craft, locking his ankles as he almost elegantly struck the water.
There was no doubt in Mac's mind. That was the plunge of Navy
SEAL used to jumping high distances into water. It was Zack! She
threw the boat into gear and raced toward the crash site, pausing only
briefly as the helicopter exploded. She gave the boat more throttle
and continued toward the exploded craft sinking into the water. As
she neared, Zack was already pulling himself to shore, his shirt mostly
torn from his body. He was bleeding and in bad shape. Mac barely

slowed the boat as she lifted the motor from the water and let the craft glide to shore. She no sooner jumped out when she saw men on ATVs racing across the beach toward them.

"Oh, that can't be good," she gasped then ran to Zack, who now collapsed on the sand. She attempted to pull him to his feet. "Zack, you have to move. They're coming for us."

He didn't verbally respond but managed to pull himself to his feet. Mac half pulled and half dragged him to the beached boat. She tossed him into the watercraft and pushed it back into the water as the men descended upon them. She could see their weapons. She cursed under her breath while starting the engine and swiftly raced back into the ocean. Once they were safely away from the island, she anchored the boat and checked on Zack's condition. With his shirt now missing, she could visually assess his injuries mostly cleaned by the salt water. He had a grazed bullet wound to his side, although the bleeding had already stopped and another bullet lodged in his left shoulder. She routed through the boat, found a first aid kit, and sterilized the small scissors within the bag.

Zack was now unconscious, so removing the bullet in his shoulder was less complicated. While he was still out, she found a sewing kit, bent the sewing needle, and stitched both wounds. She skillfully taped bandages over each wound then routed through her hastily thrown together bag and removed a large, worn sweatshirt. She slipped him into the shirt then discarded the bloodied supplies over the side of the boat. Once she had him cleaned up and looking presentable, she weigh anchor, resuming her travels to a lesser-known port in Columbia. If she were lucky, Zack would regain consciousness before they reached port. She didn't need any trouble with the authorities in Columbia.

†

Back in the present day, Jackie sat on the ground while hugging her knees to her chest and watched Mac as she listened to her story of Zack's miraculous recovery from the helicopter crash. Considering her knowledge of Zack's history with Mac, she was surprised the woman risked her life to save his.

"I ended up calling in every favor I had to get him back to the States in his condition," Mac informed her. "He was awake, but that wasn't much of an improvement. While I was debating how to contact someone from your team without involving Sal, I saw the news report from Rio." She hesitated a moment then fidgeted. "When I heard they'd found a woman's passport, I couldn't believe it was Lee killed in that blast. I'd heard she'd gotten together with Ross, and I started putting things together. I knew what I had to do. I called the FBI and asked to talk to Holden. He'd know what to do with Zack." She frowned. "When I heard about Holden's *accident*, I knew something was wrong." She finally stood and started pacing. "For Zack's sake, I thought it was best to let everyone think he was dead until I knew what was going on."

"That was less than a week ago," Jackie remarked while watching her. "What happened? What changed?"

"Beats the hell out of me," Mac launched with annoyance. "As soon as he was alert enough, he kept bugging me to call you to come for him. After learning Holden disappeared from the hospital, I refused. He wasn't strong enough to deal with whatever was going on out there." She shook her head in disbelief. "When I came back from a supply run, he surprise attacked me and took off. Some people I know told me where he was heading. I didn't know what to do, so I went after him. I couldn't contact any of you, because I didn't know how secure phones would be, and I had to find him in case someone was still looking for him."

"That was probably wise," Jackie muttered, considering her own situation.

Mac frowned while staring at Jackie. "He must have memory loss. That's the only thing that makes any sense. I caught up with him earlier yesterday before he found you at the boneyard." She became animated and slightly enraged. "The fucker nearly killed me! I know he's not in his right mind, so I've been trying to stop him without killing him. I have several non-lethal weapons to take him down quietly, but he's too clever for me." She nervously ran her fingers through her mussed hair. "I'm hopelessly outmatched and not sure what to do next."

"Sounds like you're further ahead on this than we are," Jackie remarked then studied her. "Do you know who contracted the hit on my team?"

"Jesus," Mac groaned softly while staring at her. "I was right about that? I have sources. I heard things after what happened with Holden and Ross. I didn't hear any names being thrown around, but whoever's after you has people working for him that know you and your team." She fidgeted slightly. "Zack's a ghost. No one even knows he exists since the last time he was reported dead. He's not on the same list as the rest of you. That's when a horrible thought crossed my mind. I feared his warped mind put him on your trail to collect the bounties on your heads."

"He shot Monroe twice in the chest," Jackie informed her. "He tried to kill him. It was only blind luck that Monroe was wearing a vest." She studied Mac a moment. "He could have taken me out, but he didn't. He took me down with a tranquilizer dart and stuffed me in a bag. Do you have any idea why?"

Mac snorted a sort laugh and smirked. "It's no secret, Jackie. Zack would love to have you for himself. He probably intended to stash you away someplace for his own perverse pleasure."

"I don't believe that."

"Doesn't matter what you believe," Mac remarked while cleverly raising her brows. "You just said he put two bullets into Monroe's chest." She leaned against the plane and groaned. "Look, I know you don't trust me, and I don't blame you. I'll help you where I can, but I need to stop Zack. I *saved* his sorry ass, so that makes me responsible for *stopping* his sorry ass." She again ran her fingers through her hair and appeared on edge. "It's light enough now. I need to find his tracks and figure out which way he went." She then hesitated and eyed Jackie. "If you happen to have something to eat, I'd be grateful."

Jackie felt her pockets and removed a granola bar. She tossed it to her.

Mac groaned softly and tore the wrapping from it. "You're a lifesaver," she announced then bit into the bar. "Watch your ass, okay?"

"You too," Jackie replied.

†

Jackie's plane no sooner landed in the field when Monroe appeared from the nearby woods. She wasn't exactly thrilled by the greeting she knew she was about to receive, but she'd have to stand her ground and resort to name-calling if it came down to it. Once the plane stopped close to the woods, Jackie opened the side door and casually walked down the steps where Monroe leaned against the railing at the bottom. He had his arms folded across his chest and a disapproving look on his face.

"I know what you're going to say, so save it," she immediately launched before he had a chance to speak.

As she walked past him, he hurried after her. "What the hell were you thinking?"

"I'll be honest, I hadn't given it much thought," she casually replied.

Monroe attempted to keep up with her fast pace and long strides. "Jackie, are you insane? People are trying to kill us. Zack is trying to kill us," he lashed out. "How could you go back there knowing you were possibly walking into a trap?"

She suddenly turned to face him with a wild look in her eyes. "Because, Monroe, it's Zack. I had to get answers. There had to be some explanation."

"And what did you find?" he demanded. "Nothing?"

"I wouldn't say that," she replied and showed him the picture. "I found this wedged in the passenger seat of 'Old Marge'. Does it mean anything to you?"

Monroe glanced at the picture. "That was taken on shore leave many years ago," he replied. "We all have copies of this." He then considered. "Ours all have the safe combination written on the bomb though."

"Yes, I know," she replied. "I've seen the one in my father's office, but does it *mean* anything?"

"Yeah, Zack liked to personalize gifts that went boom," Monroe remarked. "It was his idea of a joke. This is nothing more than a joke."

"Why would he leave it there?"

"What makes you think he did?"

"Because of what he said to me," she remarked. "He told me to check out that plane. I did and found this."

"You're trying to rationalize the thinking of a man who shot you with a tranquilizer dart," Monroe snarled with annoyance and glared at her. "You remember? The nice man who shot me twice in the chest."

"You said you always wear a vest after an attempt on your life," she remarked while studying him. "You expected me to know that. Is it possible he knew that too?"

"Are you suggesting he shot me with anticipation that I was wearing a vest?" he demanded. "If his intent wasn't to kill me, he took a big risk assuming I was wearing." Monroe inhaled deeply, attempting to regain his composure, and ran his fingers through his hair. "Zack's been my friend and teammate a long time, Jackie. I love the guy, but if you insist on making excuses for what he did, you could end up dead."

"I ran into Mac," she informed him.

Monroe's expression dropped as he stared at her. "Mac? The woman posing as a U.S. Marshal who attacked me while we were protecting Lee? The same woman who tried to kill Zack and make off with Sal's millions?"

"She also saved Sal's life this past Saturday and helped us last night," Jackie reminded him. "She was on Giovanni's island. She saw the helicopter crash and pulled Zack to safety. Men were coming after him. She saved his life."

"Then what happened?" Monroe asked as he folded his arms across his chest and glared at her. "Did he turn on her?"

Jackie frowned. "Well, yeah."

"I rest my case."

"She's trying to stop him," Jackie insisted. "She wants to bring him back. Something happened. She said he disappeared then returned different."

"Yeah, too many shots to the head," Monroe remarked then gestured wildly. "He's gone down the crazy path. Whatever happened, Zack can't be trusted. You need to avoid him, Jackie. You've lost whatever hold you've had on him. Maybe he only wants to play with you, but he wants to kill the rest of us." He defiantly shook his head. "Don't underestimate his devious mind. You can't trust him."

"I don't trust him," she insisted, "but I know I can bring him back."

"You are so damned stubborn," Monroe exploded then pointed a warning finger at her. "Stay the hell away from him and don't let him sucker you into playing any games with him. I'm warning you, Jackie. If I see him within twenty feet of you, I'm putting him down myself. I won't risk him hurting you."

Jackie frowned but for once had no return response. Monroe cared about her and only wanted to protect her. She knew that.

Chapter Twenty-two

The train from Chicago to Washington, D.C. was already underway that morning to its destination. It would be a long, eighteen-hour journey followed by another two-hour layover in Washington before making the connecting train to Virginia. An attractive, middle-aged woman made her way along the corridor for her sleeper cabin after breakfast in the dining car. Considering the expensive dress she wore and her designer shoes, she was obviously a woman of substantial wealth. Her make-up was flawless, and she didn't have an auburn hair out of place. She opened the door to her compartment and paused just inside to see Bogart sitting in the front facing seat by the window watching the countryside go past. She stared at him a moment with surprise.

"Who the hell are you?" she suddenly demanded, placing her dainty hands on her hips.

Bogart looked at her and appeared equally surprised. "I'm Brian," he replied then gave her an approving once over and grinned. "Who are you?"

"I'm Melissa, and this is my cabin," she informed him, matter-of-fact.

He cocked his head and smiled almost boyishly. "I don't think so," Bogart replied playing up his Southern accent. "I'm in cabin 12B."

"This is cabin 12A," she remarked.

Bogart stared at her a moment with a dumbfounded expression. "It is?" He cocked his head slightly and gave her a playful look. "Are you sure?"

"Yes, now get out."

"Well, ain't that just my luck," he replied while maintaining his charming, country boy smile. "The first beautiful woman I meet after crossing half the country and she's already mad at me."

†

Later that afternoon, Melissa snuggled against Bogart where they lay naked beneath the rumpled sheets of her sofa now converted into a bed. Melissa was pleasantly exhausted while Bogart stared at the ceiling with mild disgust at himself and mentally shook his head. She lifted her head and met his gaze. He was again smiling with all his country boy charm.

"I have a wonderful idea," she announced. "Why don't we dine in my car this afternoon and spend the entire day in bed together?"

"That's the best idea I've heard all week," he announced cheerfully.

She resumed nuzzling him. Bogart again looked at the ceiling and withheld his groan. The conman had successfully slept his way across the country in a desperate attempt to reach Virginia undetected. He was almost certain he'd seen two men multiple times now, possibly looking for him. He had to avoid the common areas at all costs and his visits to the dining car were brief to avoid anyone seeing him. He'd spent most of his travel time in the sleeper cars of several different women over the past twenty-four hours. He managed to sneak a look at the travel reservations and memorized which sleeper cars had middle-aged, solo female travelers. He sought women older than himself since they seemed to respond faster to his country boy charm. It was tough to admit that his sex drive was dwindling and he still had another ten hours on the D.C. train, followed by a two-hour layover, and then another two hours on the Virginia train. He'd spent a lot of time in bed, but what he really wanted was a little sleep.

"Why don't I grab a quick shower and then get us something to eat from the dining car?" he asked.

"Sounds perfect," she cooed.

Bogart kissed her warmly and grinned. "I'll be right back," he announced in his sexiest voice.

As he slipped out of bed, she attempted to run her hands along his naked body, but he was too quick for her. Bogart headed into the little closet, which contained a toilet and a shower in the same small cubicle. He stopped counting how many showers he'd taken in the last twenty-four hours. The wealthier the woman was, the stronger her perfume. Despite his previous fondness for expensive perfume, the overpowering scents were now enough to make him nauseous. All things being equal, he found himself longing for the company of his horse.

†

An hour later, Bogart, now dressed in a waiter's jacket, entered the kitchen and collected two covered plates of food conveniently sitting on the counter awaiting their server. He eyed the order slip then left the kitchen with the tray containing both plates. He headed straight through the dining car, not wanting to spend any more time than necessary in the common areas. As he passed, he cast a suspicious look at the two men he'd seen on the train from Colorado to Chicago. He managed to tilt his head in such a manner to conceal his face as he passed the men. Both men seemed interested in checking out other passengers more than employees. Perhaps they were looking for a certain charming country boy. Bogart slipped out of the dining car with his tray and headed up the stairs to the top-level sleeper cars. Only a moment later and stripped of his waiter's jacket, Bogart entered Melissa's cabin with their meals. She had already converted the bed back to a table and chairs for their meal. He grinned boyishly and suavely set her plate on the table in front of her.

"Your dinner, my lady," he announced and removed the lid from the plate.

"That was fast," she announced as he sat down with his plate and joined her.

"I know how to get my way," he teased while offering a boyish grin.

She laughed while studying his handsome features. "I'll bet you do."

†

It was nearly eight o'clock that night, and Bogart needed to secure his overnight accommodations with his new lady friend. In the morning, he'd only have the layover and the short two-hour ride before he was home free. Despite his lust-o-meter dipping down to less than five percent, he had to sell a night of passion in order to keep his cozy accommodations. His life might literally depend upon it. Bogart sought Melissa's leg and affectionately caressed it while pressing against her side.

"Why don't I see about locating an expensive bottle of wine and perhaps a little caviar? Then we can see where this night takes us from there," he announced in his most charming Southern drawl even if he wanted to gag on his own words. Or perhaps it was just her perfume.

She gently ran her hand along his chest and moaned softly at the suggestion. "How can I refuse that?"

He kissed her quickly on the lips and grinned. "Give me twenty minutes."

"I'll slip into something more revealing," she teased while seductively leaning back.

Bogart left the room, his smile immediately fading as he shut the door behind him. "I need to find an old man and borrow some little blue pills," he muttered aloud to himself.

As he walked along the corridor, the cabin door next to Melissa's compartment opened. An attractive woman in her mid-twenties stood in the doorway and seemingly glared at him. Her disapproving look was a bit surprising to him. Was she some religious fanatic who overheard their earlier escapades?

"If you're looking for a cougar sugar momma, you should give up now," the young woman remarked. "My step-aunt goes through dozens of pretty boys like you."

Bogart had to hide his knowing smile. He couldn't exactly tell her he wasn't interested in her step-aunt's money, just the security of her cabin for an overnight.

"I think we're both getting what we want out of this deal," Bogart casually replied.

"My step-aunt is a wretched woman," she continued without prompting. "Aside from her money, what would a handsome conman such as yourself possibly want from her?"

116

He seemed surprised by the conman assumption. Perhaps she'd met a few in her time, having traveled extensively with her step-aunt. The sassy, attractive woman was almost enough to boost his sex drive back into action.

"She doesn't seem wretched to me," he remarked while grinning.

"That's because she's not finished with you yet," the young woman remarked. "Judging by what I heard coming from her cabin half the afternoon, your charm and good looks aside, I can't imagine why she hasn't tossed you to the curb yet. She enjoys an eager young man for a one-time fling; maybe even a repeat performance, but third time's a charm? Not her style." Her look turned more commanding. "Letting you spend the night?" She shook her head. "She's definitely up to something."

Bogart suddenly felt his body twitch at the comment. Something felt suspiciously wrong. Did Melissa have her own agenda as well? He appeared moderately flustered now, but he couldn't be distracted from his plans.

"I don't have time for this," he remarked with moderate irritation. "I have an incredible night of passion ahead of me." He then glared at her as his eyes narrowed. "And no listening against the wall."

He attempted to walk past her.

"Just fair warning," she suddenly announced, forcing him to look back.

"What's that?" he snapped with irritation, tired of entertaining the young woman.

"If you're someone of any importance, she'll probably use it against you," the young woman remarked. "My step-aunt has been known to blackmail men." She folded her arms across her chest and gave him a daring look. "Among other things."

Bogart suddenly appeared curious and questioned the comment, although he hadn't intended to respond to the young woman's remarks. "Blackmail?" he asked, taking a greater interest. "Would you say your aunt has her fingers in other shady dealings as well?"

"I have little respect for the woman," she announced. "If she can profit from the blood and sweat of others, she'll do it. If you have anything to hide, you should probably run away as fast as you can."

He straightened proudly. "No, I don't have anything to hide," Bogart easily lied. "I also don't have anything worth taking." He raised a cocky brow. "So if you'll excuse me--"

As he turned, he heard the familiar voices of the two men from the dining car in the stairwell. Bogart's excessively confident expression suddenly dropped. The young woman looked toward the stairs.

"My step-aunt's entourage," she informed him then noted his look. "Something wrong?"

"No," he replied while attempting to sound confident. "I just remembered I needed something from the porter."

He turned away from the stairs to avoid the men about to appear from them. The young woman casually stepped away from her open sleeper car door and raised her brows. Bogart took his cue and darted into her car. She entered behind him then shut and locked the door.

Bogart spun around to face the young woman within her cabin then fidgeted. "You knew, didn't you?"

"I suspected you were both playing each other," she replied softly so the men in the corridor wouldn't hear them. "Are you wanted by the law or something worse?"

"The law and I get along fine," he informed her. "It's some unknown party who wants me dead."

"Dead is pretty serious," she replied.

They could hear a knock on her aunt's door. Both remained silent and listened.

"He'll be back," Melissa reported, although hers were the only words either heard.

"Yeah, you're screwed," the young woman informed him. "But if you think it'll piss off my aunt, you can stay here until we reach D.C."

"I appreciate that," he remarked then eyed her. "I don't even know your name."

"Riley," she replied and offered a pleasant smile. "Riley Pendleton. You're Brian, right? Is that your real name or just what you're calling yourself?"

"I've worn out a lot of names," he informed her. "You can call me Bogart."

She suddenly appeared interested. "I've heard that name a lot recently," Riley reported. "My aunt knows some really rotten apples. They could be the guys trying to kill you."

Bogart became exceedingly curious. "Have you met these men?"

"Unfortunately," she scoffed while casting herself onto the sofa, "but I don't know them. They stop by the house now and again." She offered an arrogant smile. "So she conned you while you were conning her, huh?"

"These guys you met might be behind those who want me and my friends dead," he informed her. "Anything you can tell me would be helpful."

"I don't really know much," she informed him. "About a week or so ago, these guys started coming to the house. Real rough types and some even worse well-dressed ones, so I avoided them. I only heard them mention one name. Giovanni. I think they meant the infamous mobster."

Bogart sank into thought and attempted to make sense of what he was hearing.

"If you want to know everything my aunt knows, you need to get your hands on her phone," Riley replied. "It has everything from recorded phone calls to files and pictures. Unfortunately, it's encrypted, and she rarely lets it out of her sight."

"Can you get your hands on it?"

"Maybe when she's in the shower," Riley replied, "but that's a pretty big favor."

"I'm no stranger to big favors," Bogart informed her. "I have an assortment of talented friends who can get things done. Name your price."

She considered the comment and raised her brow. "I want out," she announced. "My aunt will never let me leave. Get me out of her clutches, and you can name *your* price."

"People are trying to kill me," he reminded her. "You can't come with me. You can't be seen anywhere near me. They'll kill you without thinking twice."

"Then come back for me," she replied. "Send one of your *talented* friends. I'm willing to put a little trust into a stranger to keep his word."

"As long as we live through this, consider it done," Bogart informed her.

Chapter Twenty-three

Riley slipped into her sleeper car, startling Bogart. He fidgeted when the door opened then relaxed when he realized it was just her. She grinned and flashed the cell phone.

"She left it in her car when she went to the lounge for a drink," Riley announced cheerfully. "I think she may have been looking for you."

Bogart watched Riley fiddle with the phone and immediately tensed. "Maybe you shouldn't mess with that. My friend should be able to hack it."

"I'm not messing with it," she informed him. "I'm turning off GPS, so she can't locate the phone. You wouldn't want her catching you with her phone."

"Smart," Bogart remarked. "Will she check on you at any time during the night?"

"I'm twenty-four," Riley scoffed. "I'm not some teenager. No, she won't check on me."

"I don't really understand," he remarked while again making himself comfortable on the sofa. "What's stopping you from leaving then?"

"The moving train for starters," she teased then turned serious. "At the mansion, it's the estate security guards. If I'm gone longer than I say I'm going to be, they come after me. It's tough to get out of her reach. She keeps tabs on my credit cards and my associates. No matter what I do, there's a paper trail leading her right to me. I'm not chained to the wall, but the chains are still there."

"So leaving the estate grounds isn't the problem," Bogart replied while eyeing her. "It's staying off the grid that's the problem."

"Exactly."

"Well, you're in luck," he announced with his usual charming grin. "I have friends who specialize in helping people disappear." Bogart sprawled across the sofa and groaned with exhaustion. "The train reaches D.C. tomorrow morning. I'm sure they'll be watching the exits closely. Do you think you can keep them occupied so I can depart unnoticed?"

"Trust me, Bogart," she announced and smiled sweetly while studying him where he lay. "I specialize in creating scenes. No one will notice you. They'll all be watching me."

He withheld his laugh then glanced at his watch and sighed. "So that's about ten hours from now." He offered a moderately boyish grin. "I don't suppose you'd mind if I crashed on your upper berth."

"It's refreshing not having a guy hit on me for a change," she remarked.

He chuckled softly. "Darling, that's the last thing on my mind. I just want to sleep. Playing the role of a playboy is more exhausting than you'd think."

"Upper berth is all yours," she announced with a humored laugh.

†

It was early Saturday morning just a little after sunrise.

Pinto stood on the porch dressed in a pair of shorts and a sweatshirt. It was another chilly morning outside the small, remote cabin. She leaned against the support beam and stared seemingly at nothing. Perhaps she was waiting for Beck to return from his 'bring back Bogart' mission. Monroe appeared from the cabin and picked up two buckets from the porch. He eyed Pinto and seemed to consider her mood.

"Worried about Beck?" he finally asked, bringing her out of her trance.

Pinto looked at him while straightening and offered a pleasant smile. "No, I know he's fine," she replied with a sigh. "I was just watching."

"Watching what?" Monroe asked and looked in the direction she stared.

Across the field not far from the cabin, Jackie assaulted a makeshift punching bag she hung from a tree. Monroe sighed and shook his head.

"She's got to let it out some way," he replied. "Better that bag than my face."

"She wouldn't do that," Pinto scolded. "You're being dramatic."

"I've worried about her doing stupid things in the past," Monroe informed Pinto. "Adopt-a-fed was probably one of the stupidest things, but this week has pushed her to the edge. I've never seen her so hurt and so angry at the same time. She's at peace with Holden safe in Othello's capable hands, but this Zack thing is killing her."

Pinto stared at Monroe and appeared curious by his reaction to Jackie's state of mind.

"She's treating it like it's all some sort of game," he remarked with frustration. "She trusts Zack to do the right thing, and I'm afraid it's going to get her killed."

"If she trusts him, why is she hurt and angry?" Pinto asked.

"Because somewhere deep inside, she knows he's betrayed her and us," he explained. "There's that small part of her that wants to kill everything in her path."

"Maybe I should talk to her," Pinto suggested.

"I've tried," he remarked. "She's too damned stubborn to listen to anyone."

"No offense, Monroe," Pinto announced and offered a sweet smile, "but I think this needs a woman's touch."

"Good luck with that," Monroe muttered then snorted a laugh. "Jackie's not familiar with the sisterhood concept. I'll be at the stream."

As Monroe walked off the porch, Pinto headed across the field and joined Jackie. She watched in silence as Jackie kicked the crap out of the makeshift punching bag. Jackie took a moment to eye Pinto then continued her assault.

"Monroe send you to talk me off the ledge?" she finally asked and again kicked the bag.

"No," Pinto replied as she leaned against a nearby tree. "I was just wondering if you'd be willing to teach me a few life-saving moves."

Jackie straightened and looked at Pinto with some surprise. "Really?"

"It's recently occurred to me that being Beck's girl comes with its own set of challenges," she informed Jackie. "If I want to survive the experience, I need a little more protection than a handgun."

"Assault rifles are extremely empowering," Jackie reported with a sly smile.

"I want to learn to defend myself using my own body," Pinto countered. "I've never thrown a punch in my life. I'm not even sure I've ever made a fist."

"With your shoulder injury on the mend, I don't recommend too much hand-to-hand combat," Jackie informed her. "Why don't I show you some kicks?"

"Yes, kicks," Pinto practically cried out with enthusiasm and straightened. "I want to kick some bad guy ass."

"You've come to the right place," Jackie teased.

✝

The commotion coming from the train at eight o'clock Saturday morning was enough to clog up the aisle for departing passengers allowing Bogart to slip off the train unnoticed. Riley stood in a face-off with one of the two men who'd been following Bogart that she claimed worked for her aunt.

"What the hell is wrong with you?" Riley demanded, shouting loud enough for the passengers in the aisle to hear.

"What are you talking about?" her aunt's guard asked with surprise.

"Don't act innocent," she snarled. "You put your hand on my ass. My God, you must be twice my age!"

"What's going on?" another male passenger suddenly demanded and shoved the guard. "Are you copping a feel? Leave the girl alone and pick on someone your own size!"

"She's making it up," the guard informed the man. "She enjoys causing a scene."

"Oh, sure," a woman a few feet away declared. "Blame the defenseless girl."

"She's hardly defenseless," the guard launched back.

Melissa pushed her way through the congested train aisle with the second guard on her heels. She grabbed Riley by the arm and looked at the massive crowd stranded in the aisle coming to Riley's defense.

"My niece is only seeking attention," Melissa informed them. "She's under the care of a psychiatrist for this sort of behavior. Everyone needs to go about their business, or I'll be the one calling security."

One of the porters pushed his way through and successfully broke up the crowd, directing people from the train. Riley gave Bogart nearly twenty minute's head start, which would be plenty of time for the conman to make his escape. Bogart still had a two-hour layover at the train station before hopping a train to Virginia. It would be a much smaller train, forcing him to find somewhere cramped to hide. If the men somehow knew he was heading to Virginia, they'd likely be casing that train. It was in his best interest to find a ride to the next town and, as much as he hated to admit it, he'd need to steal a car to reach his final destination.

Bogart checked a map within the station and discovered a subway, which ran passengers from the train station to a long-term parking lot. He was familiar with the parking lot. It was free to park, which meant there weren't any tolls or security officers to check his identity. He just needed to slip across the large waiting area and head toward the ground transportation. With only his duffel bag that he'd reclaimed from Melissa's cabin, he was making good time. Halfway through the train station, he had the sense he was being followed. His two stalkers had somehow found him despite his head start. He had to lose them before they discovered he was heading for the shuttle. They'd easily figure out his new plan from there. He preferred they continued to believe he intended to hop another train.

He left the station and headed across the train platforms beyond the passenger area. If he were correct, they'd assume he was going to hop a train, and he needed to sell it. The men followed him into a less populated area near the large assortment of tracks with trains arriving and departing. Unfortunately, he was also giving them the opportunity to take him out unnoticed. When he saw them reaching for their guns, he knew he was in trouble. There were still security cameras along the back portion of the station, so they weren't in any hurry to pull their weapons and shoot him on camera. Their window of opportunity was coming up. He had seconds; not minutes to get away from them. Several trains were coming and going along several lanes of tracks.

Bogart watched the trains as he hurried along the tracks. His timing had to be perfect. He now ran parallel with the tracks and waited for his opportunity. When a train heading south was close enough with another train heading north, Bogart ran across the track in front of the first train and immediately crossed the track in front of the second train heading in the opposite direction. The men attempted to follow him, making the first train, but they hadn't been aware of the northbound train. It was suddenly upon them. The first man was struck by the train while the second man managed to stop in time. By the time the train finished passing, Bogart was gone, leaving his stalker one man short and alone.

Chapter Twenty-four

Gil, Beck, and Darth waited by the plane in a secluded field. It was a little after ten o'clock that morning, and they had another two hours before Bogart's train would be arriving at the train station, which was only thirty minutes from their location. They'd secured a car to meet him at the station for their return to the plane. The satellite phone rang, surprising both. Beck grabbed the phone and placed it to his ear.

"Yeah," he replied, slightly concerned someone else got the satellite number.

"I was at the rendezvous," Bogart announced from the other end. "Where the hell are you guys?"

Beck sighed with relief. "We thought you weren't getting in until noon," he informed him. "There were some complications at the rendezvous. Where are you now?"

"I decided to borrow a car. I made better time driving," Bogart informed them. "I'm outside a diner in town."

"Wait there," Beck announced. "We'll be there in twenty minutes."

"Take your time," he replied. "Some pretty lady offered to buy me breakfast."

Beck rolled his eyes. "Twenty minutes," he reconfirmed then disconnected the call. He glared at Gil, who still stared at him awaiting acknowledgment. "How many lives does that boy have?" Beck demanded.

"You have to give him credit for surviving this long," Gil casually replied.

"Let's go get him."

✝

Sal walked onto the cabin porch later that morning and saw Monroe leaning against the support post with his arms folded across his chest. He stared across the field with a disapproving look. Sal glanced in the direction he stared. Pinto kicked at Jackie, who blocked the same kick repeatedly. They then moved on to a different kick.

"Is that my daughter?" Sal asked with surprise.

"Yep," Monroe muttered with little emotion. "Beck's not going to like it."

"Well, the last week has proven she should learn to defend herself," Sal insisted.

"Learning self-defense is one thing," Monroe remarked. "Learning Jackie's 'kick ass' karate is totally different. She's not teaching her to defend herself. She's teaching her how to maim someone."

Sal gave him a look of disinterest and shrugged. "If it saves her life, I'm not too particular the manner in which she learns or how she defeats her attacker."

✝

An hour later, Jackie and Pinto walked barefoot through the stream to cool off after their training session. Pinto had shed her sweatshirt to reveal a tank top, giving her the same moderately dangerous look as Jackie.

"Have you considered the possibility the guys are right?" Pinto asked, attempting to approach the subject delicately. "I mean, after what he did to Monroe. Aren't you the least bit worried he might actually hurt you?"

"Zack's not crazy," Jackie insisted. "I don't know what's going on with him, but he has his reasons for doing what he did. He

127

left me some clues. I just need to figure out what he's trying to tell me."

"But Mac said he was fine one day and over the edge the next," Pinto protested. "Isn't it possible he's seen too much action and has finally lost it?"

"A normal man could never have survived what's in Zack's head," Jackie informed her. "He has his shit together. He operates on a completely different level than the rest of us."

"But doesn't that also mean these secret messages he's leaving for you could be his way of bringing you to him?" She fidgeted slightly as her look turned concerned. "He knows you, Jackie. He knows how you think. He can easily prey on your emotions, particularly for him."

"That's a two-way street, Pinto," she remarked and eyed her slightly baffled counterpart. "I know Zack better than most women know their husbands. I could tear him apart from the inside if it were my intent." Jackie sank into thought. "I just need something that will throw him off his game."

"Like what? Fishnet stockings and a garter belt?" Pinto remarked under her breath.

"Close," Jackie replied, surprising her with the comment. "I need to learn some superhero moves."

Pinto stared at her with confusion. "Superhero movies?" she asked. "What does that even mean?"

"Certain gymnastic flips I could incorporate into my kicks," Jackie replied. "Zack became obsessed with me learning gymnastics so I could do flips. He also had this thing about me trading in my tactical batons for swords." She attempted a smile. "Zack has a warped sense of desire." She sank into her own thoughts and made a face. "I swear he got some sort of perverse pleasure whenever I kicked him in the groin."

"Yeah, Beck sort of mentioned Zack's unusual obsession with you," Pinto muttered.

"Well, I'd like to use that unusual obsession to pull him back," she announced.

"And you think a few gymnastic flips will make the difference?"

"I'm willing to try anything," Jackie replied.

Pinto fidgeted as if holding back then groaned. "I took a few years of gymnastics," she reluctantly informed her. "I could teach you some of the flips."

Jackie stared at Pinto with surprise. "Really? All things considered, you'd do that?"

"You have your own demons to fight," she remarked. "It's really not my place to question why you feel you must fight." Pinto then ran her fingers through her hair and groaned. "Beck's going to kill me if he finds out."

"You won't be doing anything wrong," Jackie informed her. "Just because I want to learn some gymnastics that doesn't mean I have any intentions to confront Zack. Even if you suspect I do, I have absolutely no idea where to find him."

"That is true," Pinto countered then appeared more confident. "There's nothing wrong with you learning a few flips. I mean, it'll benefit you in the long run just as learning a few self-defense moves will help me. No big deal, right?"

"Nope, none at all," Jackie announced while grinning slyly.

Chapter Twenty-five

Later that afternoon, Gil's plane touched down in the field and taxied behind Jackie's plane. The four already at the cabin crossed the field to greet the rest of their team in hopes they were able to connect with Bogart at the train station. Pinto jumped into Beck's arms and enjoyed a long, warm embrace while Darth made rounds with joyful tail wags and playful jumping. Bogart and Jackie exchanged a long, warm hug, which caught Monroe's attention. He took note of their newly found connection but didn't comment on it. The mood immediately turned dark when they noticed Kirk hadn't returned on the plane with them.

"Where's Kirk?" Monroe was first to ask.

Beck, Gil, and Bogart looked away with mixed feelings of sorrow and anger almost unable to answer. Beck finally looked back, placed his hands on his hips, and appeared enraged.

"Fucking Zack killed him," Beck nearly shouted.

The others stared at Beck with surprise and horror, shocked by the announcement.

Jackie felt her entire body turn cold as she stared at Beck. She couldn't believe it. It couldn't be true. "Are you sure?" she gasped.

Beck glared at her with limited patience. "Yes, Jackie, I'm sure," he snarled, holding nothing back. "He shot Kirk with an assault rifle at close range through the back of his head right before he took pot shots at me."

Jackie tried to let the information sink in, but she couldn't process it. She just couldn't believe it. She ran across the field for her plane. Her intentions were alarming to the others. Monroe turned to follow when Bogart stopped him.

"I've got this, Monroe," Bogart announced then hurried after her.

Monroe stared after him with disbelief. "What's with the two of them?" he remarked more to himself.

"We need to discuss our options regarding Zack," Beck boldly announced. He then demandingly pointed toward Jackie's plane. "I don't want her anywhere near Zack or our plans for dealing with him."

Monroe frowned and reluctantly nodded. "I absolutely agree," he replied with little enthusiasm.

✝

Jackie sat slouched in the pilot's seat staring at nothing in particular. Bogart joined her and slipped into the co-pilot's seat. She didn't bother looking at him.

"Is Beck sure it was Zack?" she finally asked in a moderately sedate tone.

"Yeah, he's sure," Bogart gently replied while studying her. "It doesn't make sense, does it?"

"No, none," she replied feeling as if her entire world had crashed. She could no longer explain away Zack's behavior. "I almost wish Zack had killed me when he had the chance," she muttered. "It'd be better than feeling this way."

"Don't say that," Bogart remarked in a sympathetic tone while placing his hand on hers.

She let her head fall back against the headrest and shut her eyes while exhaling. "They're going to put him down," she whispered. "The next time the guys catch so much as a glimpse of Zack, they're going to kill him. They won't attempt to take him alive. No questions asked."

"I know it sounds harsh--" Bogart began.

She looked at him with surprise. "They already told you their plan, didn't they?"

Bogart allowed his head to fall back against the seat as he groaned softly. "Yeah, they discussed it," he gently replied then looked at her. "He shot Kirk in the back of the head with an assault rifle." There was a pause. "At close range. Beck was pretty traumatized seeing Kirk, well, messed up like that. Makes it tough to argue Zack's case."

She again let her head hit the back of the seat. "If they kill him without asking why, we'll never know what happened. I'll never have any closure."

"If any of us run into him again, I doubt we'll be given much choice," Bogart remarked and gently tilted his head. "You know that."

"He didn't kill me," she insisted.

"Of course he didn't," Bogart suddenly lashed out. "He wanted to keep you as his plaything. Everyone knows Zack has a hard spot for you. What did you think he wanted?" He immediately fidgeted and reined in his emotions.

Jackie sat forward with a sense of urgency and stared at Bogart. "I need to talk to him," she insisted. "The guys aren't going to support my decision. You have to help me."

"Are you kidding?" he demanded with surprise then shook his head. "No way, Jackie. I'll end up dead, and you'll be chained to his bed in some basement."

She wanted to lash out at the country boy, but she couldn't be mad at him for wanting to protect her. She felt completely helpless. They heard someone running up the steps to the fuselage, immediately alerting both. Jackie and Bogart looked past the cockpit as Monroe entered with renewed enthusiasm.

"We got an encrypted message from Othello on the satellite phone," Monroe announced barely able to contain his excitement. "Gil already deciphered most of the message. They're coordinates to a safe house. It's an abandoned ranger's station in the woods. Gil found a place for us to land. It's a small hike up a footpath to the station."

"I could kiss that man," Bogart cheerfully announced while grinning.

"Sounds like everything is set up for our arrival," Monroe informed them. "That's what took him so long to get in touch with us."

"Did he say anything about Holden?" Jackie asked with enthusiasm.

Monroe suddenly hesitated and tensed slightly. "No, he didn't say either way, but it was a short message."

She stared at him with some concern. She couldn't be the only one who had her suspicions. "How do we know it was really Othello? Was it his voice?"

"Well, no, it was a computerized message," Monroe remarked.

"So how do you know it was him?"

"I've had a long-standing relationship with Othello," Monroe reported. "He's sent me similar messages before. Obviously, we'll be cautious, but I'm sure it was him."

"We could go in two teams," Jackie suggested.

"Good idea," Monroe announced then eyed her. "Beck and I will stay with you."

She sneered at him realizing why he made the comment. "Where the hell do you think I'm going to go?"

"Just looking out for you," Monroe casually replied then turned stern. "We move out in twenty."

Chapter Twenty-six

Once both private planes landed in the secluded field, using an old road as their landing strip, they found an area large enough to keep them hidden beneath some trees. With little effort, they found the path leading up the hillside to the abandoned ranger's station. Although the hike only took a little over fifteen minutes, they separated into two groups to prevent an ambush. Each group was within eyeshot of the other, and everyone was armed and prepared. They said very little to one another on their trek and listened for any sounds that didn't belong. Gil and Darth took the lead of the first group while Beck brought up the rear of the second group.

The abandoned ranger's station needed some work, but it looked to be in fairly decent shape. There were two newer ATVs parked outside the building, alerting the group to potential danger. Perhaps Othello was waiting for them, but they weren't taking any chances. Monroe and Bogart scouted out the back of the building. When nothing moved, they gave their signal to the first team. Gil, Beck, and Darth approached the main entrance to the building and tried the door. The door was locked, but the key was where they were told it would be.

The first team unlocked the door and entered. When they gave the 'all clear', Jackie and Monroe entered next, leaving Bogart to keep an eye on Sal and Pinto until they were certain the entire building was clear. The five made their way across the large lobby area of the ranger's station and headed into the living quarters. Darth suddenly started whimpering and ran through the building, surprising the team. They hurried after the dog while watching doorways and their backs. Darth scratched at one of the doors and whined loudly. Gil pulled Darth back. He tried the door, but it was locked. He drew a deep breath then stepped in front of the door and kicked it in. There was a loud crack as the frame splintered and the door struck the opposing wall. Gil aimed his weapon into the room while Beck took a low position on the opposite side of the doorway and aimed his weapon as well. A gun fired, nearly clipping Gil in the head. Darth bolted past them and into the room while everyone else ducked and aimed their weapons.

Gil stared down the barrel of his assault rifle at Ellie, who held a semiautomatic aimed at him. They stared at each other a moment with surprise. Ellie suddenly screamed with delight and ran for Gil. He pulled her into his arms and held her while sobbing softly.

"I thought you were dead," he cried out without releasing her.

She managed to pull back just enough to look into his eyes while smiling. "No, this guy with wild, curly black hair showed up," she announced. "He said he was your friend, but I didn't trust him. He practically abducted me." Her eyes widened as her look turned serious. "We were only a few houses down when these men broke into the house."

"I know," Gil announced while wiping his tears. "I thought they got you. The neighbors said they didn't pull anyone out of the ash."

"They burned my house?" she gasped.

The others entered the room, relieved to see Ellie was alive. They then saw Darth jumping on a man by the foot end of the bed. Holden attempted to hold himself up while the dog excitedly stood on his hind legs and licked his face. He had a semiautomatic in one hand and a cane in the other. Jackie saw Holden and felt her heart nearly explode. He grinned when he saw her and attempted to take a step toward her, but he was obviously having difficulty walking. Jackie ran to him and gave him the same reception Ellie gave Gil. Holden tossed the cane and gun onto the bed and pulled her into his arms. They kissed passionately then pulled away when they realized they were being watched.

Beck smiled with some awkwardness at the happy couples. "I'll, uh, get the others," he announced then hurried from the room to allow them some privacy.

Monroe fidgeted. "I'll, uh, help him," he announced and disappeared.

Jackie looked over Holden where he stood with some difficulty. He had a healed wound on his temple with freshly removed stitches.

"Are you okay?" she asked when gingerly touching his forehead then met his gaze. "Blake told me what happened during the raid."

"It was an ambush," Holden replied while frowning. "They were professional killers. They waited for my team and then gunned us down. I wanted to call you, but it wasn't safe."

"The bad news doesn't end there," she informed him with added anxiety.

"Ellie told me about Ross, Lee, and Zack," Holden gently responded while caressing her shoulder. "I can't believe it. They were after the entire team?"

"Yes, they came after all of us. They trashed our house." She grimaced slightly. "They also broke the glass door on the grandfather clock."

"The house isn't important," he informed her. "I'm just happy you're okay."

Jackie resumed her concern for him and his condition. "What happened?" she asked while again looking over him. "We haven't seen on spoken to Othello."

"I was half doped one night, and Othello enters my room," he announced with disbelief. "I was lucky I even recognized him. He said 'Holden, we have to go'." Holden casually shrugged. "So we went."

"That's it?" Jackie nearly gasped with surprise. "You didn't question him or anything?"

"My team was gunned down by professional killers," Holden remarked. "When Othello showed up and said we had to go, I knew we had to go. If Othello got involved, it had to be bad. He left me here and then returned with Ellie. Although I'd never officially met her, I knew she was Gil's ex-wife and a nurse. She took care of my injuries while Othello ran errands and brought supplies to the station. He said it was too dangerous to contact you or the rest of the team. I had no choice but to trust him and your ability to take care of yourself."

She again hugged him and sobbed freely. "I'm just glad you're okay," she gasped, no longer fighting the tears that flowed. "I was so worried, even after I knew Othello was the one who took you from the hospital."

"You were worried?" Holden gasped while clinging to her. "You have no idea what I went through having no way of contacting you. I couldn't even get out of bed without assistance, let alone try to find you. I had no idea where you were, what was happening, or if you were even okay."

She looked into his eyes and drew a deep breath. "Zack didn't die in the crash," she announced gently and nearly choked on the rest of her words. "He attacked us at the boneyard." She hesitated while trembling. "He killed Kirk."

"Zack?" Holden gasped while staring at her. "That's impossible. He wouldn't do that."

Jackie sank into Holden's arms and clung to him. "I'd rather not think about it right now. I just want you to hold me," she whispered.

"We'll get through this, Jackie," he announced softly in her ear while gently caressing her back. He then looked past her. "It would seem we cleared the room."

Jackie glanced across the room and realized the others had left, leaving them alone. She never even heard them close the door behind them. She smiled gently, knowing the guys wanted her to have a few minutes alone with someone who could bring her back to rational thinking. Now that she was alone with Holden, another thought crossed her mind, and it was the most pleasant thought she'd entertained in a while. Jackie gently caressed Holden's chest while giving him a sympathetic once over.

"How *are* you feeling?" she asked delicately, although the moderately mischievous look in her eyes expressed her lustful thoughts.

He stared into her eyes and raised his brows. "*Happy* to see you."

Jackie hid her knowing smile then kissed him warmly but passionately. He eagerly returned the kiss, encouraging her rising aggression, but his unsteadiness was obviously an issue. Holden broke off the kiss and leaned heavily on her while attempting to regain his balance.

"A little like china though," he informed her with an embarrassed chuckle. "You should probably use the kid gloves."

Jackie laughed while fighting her tears then kissed him quickly on the lips and met his gaze with a sly smile. "Let me help you to bed then you can show me which boo boos to kiss."

"Hmm, I like the sound of that," he murmured as she helped him to the edge of the bed.

Jackie gently pushed him back while climbing on top of him as she affectionately kissed him. As she worked on unbuttoning his shirt, he kissed her chest above her tank top.

"We should probably keep it down," he announced. "The walls are thin, and I wouldn't want the guys to think we're being disrespectful--"

There was banging against the wall across from them as the bed in the next room creaked loudly. Ellie cried out Gil's name followed by loud moans. Jackie sat up while straddling Holden's hips and both looked to the connecting wall with surprise. They then exchanged bewildered looks.

"Didn't they just leave the room two minutes ago?" Jackie asked with surprise.

"I guess that settles that," Holden remarked then pulled Jackie down on top of him and kissed her passionately.

Chapter Twenty-seven

The team and their new recruits searched the large building to familiarize themselves with their surroundings, exits, and weaknesses. In addition to the building itself, they conducted a thorough inventory of items within the ranger's station. Despite being abandoned for five years, the building had a lived-in feel. Othello brought supplies on his return visit with Ellie, being the last time anyone actually saw him, but there were also other non-perishable supplies already stored. Some of the items seemed to have been stocked a year or longer. While the guys looked for anything useful, Jackie wanted to learn a little more about the actual owner. Monroe was on a need-to-know basis with Othello, so he didn't readily know all his connections.

The living quarters within the ranger's station contained several bedrooms, kitchen, lounge, and laundry room. As far as safe houses went, it was quite comfortable. The public area of the ranger's station itself consisted of a large lobby with information desk, ranger's desk, and exhibits on display. Some exhibits contained preserved, mounted wildlife found in the woods. Jackie and Bogart explored the back of the living quarters and came across a locked door. Since they didn't have a key, Bogart accepted the challenge to pick the lock. He had the door open in under two minutes. The door led to the basement, although it seemed odd to lock a basement. Being the suspicious type, both drew their semiautomatics before exploring.

When they reached the bottom of the stairs, they stopped and stared with identical looks of shock. The large weapon's room was lined with rows of open cabinets containing rifles, shotguns, and automatic weapons. In the smaller cases beneath, there were hundreds of handguns ranging from derringers to Uzis. Another case contained dozens of knives in varying sizes. There was a wall with crossbows, hunting bows, and over a dozen swords. As they looked around with astonishment, Bogart shook his head.

"So this is what Zack heaven looks like," he teased.

"We'd never get him out of this room," she muttered.

Jackie approached the swords and removed one from the case. She touched the sharpened edge then frowned.

Bogart caught her look as she seemed to drift off into her own world. "What is it?"

She replaced the sword and shook her head. "Zack would tease me about trading in my 'wuss sticks' for swords," Jackie remarked. She cast her back against the wall and groaned. "What should I do, Bogart?"

"There's nothing to do," he replied. "We sit here and ride out the storm. Beck has that cell phone I liberated off Melissa Pendleton. Maybe it has some answers. This place has a satellite dish, and he got some information on those dead guys from your house." He offered a tiny smile. "All we can do is hope for a miracle cure that gets us home in one piece."

"And what about Zack?" she asked with a curious look. "Does he get home in one piece?"

"I don't think there's any home for him to return to," Bogart replied, attempting to sound sympathetic for her sake. "He killed Kirk. It's pretty much game over for him." He sighed deeply and leaned against the wall alongside her. "I'm afraid that's just the way it is, Jackie. You know that."

She insecurely folded her arms across her chest and shivered slightly. "I know you're right, but I don't want to admit it."

Bogart attempted a smile and pulled her into his arms. She placed her arms around his waist and rested her head on his shoulder as he held her. She never thought she'd find comfort in Bogart's arms, but with the possibility of him being her brother still hanging in the balance, their relationship changed drastically and definitely for the better. Monroe appeared at the bottom of the stairs within the room and saw them in a warm embrace. They pulled apart when they saw him and noted his strange look. His attention then focused on the amazing weapon's room.

"Stumbled into Zack heaven, huh?" Monroe remarked and nodded his approval.

Jackie and Bogart laughed at the irony of the comment.

†

Bogart fiddled with a gas powered weed whacker he'd found in the small, detached garage. The guys made their way outside and watched him manage to start the unit. Gil, Beck, and Monroe folded their arms across their chests and shared the same broad stance while watching the conman, wondering what he was up to this time. They watched with mild surprise as he cleared the entire backyard, taking it from a wild jungle to a semi-neat picnic area.

"He never willingly lifts a finger to do yard work at the lodge," Beck remarked.

"Does he expect us to have a barbeque?" Gil muttered under his breath.

"Nah," Monroe casually remarked. "I checked. There's no propane for the grill."

Gil and Beck eyed Monroe, who continued to watch Bogart. Of course, Monroe checked the grill. His obsession with outdoor grilling was beyond comprehension. Once the area was cleared, Jackie walked past the guys and joined Bogart. She looked around and nodded her approval.

"Looks good," she announced and patted his arm before walking away.

All three men stared at the scene with puzzled looks.

Monroe was beyond astonished by what he'd been witnessing between Jackie and Bogart. "What's with those two lately?" he demanded although it sounded more like whining.

"They have been oddly chummy," Gil added then hid his teasing smile. "Maybe they're having an affair."

Beck and Gil cast secret looks at Monroe to witness his reaction to the comment.

Monroe sneered at them. "Never in a million years," he snarled.

Beck shrugged it off. "Jackie needed a pet project," he replied without care then headed inside.

Monroe frowned and continued to watch the couple interact by the tree line.

Gil noted Monroe's moderately jealous expression then with all seriousness patted him on the back. "Don't take it so hard, Monroe," he announced. "I'm sure you're somewhere in her top ten list if she ever trades in Holden."

Monroe glared at Gil then smirked. "Is that all? I made Ellie's top five."

Gil's eyes suddenly narrowed. Monroe scratched his brow with his middle finger and grinned, mocking him. Gil threw a punch for Monroe's face, but he was already ducking and running. Gil chased after him even though he'd never catch the lanky, faster man.

✝

It was just before nightfall. Beck returned to the backyard to find Sal sitting on one of the old picnic table benches. Sal casually sipped tea from a cup while watching Jackie and Pinto in the cleared area. Pinto was instructing Jackie on how to do basic forward flips while using her hands then quickly graduated her to flips without the use of her hands. Beck remained puzzled as he watched the women. Sal seemed entertained by the show.

"What's happening out here?" Beck asked, indicating the women.

"Jackie needs to burn off some steam, so Pinto is teaching her some new tricks," Sal casually replied. "It's nice to see them bonding."

"Pinto didn't mention she was showing Jackie her old gymnastics moves," Beck remarked.

Sal shrugged it off. "Just something for them to do, I suppose. Some women gossip, others like a little more physical activity."

Bogart casually walked across the backyard carrying a large punching bag he'd found in the maintenance shed. It was covered in duct tape to plug up multiple holes. Beck watched as Bogart attached it to some hardware he'd rigged on one of the nearby trees.

Beck placed his hands on his hips then shook his head while watching. "Jackie certainly has him whipped these days," he remarked.

"I think it's great they're keeping busy," Sal replied. "I think between the exercises and finding Holden, Jackie's in a much better place."

"Getting Zack and Kirk laid usually made them more tolerable," Beck remarked then shook his head. "Who knew it'd work with Jackie."

Sal cast a disapproving look at Beck, although he didn't seem to notice it. "And sometimes a woman just needs to be held," Sal countered.

"Obviously, you've never had a bedroom next to hers," Beck remarked. "She's as aggressive in bed as she is in combat. Honestly, she can be a little scary at times."

Sal fidgeted in his seat and seemed uncomfortable by the conversation. "Women are like Mutual Funds. You only get out what you're willing to invest," Sal informed him.

Jackie made a few attempts at backward flips, failing miserably. She became disgusted and gave up for the evening. Bogart proudly displayed the punching bag, grinned boyishly, and took a few steps back. Beck watched with great interest. Jackie kicked the bag then stepped back and instructed Pinto. As Pinto kicked the bag, Beck's hands fell from his hips, and his expression immediately dropped.

"Oh, no," he suddenly cried out while headed across the yard toward them.

Jackie and Pinto stopped and looked at him with surprise.

He approached Jackie and gave her a warning glare. "You're not turning my girlfriend into a little Jackie clone," he huffed. "I like her the way she is. Particularly the non-lethal part."

"You're being ridiculous," Pinto informed him. "She's not training me to kill. She's just teaching me some self-defense moves. We discussed my learning to defend myself, remember?"

"And I think I should be the one to teach you," Beck firmly insisted.

Both stared at him with surprise.

"Why's that?" Jackie demanded while folding her arms across her chest as she glared at him. "I'm the better ass kicker of the two of us."

"That's exactly why," Beck announced. "I don't want this--" He indicated his girlfriend. "Turning into this." He then pointed at Jackie.

"You're being overly protective and royally annoying," Jackie informed him. She then pointed to his lips. "And that can kiss this." She then indicated her backside.

Beck glared at her without humor.

"I want to learn martial arts," Pinto informed him. "Jackie's the most qualified to train me, and we've got nothing but time on our hands."

Beck was about to speak.

143

"Ultimately," Pinto boldly continued, stopping him before he could speak, "it's my decision."

He immediately backed down and nodded. "Yes, it's your decision," Beck gently replied while attempting to relax. "It's been a bad week. I just don't want you following in our footsteps. I don't want you putting yourself in harm's way because you have a false sense of fighting skills. Just like shooting. I taught you how to shoot for defense only; not so you can fight alongside me and risk your life."

"That's not what's happening, Beck," Pinto insisted. "I know it takes years to get to Jackie's level. I just want to be able to defend myself. I don't want to be 'the woman who screams' anytime there's danger."

Beck kissed her warmly on the forehead. "Forget I was here," he announced. "Just watch your injured shoulder."

"Thanks for worrying," Pinto replied warmly.

"Yeah, yeah," Jackie scoffed and waved him off. "Save it for the bedroom. Back to work, princess."

Beck stopped in his tracks and stared at Jackie with surprise. She saw the look he gave her then realized what she'd said. She managed a tiny smile.

"Sorry," she replied gently. "Having a Zack moment."

Beck eyed Pinto and indicated Jackie. "Don't turn into that."

Chapter Twenty-eight

The following morning, everyone woke early to the sound of an ATV. They were quick to grab their weapons and secure the ranger's station. Gil, Darth, and Monroe took the back exit and made their way around the building while Jackie, Beck, and Bogart secured the front door. Sal, Pinto, and Ellie remained toward the back of the lobby area with their weapons handy. The sound of the approaching ATV got louder. Othello appeared on the path riding his four-wheeler. Given his size, they easily recognized him from afar. Everyone relaxed and lowered their weapons. Since they were already outside, Monroe and Gil approached the front of the building to greet him. Othello dismounted his ATV, saw Monroe, and grinned with enthusiasm. They shared a manly hug.

"Glad to see you in one piece, dude," Othello announced then accepted Gil's hand and gave him the official 'chest bump' greeting.

Darth greeted him with enthusiasm, and Othello was almost happier to see the dog. He gave Darth a good scratching then eyed the others as they stepped onto the porch. Othello saw Jackie and immediately beamed with joy. She met him halfway and hugged him. He gave her a big bear hug in return.

Othello then looked around. "Where's Kirk?" When he was met with silence, he immediately groaned and shook his head. "I'm so sorry."

"It's a long story," Monroe informed him with disgust and uncertainly scratched his brow while avoiding making eye contact with Jackie.

Othello looked back at Jackie and managed a smile. "How'd you like the present I'd left you in the back bedroom?" he asked, attempting to change the subject to something more pleasant.

"I'm eternally grateful," Jackie replied while returning the smile. "I should help him out of bed. He'll be happy to see you."

Othello entered the building with them and was immediately inundated with questions. He retold the same story Holden and Ellie had given about how he learned they were in danger. They gathered in the kitchen for coffee and fresh pastries he'd picked up and brought with him.

"I didn't know what to do with Holden after I'd nabbed him from the hospital, so I got a friend to fly us back to Virginia thinking we'd hide out at my house," Othello informed them. "Another friend then tells me there were guys casing my house. I was scrambling. I mean, for a big guy, I'm pretty much a shadow. How did they even know about me? Thankfully, I never leave home without my equipment." He managed a tiny smile. "I did have to 'borrow' a few things. I can't tell you how lucky I was when a friend found this place for me."

Jackie helped Holden into the kitchen where they joined the others for coffee and pastries.

Othello then indicated Holden. "I brought Holden up here, hacked into the satellite dish, and heard what was happening. I figured the only soft target was Gil's wife." He then indicated Ellie. "She was also closest, so I went after her. I was thrilled to learn she was a nurse. I didn't know what to do with Holden's injuries, but she did. I found her a medical bag full of supplies just sitting in the back of this ambulance on our way here, so I was able to borrow that too."

There was some soft chuckling.

"I didn't know what to do for you guys," Othello continued. "I was terrified to attempt a message of any kind. I was hearing all sorts of chatter from the underground. Someone is offering a million dollars on each of your heads."

A round of groans followed as they learned of the actual dollar amount on their heads.

"Who the hell did we piss off?" Bogart demanded becoming defensive. "We've kissed every connected ass from here to Columbia. It can't be a mob hit, can it?"

"No," Sal announced with confidence while shaking his head. "This started while we were on Giovanni's island. If it were mob related, he'd have warned us and possibly handled the situation himself."

Beck leaned across the table while staring at Othello. "Any idea who?" he asked.

"If anyone knows, they aren't talking," Othello replied. "I met with a few of my underground friends, but they couldn't give me anything."

"That's probably why I came up empty with the men identified at Jackie's house," Beck replied while sitting back in his chair. He tapped his fingers on the table. "They were independent contractors looking for a big payday. I couldn't connect them to anyone from our past."

"What about Melissa's phone?" Bogart asked with enthusiasm. "She was traveling with two men who wanted me dead. Her niece thinks she knows people."

"I'm still trying to hack her email on the cell phone," Beck replied with disgust. "Her contacts revealed nothing interesting. Her social calendar listed some events that all checked out. I started sorting through pictures on her phone, but there are tons to go through."

"I can hack her email account," Othello informed him. "Cracking into electronics is my specialty."

"Maybe you'll have better success with her email than I did," Beck replied. He then became uncomfortable. "I have to ask, Othello. Have you had any contact with Zack?"

Othello stared at him with a strange look. "Dude, Zack's dead."

"I'm starting to wish that were true," Beck muttered under his breath.

✝

Early the following morning, Jackie slipped out the back door with a blanket neatly rolled and tucked beneath her arm. She cast looks around the area, even though she was moderately certain no one else was up yet. She headed across the neatly trimmed backyard, passed the punching bag, and walked along a path in the woods. Jackie reached a clearing nearly one hundred yards from the ranger's station and unfolded the towel to reveal two samurai swords. She drew a deep, cleansing breath then took her usual karate stance with a sword in each hand. She attempted to use the swords in the same fashion she used her tactical batons. Shortly into her routine, one of the swords flew from her hand and struck the ground not far from Othello's feet.

Jackie stared at Othello and gasped with horror. "Oh, are you okay?"

Othello eyed the sword embedded in the ground an inch from his feet and made a face. "Missed me by a mile," he replied then gave her a strange look. "What are you doing?"

"Entertaining myself," she replied then frowned with defeat. "Doing a poor job too. I thought swords would be the same as batons."

"Different animal," he remarked then appeared curious. "So why did you sneak out here?"

"I wasn't sneaking," she insisted.

"I saw you," he replied and raised a dark brow. "You were sneaking. You could have practiced in the yard behind the house, but you came out here where no one would see you. I'm just wondering why."

Jackie groaned softly, approached him, and collected her discarded sword. "Because they're all a bunch of uptight pussies," she scoffed. "Monroe and Beck have been riding my ass whenever I make a move without checking with them first. Because of this whole Zack thing, they don't trust me. They seem to think I'm up to something."

"Those bullies," Othello scoffed dramatically then turned serious. "You're obviously up to something, dude."

"You too?" she snapped and returned to her original position. "I just need something to keep me busy. I wish people would understand that and just leave me the hell alone."

She took her karate stance and once again held the swords in position.

"I totally understand," he announced, "but I also don't want to see you slicing off a toe with those things. They're not tactical batons, and your grip is all wrong." He motioned for her. "Let me show you the proper way to hold them."

She stared at him with surprise. "You know something about swords?"

"Don't let my size fool you," he announced and took one of the swords from her. "I loved swords growing up. Playing with them in games wasn't enough. I did everything from fencing to broadsword battle re-enactments at Renaissance fairs."

She watched as Othello twirled the sword like a Ninja master. The way he handled the sword was almost graceful. He added a yell as he went in for an imaginary kill. He straightened and grinned proudly.

Jackie stared at him with amazement as her mouth hung open. Her look suddenly turned serious. "Teach me."

He nodded with little hesitation. "Sure, I'll teach you," he remarked. "You know most of the moves already. You just need to change the way you strike."

"Thank you," she gasped with relief, although she realized it sounded a little too eager.

"I'll teach you," Othello reiterated. "If you tell me why you want to learn and why you really snuck away from the house to do it."

She huffed while folding her arms across her chest then groaned with defeat. "Zack wanted me to learn to fight with swords. I guess he didn't think my 'wuss sticks' were lethal enough." Jackie allowed her arms to fall to her sides. "With everything that's happened, I guess I'm just feeling a little sentimental. He may not actually be dead, but I have to admit that he's gone."

Othello smiled and nodded with understanding. He placed the sword under his arm and slowly clapped his hands together. "Lovely speech," he announced. "Such a sentimental piece of bullshit."

She stared at him with surprise then immediately became defensive. "It wasn't bullshit!"

"No, I'm sure the truth was in there somewhere," Othello remarked. He flipped the sword in the air and gracefully caught it. "Fact. Zack betrayed you, the team, and killed Kirk. Fact. Beck intends to kill Zack the next time he sees him. Fact. You need closure, and the only way for that to happen is for you to confront your monster."

Jackie grumbled under her breath and again turned defensive. "Are you going to run off and tell Beck?"

"No, I'm going to teach you how to use swords properly," Othello informed her. "I have no loyalty to Beck, and Monroe's friendship doesn't mean he gets to dictate my actions. You may never run into Zack again, but if you do and you confront him, I'd feel better knowing you have enough skills to survive that confrontation."

She sighed with relief and smiled more naturally. "Thank you, Othello."

"Besides," he remarked while shrugging. "It's not like I have anything better to do around here either, and I like playing with swords." A twisted smile crossed his face. "Besides, women with swords are hot."

Jackie hid her smile and laughed softly. "Yeah, I've heard that before."

"Damn," Othello gasped. "All the good pick-up lines are already used."

Chapter Twenty-nine

One week later. Despite the comfortable quarters at the ranger's station, everyone was becoming restless. Their situation was the same as it had been the week prior. Jackie kept busy with learning new tricks and teaching Pinto karate moves under Beck's watchful eye. Bogart spent a lot of time with them during practice and even attempted a few of the kicks as well. He usually ended up falling on his backside. Holden was recovering nicely from his injuries and was starting to get around better on his own. The guys were fighting more than usual despite Pinto and Ellie's efforts to keep peace while Sal assumed a fatherly role and broke up more than his fair share of fights.

Even though Pinto and Ellie attempted to include Jackie in 'girl time', Jackie remained distant and spent most of her time either training or taking out her frustration on Holden in bed. Jackie didn't mention Zack to the guys, and his name didn't come up in conversation. She knew they were secretly plotting, but she couldn't blame it all on Beck because Ross would have done the same thing had he been there. If they suspected she'd protest, she was automatically excluded. She tried not to take it personally, but sometimes it was difficult.

t

Jackie sat behind the desk in the weapon's room with a bored expression as she flipped through a book on World War II. The extreme man cave was filled with books on war, magazines on hunting, and everything in between. Since the reading material didn't interest her, she decided to do a little more poking around. Othello's friend didn't leave anything personal in his secret hideaway. She understood the need for secrecy, as it wasn't an actual residence, but since she was now bored, it seemed like a fun pastime. She still had an hour before bedtime when she would take out her frustration and boredom on Holden. He actually enjoyed when she unleashed her aggression on him in bed, especially now that he wasn't nearly as sore from his injuries.

She opened each drawer and removed the few items, going through each thing in her attempt to snoop. Sadly, she wasn't given much to work with. She removed another war book from the drawer and saw a bookmark sticking out. Jackie wondered who was reading what last. She opened the book to the marked page and nearly dropped the book. She stared at the piece of paper used to mark the reader's place and immediately recognized her father's handwriting. As she stared the note, she realized she recognized the note as well. It simply read, 'Jackie, I'll be at the airfield this afternoon. Giving flying lessons to an old friend. Love Dad.'

Her entire body tensed as she held the familiar note. The last time she'd seen that note was exactly where she'd left it on the refrigerator in her father's house, the same place he'd put it the day he died. She'd purposely left it there for sentimental reasons and didn't even like anyone commenting on the note let alone touching it. She dropped the note and sprang up from the chair while looking around the room. Her heart was now racing as she scanned the room, eyeing the weapons and the setup. How could she have been so blind? She needed something concrete to prove her theory. Jackie nearly knocked the chair over while hurrying to the shelves of weapons. She frantically scanned the shelves, not entirely sure what she hoped to find.

Jackie then caught a glimpse of something behind the guns in the cabinet. She opened the glass cabinet door containing the handguns meticulously placed on their pegs. She carelessly tossed the guns from their pegs, allowing them to clatter and collect on a pile on the bottom of the cabinet. Scribbled on the wall behind the guns was a drawing of Kilroy peeking over his wall. Jackie could feel her heart pounding as she stared at the familiar drawing with a 'Z' in the corner. She took a step away from the cabinet and attempted to catch her breath. It couldn't be! Jackie scanned the room, finally able to put it all together. There was a reason why the room was so comfortable and familiar to her, but it almost seemed impossible to believe.

She could hear someone on the stairs. Jackie lunged back to the cabinet and hastily replaced the carelessly discarded guns to random pegs, covering the drawing. She just finished replacing the last gun when she heard someone enter the room. Jackie looked up and saw Bogart in the doorway. He had a solemn look on his face, immediately setting her on edge, although she was halfway there already.

"I thought you'd like to know Othello cracked the email on that cell phone," he announced while frowning. "I saw the look on Othello's face when he told Beck. I think he saw something, but he didn't want to say anything."

Jackie casually closed the cabinet while attempting to sort out what he'd just said along with what she'd just found.

"Oh, uh, I don't suppose he intends to share that information with me anyway," she replied as she attempted to slow her heart rate.

Bogart eyed the note on the table a few feet from him. Jackie saw him looking at the paper. She casually approached the desk, opened the book, and placed the paper between the pages. She replaced the book to the drawer then looked at Bogart.

"I think I'm going to take a shower then go to bed early," she informed him. "You'll tell me if they find anything in the emails, won't you?"

"Yeah, sure," Bogart replied while giving her a strange look. "Is everything okay? You look a little flushed."

"Yeah, everything's fine," she replied despite feeling her body trembling inside. "I mean, as good as it gets."

Bogart attempted a smile and nodded. Jackie returned the smile as she passed him, gently patted his arm, and then headed up the stairs. Bogart watched her leave then glanced back at the desk drawer.

†

Jackie sat on the bed in her sleep tank top and floppy shorts while brushing her wet hair. She was deep in thought and couldn't seem to shake what she'd seen. Her heart was still racing, and every nerve in her body seemed to twitch. The door opened startling her. Holden limped into the room and immediately looked at her as he closed the door behind him.

"Well, Beck's being a prick," Holden remarked.

Jackie's heart sank along with her shoulders. "They wouldn't share any information with you?"

"Share?" he remarked and laughed. "They stopped talking the moment I entered the room. They must have found something important in those emails, and neither of us is privy to the new information."

"I'm not surprised," she muttered. "They must suspect you'd share that information with me, and I'm on a 'you don't need to know' basis."

Holden limped toward her and sat on the edge of the bed near her. He gently caressed her bare leg while staring sympathetically into her eyes. "I know this is killing you, Jackie," he remarked timidly then drew a deep breath and held it. "You realize you don't need them, right?"

"This isn't about how they're treating me," she replied. "You know what this is about."

"Yes, I do," he remarked while staring at her with a serious look. "You're part of the team. If they won't take your opinion into consideration and feel the need to exclude you from something as serious as killing one of your own, then you have every right to tell them you're through with them and the team. They need you more than you need them."

"Without Ross, Kirk, and Zack there may not be a team," Jackie replied sadly. "What I think doesn't really matter. They're hell bent on putting Zack down, and there's nothing I can do to stop them if they attempt it."

Holden groaned softly. "Jackie, I know you," he announced simply. "We both know you intend to go rogue."

She stared at him with surprise, but it was too late to hide it from him. Jackie groaned and held her head. "I'm a horrible person."

"No you're not," Holden replied and caressed her leg. "You're looking for the same answers we all want. I just hope if the time comes, you'll have the good sense to take him down before he takes you down."

Jackie was slightly stunned by his words. He knew what she intended to do, and he didn't intend to stop her. She placed her arms around Holden's neck and hugged him while trembling.

"I'm sorry."

He held her in his arms as if he'd never let go. "Don't be sorry. I knew what I was getting into when I married you." He pulled away and looked into her eyes. "Just don't get killed trying to bring him back, because then it's my turn." His look was serious. "If he hurts you and I get him in my sights, I'm not asking questions."

She attempted a smile and nodded while wiping the tears from her eyes. "I know, but I promise it won't come to that." Jackie pulled away and revealed her shaking hands then smirked. "I'm afraid I have a lot of anxiety and aggression to work through tonight."

"Well," Holden announced with a sigh. "You can beat the living crap out of the punching bag if you'd like." He then hesitated. "Or grab my handcuffs from my jacket pocket."

Jackie eyed him and grinned. "I'll get the handcuffs." She sprang up from the bed and ran for the closet.

Holden groaned and fell back on the bed. "The things I do for that girl--"

Chapter Thirty

It was nearly midnight when the team gathered in the weapon's room. Beck wanted to inform them what he'd found on Melissa's phone and discuss their course of action. Beck, Gil, Monroe, and Bogart were the only ones allowed to attend the secret meeting. Othello was already in bed as were Jackie and Holden. Sal, Pinto, and Ellie were outside enjoying the pleasant night air while having a drink before heading to bed. Beck chose the weapon's room for its basement location, which would reduce the likelihood of anyone overhearing their conversation.

"I found dozens of emails on the phone Bogart snatched," Beck informed them where they gathered around the desk. "This woman Bogart ran into must know the man who put the bounty on our heads. Her emails are loaded with reference to him without directly coming out and naming names. The emails are all rather vague, but they were designed that way to keep anyone from fully understanding their nature." He glanced at the remaining team. "We need a plan to infiltrate this woman's mansion and find out who's behind the hits on us."

"Question," Bogart immediately spoke up then looked around the room. "Why isn't Jackie part of this meeting?"

Beck inhaled deeply and seemed to drift out a moment. Monroe and Gil fidgeted simultaneously at the question. Beck looked back at Bogart.

"According to the emails, there's a Russian bounty hunter new to the scene," Beck informed him. "A more recent email indicates he's submitted a request for payment on Kirk's head." He shifted uncomfortably. "There was an attached photo of his kill. I couldn't look at it, but Gil confirmed it was Kirk in the photo. That means our Russian bounty hunter is Zack. He's been spending a great deal of time at this woman's mansion. If she's as loose as you claim she is, I wouldn't doubt he's conned his way into her bed already."

Bogart groaned and looked away. He cursed softly under his breath, hesitated, and then looked back at Beck. "So we're excluding Jackie because we might run into Zack?"

"Yes, Jackie's officially off the assignment due to conflicting interests," Beck replied.

"You know," Bogart began with some irritation. "I realize I'm not officially one of you, and I never will be, since I wasn't part of your little boy band back in the day, but I'm a little uncomfortable with you plotting Zack's assassination."

"He killed Kirk in cold blood," Monroe snapped, becoming animated. "Do you honestly think he won't do the same to you or the rest of us?"

"It's the only way," Beck insisted, attempting to remain calm. "Zack is very good at what he does. If we don't attack first, our chances of beating him are slim. Do you get it?"

Bogart frowned. "Yeah, I get it." His anger then returned. "It's still wrong to exclude Jackie. She's the only one here he might listen to. He'd *never* hurt her."

Beck suddenly slammed his hands on the desk. "I'm not willing to risk her life to find out," he launched back then attempted to compose himself. He ran his fingers through his hair and held his breath. He calmed slightly. "You weren't at the boneyard, Bogart. You didn't see the things we saw. Zack turned on us. We can't let him harm anyone else. That's just the way it has to be."

Bogart maintained his frown and nodded even if he didn't necessarily agree with him.

Beck rubbed his eyes and appeared upset with their decision as well, but there was no turning back. "According to another more recent email, they're having a meeting to discuss the bounties at the Melissa Pendleton's mansion the evening after tomorrow. That gives us forty-eight hours to come up with a plan. The email was forwarded to nearly two dozen men, whom I'm assuming are all bounty hunters and professional hitmen. There's an excellent chance Zack will be among them." He casually sat on the desk and looked at the others. "We'll stake-out the meeting, get eyes on Zack, and see if we can figure out who's in charge. We find out who put the hit on us, and we take him out."

"We're going to storm a fortress containing over two dozen men who want our heads?" Bogart blurted out then grinned nervously. "Four of us against two dozen of them? Meanwhile, our best fighters are either sidelined or playing for the other team. That's suicide."

"We'll go in after the meeting breaks up, genius," Beck snarled while glaring at Bogart. "Two of us will keep eyes on Zack and handle that while the other two take care of the man in charge of this little 'farewell to us' party."

Bogart shook his head defiantly. "I'm sorry, Beck," he announced with little hesitation. "I won't be a part of killing Zack in cold blood."

Beck glared at Bogart and stood. "Do you want to sit this one out?" he demanded. "Because you're more than welcome to sit this one out."

"I'll need time to think about that," Bogart snapped in response then turned to leave. He hesitated then looked back at Beck while cocking his head. "You know, Ross was a ballbreaker, but I can't imagine he'd approve any of this behavior."

Bogart turned and left. Gil, Monroe, and Beck avoided looking at one another while sinking into their own moral dilemmas regarding Zack.

Chapter Thirty-one

The following evening, Jackie hugged her knees to her chest while sitting on the decorative concrete bench in the backyard behind the ranger station's living quarters. She stared toward the slowly darkening woods. They still had an hour before the sun officially set, but the forest was already becoming dark. Monroe stood in the doorway a long moment watching her then finally approached. He sat on the bench alongside her feet and stared in the same direction she stared.

"You okay?" he gently asked.

She didn't bother looking at him. "I don't want to argue with you anymore," she replied with little emotion.

"I'm not here to argue," he informed her.

"If we continue talking, it'll turn into an argument," she countered.

"Yeah, you get that from your father," Monroe replied. "He loved a good debate."

"I believe the term is pissing match," she corrected then cast a glance at him.

They exchanged tiny smiles for the first time in a while. Monroe cast her feet from the bench, moved closer to her, and pulled her into his arms. She tensed at first then allowed him to hold her in a warm embrace.

"Don't be mad at me, Jackie," he announced softly. "We sometimes have to do things we don't want to do."

159

"I know," she replied into his shoulder while clinging to him as if her life depended on it. She drifted off into her own world. "We've been through a lot, and I wouldn't want us to be angry with each other with things being so uncertain."

"Yeah, me too," he replied then finally pulled away and smiled at her. "Bogart told you we were leaving tomorrow afternoon, didn't he?"

She managed a smile and nodded. "I guess my invitation got lost in the mail."

"You know why you weren't included."

"I know," she replied, taking on a callous attitude. "You can tell Beck if he intends to fill Ross's shoes, he'd better grow a pair and tell me to my face."

Monroe drew a deep breath while taking her hands in his. He stared into her eyes. "Jackie," he announced gently. "You're scary. Even Ross was a little afraid of you at times."

"Then take a vote and let me come along," she replied in a firm tone.

"I don't have that sort of power," he remarked. "And even if I did, I wouldn't want you going. If we run into Zack, you're going to let your feelings get in the way."

"He won't hurt me."

"Damn it! He held a gun to your head!" Monroe took a deep breath and resumed his gentle tone. "We've been through all this already. Even if you're right, he'll kill the rest of us just for standing in his path to you. You need to stay out of this battle for your own good. If you put yourself in harm's way, you could endanger all our lives."

Jackie fought her tears so that she wouldn't show her emotions in front of Monroe. She hesitated and drew a deep breath. "Deep down inside, I know what needs to be done," she informed him while drifting into her own thoughts. "It may not be rational, and it may cause some hostility among us, but we need to trust one another in the end. Ultimately, we need to do what's best for those we love and worry about the cost later."

Monroe smiled and hugged her. She returned the embrace. "Thanks for understanding, Jackie," he replied warmly. "I promise we'll do what's best." He finally pulled away and attempted to lighten the mood while patting her hand. "We're playing poker tonight. It'd be nice if you joined us and showed the guys there are no hard feelings."

"Thanks, but I already made plans with Holden," she replied. "We had a bet. He lost, so I'm collecting tonight."

"More information than I needed," Monroe replied then smiled and kissed her quickly on the lips. "I'll see you in the morning then."

She nodded then returned to watching the woods as he walked away. As Monroe approached the building, Beck walked out and stopped him.

Beck indicated Jackie while fidgeting. "How is she?"

"Calm before the storm," Monroe casually replied then pat him on the back before heading inside. "Good luck."

Beck took a deep breath then approached Jackie where she sat with her back to him. Despite facing away from him, her eyes were on him as he got closer. He slowed his approach, feeling her stare out the corner of her eye.

"May I join you?"

"It's a public place," she replied.

Beck sat on the bench near her, immediately hunched over, and clasped his hands between his knees. He was obviously uncomfortable.

"This is ridiculous," he blurted out while sitting up straight. "I know you're pissed and most of it is directed at me. I'm sorry we can't include you, but you already know why."

She cast a look at him. Beck tensed as if waiting for her to erupt.

"It's okay, Beck," she replied, surprising him. "Holden and I had a long talk. He made me see things differently, and I've come to terms with the way things are."

Beck stared at her a moment with a look of disbelief. "Oh? Well, I'm glad he was able to make you feel better about the situation."

"Yes, he's very supportive," she informed Beck. "He offered to arrange a transfer back to the east coast Bureau, and we can move back into my father's house here in Virginia. Without a mortgage, I wouldn't even have to work if I don't want to."

Beck's mouth fell open as he stared at her. "You're moving back home?"

"Yes," she replied simply. "I thought I'd earned my way onto this team, but I recently discovered the only two men who actually respected my position are gone."

"You're threatening to quit if I don't let you come along?" Beck almost demanded.

"No, that's not what I'm saying," she announced firmly then groaned. "I'm saying my services to the team are officially discontinued."

He was at a loss for words as he stared at her. "Jackie, please reconsider. Of course, I respect you," Beck insisted then practically pleaded with her. "We've all been under a lot of stress recently. Take time to give this some serious thought before you do anything rash like moving back to Virginia."

"Obviously, I have plenty of time while we're stuck here," she informed him. "But I doubt I'll change my mind. Without Ross, Kirk, and Zack, this team will never be the same."

"You're absolutely right. It won't be the same," Beck agreed with rising tension, "but we'll make it work. Jackie, we need you. I need you."

"I'm having a difficult time sorting out everything that's happened the last couple of weeks," she informed him. "I'm feeling confused, betrayed, and unappreciated. Those feelings don't just go away overnight."

Beck fidgeted and briefly sank into thought. He turned on the stone bench to face her. "What if I promised to find you some answers?"

"How?"

He groaned then ran his fingers through his hair. "If possible, we'll try to take Zack alive." His enthusiasm suddenly returned. "You could interrogate him however long you want and use him as your personal punching bag."

Jackie considered the suggestion and gave a slight nod. "If I couldn't get answers, I'd at least have someone to direct my aggression toward."

"I promise I'll try to take Zack alive," Beck announced. "We may have to plug up a few holes, but we'll attempt to take him alive."

She considered the comment then nodded. "I can live with that," she replied and managed a tiny smile.

Beck appeared relieved then softly laughed while shaking his head. "I don't know how you do it, but you always somehow manage to get your way, don't you?"

"If I got my way, I'd be going along tomorrow afternoon," she replied.

"No amount of manipulation would get you that," he replied with a slight chuckle. They sat in silence a moment before he eyed her with a curious look. "What happened to the third ATV? I noticed it was missing."

She cast a sideways glance at him and smirked. "Did you think I took it?"

"It crossed my mind," he replied.

"You were watching the wrong girl," she casually informed him. "Sal and Pinto took one of the ATVs a little while ago to pick some blueberries. I heard mention of blueberry pancakes tomorrow morning."

Beck groaned softly. "Yeah, she mentioned they were going to pick blueberries," he muttered. "I just assumed they were walking."

"I think the bushes are a bit of a trek from here," Jackie replied. "It's getting close to dark too. They may have some competition for those berries. They'll want to get back as fast as they can."

"Yeah, neither of them are exactly the outdoorsy type," Beck added.

Jackie glanced at her watch then looked at Beck and grinned. "I'm late for my date," she announced. "Holden lost a bet, and I'm collecting."

Beck groaned as she sprang up from the stone bench. "I wish you wouldn't announce those things."

"Beck, you're a prude," she announced then kissed him on the cheek and hurried inside.

He leaned back on the bench after she'd gone and stared at the darkening woods. "No, just a little jealous that Pinto doesn't brag about our evening plans," he muttered.

Chapter Thirty-two

Jackie entered her bedroom a few minutes later and found Holden comfortably sitting reclined on the bed leaning against the headboard as if he'd been waiting for her arrival. He was still fully dressed, but he'd taken off his shoes. He glanced at his watch then eyed her.

"Cutting it a little close, aren't you?" he asked with some arrogance.

Jackie approached the bed and leaped on top of him. He cried out with surprise as she tackled him to the bed. She straddled him while on all fours and kissed him quickly but passionately on the lips. Holden returned the kiss then pulled away and met her gaze as she hovered over him.

"Aren't you forgetting something?" he asked.

She moved onto her knees and hurriedly removed her tank top. Jackie cast her shirt aside and lowered herself on top of him, allowing her hands to travel his body.

"There's something very important we need to discuss," she announced then kissed him aggressively while running her hand along his body toward his crotch.

Holden groaned and flipped her onto her back while attempting to slip her out of her pants. "I'm listening," he moaned softly.

t

A short while later, Jackie and Holden lay naked beneath the sheets while in each other's arms as they panted, attempting to catch their breath after their aggressive lovemaking.

"I swear you're going to kill me one day," Holden remarked then gave her a curious look. "Death by sex. Do you suppose that's possible?"

Jackie rolled onto his chest, smiled lovingly, and kissed him quickly on the lips. "I'm not sure, but I'm willing to explore it further any other time."

Holden glanced at his watch then gave her a moderately stern look. "Yes, you're definitely going to be late now," he announced in a firm tone.

"Yeah, yeah," she muttered while jumping up from the bed and slipping into her clothes. "Late for my own funeral. I don't really see the rush."

"Don't even joke," Holden warned while slipping into his boxer briefs.

He sat up on the edge of the bed and watched her pull on her boots. His look was concerning. She slipped into her leather jacket then caught his look. She gave him a warm, reassuring smile and kissed him quickly.

"I'll be back," she announced. "I promise."

"I know," he replied, almost successfully hiding his concern. "Just remember our deal."

"I promise to do what has to be done," she replied then hugged him.

He held her in a warm embrace and sighed into her shoulder. "Be careful."

She kissed him quickly, flashed a tender smile, and then hurried to the window. Holden watched Jackie climb out the window and disappear into the darkening evening. He allowed his head to fall into his hands as he groaned.

"I must be out of my mind," he muttered.

$\dagger$

Jackie slipped away from the ranger's station unnoticed and hurried into the woods finding the path despite the rapidly darkening woods. She ventured only one hundred yards from the ranger's station when she heard movement within the shadows. Jackie paused and looked around. Othello appeared on the path holding a duffel bag.

"You're late," he scoffed. "I've been waiting nearly fifteen minutes."

"Sorry," she announced and took the bag from him. "I was unavoidably detained."

"More fancy talk alluding to servicing your husband," Othello muttered. "While you were off riding the wild fed, some of us were being eaten alive by mosquitos."

"I said I was sorry," she replied then eyed him suspiciously. "I thought Bogart was meeting me with my bag."

"He was but something came up, so he sent me," Othello replied.

"Something came up?" she muttered and looked around. "We're in the middle of the woods. What could possibly have come up?"

"The male plumbing is a complicated piece of machinery," Othello informed her.

She groaned and held up her hand. "Never mind. Sorry I asked."

Othello handed her a set of car keys. "The jeep is parked near the planes. Just follow the thing that looks a little like a road. It'll bring you out to some dirt road. You'll figure it out from there."

"Thanks, I appreciate this," she announced.

"Yeah, just don't tell the guys I gave you the information from those emails," Othello replied and gave her a stern look. "I bruise easily."

"They didn't want to include me," she remarked with irritation. "Sometimes a woman has to take matters into her own hands."

"Just be careful, okay?"

"I won't be anywhere near that mansion tomorrow night," she informed him. "I intend to case the place in the morning and be gone before the team shows up."

"And if you find Zack?"

Jackie held her breath then managed a smile. "That depends on what hand he's playing," she replied. "If he doesn't fold willingly, I promise he'll be drawing dead."

Othello tensed at the comment. "Good luck, Jackie," he announced reluctantly.

She kissed him on the cheek. "I'll see you in a few days." She hurried down the path.

Othello watched her leave and frowned as she vanished into the woods. "I hope so."

✝

Pinto and Sal picked blueberries from a large blueberry bush in a small clearing. Sal glanced at his watch several times while Pinto listened to strange sounds coming from deep within the woods. She seemed concerned about their location and safety.

"It's getting dark," she informed her father. "How much longer?"

"Another ten minutes," he assured her. "Then we'll head back."

They heard some rustling in the woods. Pinto gasped and nearly dropped her basket of blueberries. Jackie appeared in the clearing while panting from her lengthy sprint.

"You're late," Sal announced.

"By ten minutes," she scoffed. "Is everyone the time police?"

Sal indicated the nearby ATV then hurried for it. Jackie slung the duffel bag over her shoulder and jumped on the back behind Sal. He looked at Pinto near the bushes.

"I'll be back in twenty minutes," he announced. "If you see a bear, throw the basket and run."

The ATV took off down the path. Pinto nervously looked around the darkening woods then eyed the basket of blueberries she held.

✝

The ATV raced along the woods edge toward the parked planes. The jeep was located alongside the last plane where Othello said it would be. Sal pulled up next to the jeep, allowing Jackie to jump off the back with her duffel bag. He looked at her and forced a tiny smile.

"Be careful, okay?"

"I'll be fine," Jackie gently replied while returning the smile. "I just need some answers, that's all. When I get them, I'll be back."

Sal raised his brows above his round, wire glasses. "If it comes down to him or you--"

"Way ahead of you, Sal," she replied. "Thanks for your help."

"You've got to at least try," he remarked. "You'll never forgive yourself if you don't do that much."

She nodded then managed a tiny laugh. "Go get Pinto before she's eaten by Boo Boo."

Sal smiled and raced back for the path in the woods. Jackie hurried to the jeep and tossed her duffel bag into the back of the open vehicle. She jumped into the driver's seat and turned the key. The engine wouldn't turn.

"No," she groaned and tried again. Nothing happened. "This can't be happening!"

Jackie popped the hood and jumped out the driver's side door. As she hurried to the front of the jeep, she saw Bogart leaning against the nearby plane casually tossing the spark plug in the air and catching it. He revealed the spark plug and grinned.

"Won't get far without this," he informed her.

She groaned and glared at him. "Give me the damned spark plug."

Bogart approached her and the jeep. He raised his brow while tilting his head and offered his most charming country boy grin. "What's the magic word?" he teased.

Jackie sneered at him and growled her response. "Fine, you can come along."

"I thought you'd never ask," he teased.

"Just replace the damned spark plug so we can go," she scoffed then headed for the driver's seat.

"Acht," he announced catching her attention.

She looked back at him. He beckoned her toward him. Jackie frowned and approached. He pointed to the spot alongside him. She stood on the spot, relaying her irritation, and then folded her arms across her chest.

"Now you stay right there and don't move until I say you can," he informed her.

She rolled her eyes and muttered a curse under her breath. He wasn't as dumb as he'd have people believe. He knew she'd take off the moment he shut the hood, leaving him behind. She didn't want to take him. She didn't want to put anyone else at risk for her fool's errand, but he was forcing her hand. He slammed the hood down, grinned, and politely extended his hand to the driver's seat.

"After you, my dear."

Chapter Thirty-three

The old split-level home belonging to Jackie's father was nestled in a quiet development with other country homes in the upper middle-class neighborhood of Vernon Heights, Virginia. Despite her absence, the yard was meticulously manicured. The home appeared to be in excellent condition since she paid to have a service tend to the yard and garden. After Holden had received his promotion to the Colorado FBI Bureau, they kept her father's home as a layover for the guys while they were traveling. It was midnight by the time Jackie and Bogart reached her old neighborhood. Although streetlights dimly lit the small development, the homes were mostly dark since it was a weekday. Othello's jeep was parked two homes away along the curb. There were few vehicles parked on the street, since most of the homes had large driveways, so they had to stay far enough away to remain out of sight.

Once they were sure no one was watching the house besides them, they headed for the back door. Jackie removed the hidden key and let them in through the kitchen.

Bogart looked around the familiar, tidy kitchen and grinned. "Haven't been here in a while," he remarked.

"Don't get comfortable," she announced and turned on a small light above the stove.

"Remember the time I saw you naked in the shower?" he teased.

Jackie glared at him.

"So if I saw my sister naked in the shower, does that make me a hillbilly?" he joked while grinning.

She continued to glare at him and folded her arms across her chest with limited patience. "Trust me, Bogart. You're a hillbilly either way."

He laughed at the comment. "You know what you're looking for?"

She nodded.

"Can I assume this has to do with the note from the frig?" he questioned.

Jackie stared at him with surprise as her arms fell to her sides. "How'd you know?" she asked. "Even if you saw the note in the weapons room--"

"Come on, Jackie," he announced with a groan. "I'm not as stupid as most people think. I recognized that note from the last time I was here with you. You were very protective of your father's note. I knew it didn't just find its way into the ranger station. It was planted there."

She fidgeted slightly and remained stern. "I know what I'm doing, Bogart."

"I know," he replied simply with little concern. "I'm going to take a quick look around and make sure everything's clear. Don't be long."

As Bogart left the kitchen, Jackie approached the refrigerator and looked at the spot beneath a helicopter magnet where her father's note was last hanging. Jackie stared at the piece of paper with Kilroy drawn on it now beneath the magnet. She removed the paper and studied the drawing as her heart pounded. She took a moment to stare at the newly added paper then removed her father's note from her jacket pocket and lovingly replaced it to its rightful spot on the refrigerator. She took the Kilroy drawing closer to the small light over the stove and studied the paper both front and back. On the back was handwritten, 'love always'. She didn't know how long she stared at the paper before carefully folding it and placing it in her pocket. She gently wiped the tears from her eyes. She didn't know what to make of the clue. Was Zack playing games with her emotions? What did it mean?

†

The light came on within the two-car garage to reveal the neat and tidy interior. Bogart eyed the familiar older sports car, which belonged to Holden. He didn't recognize the brand new, black sedan. Someone was obviously using Jackie's garage to store his car. The sedan definitely didn't belong to her or Holden. Bogart entered the garage from the mudroom and approached the sedan parked in the farthest bay from the house door. He ran his hand along the hood of the car then hesitated when he felt the warmth from the engine. His eyes suddenly widened in horror.

Bogart turned toward the house entrance and came face-to-face with a tough looking man in a dark suit. His neatly pressed shirt told Bogart all he needed to know about this man. The neatly dressed intruder punched Bogart in the face, knocking him back against the sedan. As Bogart straightened and was about to go for his gun, the intruder pulled his own gun with a silencer affixed to the barrel from his shoulder holster.

"Well, this isn't going to end well," Bogart muttered while staring at the gun in the man's hand.

†

Jackie leaned on the counter and stared outside through the small part in the curtains covering the sink window. Her thoughts were all over the place, and she suddenly wasn't sure if she could do what needed to be done. Her self-pity was cut unexpectedly short when she heard a faint clunk from the garage. She was about to turn around when she saw the reflection of a man behind her in the window glass. Jackie suddenly leaped onto the kitchen counter and back flipped over the man. He spun around with his gun in his hand, obviously stunned by her ability to leap over him.

By the time he turned, Jackie was already spinning into a kick, knocking the gun from his hand. The gun flew across the room and struck the wall with tremendous force. The well-dressed intruder stared at her with some surprise. The rage on her face was possibly more frightening than her last two moves.

"It was you," he suddenly declared. "You're the bitch who killed my friend."

A devious smile crossed her face. "Oh? So you got my message?" Her eyes suddenly narrowed while glaring at him. "That makes you next."

A knife suddenly appeared in his gloved hand as he lunged for her. Jackie caught his wrist and twisted his arm completely around while spinning his body along with hers, placing his back to hers. She flipped him across her back, over her head, and threw him to the floor. He landed with a little more grace than she'd anticipated, allowing him an opportunity to return to his feet. With the knife still in his hand, he slashed at her. Jackie leaped to the floor in a forward roll to avoid the blade. She sprang up and leaped into a backward flip while kicking mid-air. She struck the man in the chest and knocked him clear across the kitchen. He struck the kitchen table with enough force that it slid across the floor nearly a foot. Jackie crossed the kitchen and paused before the man writhing on the floor with disorientation. He saw her coming for him and immediately waved his hands defensively.

"I'm not here for you," he announced in panic. "Let's talk about this."

"I'm tired of playing with you," Jackie informed him with little emotion. She removed her semiautomatic from her concealed shoulder holster beneath her leather jacket and aimed it at him. "I've got more important things to do than waste my time and energy on you. A bullet is faster and cheaper." Her finger tightened on the trigger.

"Who the hell are you?" he suddenly gasped with horror. "Are you CIA or something?"

"I'm the daughter of Lieutenant Commander Jackson Remus, United States Navy SEAL team Whiskey Tango Foxtrot," she announced while proudly straightening. "And your friends killed my friends. *Now* you're going to die." She cocked her head and offered an unsettling smile. "Any questions?"

He again waved his hands defensively. "Wait, wait," he cried out fearfully. "I didn't kill your friends, I swear. It was the Russian."

Jackie's heart skipped a beat. She didn't want to show any emotion, but he had to see the shattered look in her eyes. She felt the gun tremble in her hand as her concern replaced her hostility. Jackie held her breath and attempted to resume her authoritative position over the man.

"Yes, the Russian," he explained with renewed enthusiasm, almost certainly reading her expression. "You want the man who killed your friend, don't you? I can give you the Russian. Let me go, and I'll give you the Russian."

"You know where to find him?" she asked while attempting to conceal the quiver in her voice.

"Yes, I know where he is," he reconfirmed. "I can take you there tonight. That's why we were here. He's been here several times. We were told to keep an eye on him." He again waved his hands. "We're not hitmen, I swear. We aren't after the bounty on you or your friends."

"We?" she suddenly gasped.

"My co-worker," he announced.

Jackie felt horror sweep through her body. "Bogart!" There was no response. "Bogart!"

Bogart ran into the kitchen while gasping for air. She saw his shirt was covered in blood and his expression was almost panic-stricken. "There was a small accident in the garage," he announced while pointing.

She stared at him and the blood covering his shirt and arms. "What happened?" Jackie cried out.

"I don't know," Bogart pouted. "This guy came after me, and I tried to do what you guys do, and he just sort of died." His look was serious. "I'm telling you, Jack. They drop like flies around me." He eyed the gun in her hand aimed at the man on the floor. "Who's that?"

"Oh, that's maggot bait," she announced simply. "He's going to tell us where to find the Russian."

"The Russian?" Bogart questioned.

Jackie raised her brows demandingly while glaring at Bogart. "Yes, the *Russian*."

Bogart then appeared to understand what they were talking about. "Oh, the Russian." He gave the guy a serious look and nodded. "Smart move," he informed the man on the floor then indicated Jackie. "That bitch be crazy."

"Why don't you clean up while I finish my conversation with maggot bait," Jackie remarked while eyeing his shirt and nodded him from the room.

Bogart eyed his shirt and grimaced. "Good idea." He headed for the downstairs bathroom.

Jackie looked back at the man on the floor. "Who's your boss?"

"If I tell you I'm dead."

"If you don't tell me you're dead anyway," she replied and raised a cocky brow along with a tiny smirk. "You may want to consider a new career."

"Melissa Pendleton," he blurted out.

"Who put the hit on my team?"

He shook his head. "I don't know," he informed her with sincerity. "She spoke of 'the boss' to others, but I'd never met him. None of us have."

Jackie gently scratched her temple with the barrel of the semiautomatic handgun. "You're surprisingly cooperative for a killer."

"I told you," he announced seeming to relax. "I'm not a hitman. I'm just one of Ms. Pendleton's guards. She always sends us to keep an eye on the new guys. The Russian is sneaky. She doesn't trust him. There's a guard keeping an eye on him where he's staying. My co-worker and I were supposed to find out what he was doing here. We didn't find anything." He then appeared curious. "Is this your place?"

"It's a friend's," she replied and offered nothing more to the stranger. "What else do you know about the Russian who killed my friend?"

"He's highly skilled," he informed her. "You could have your hands full if you go after him. He came highly recommended by another known associate."

"Who?"

"I don't know," he replied seeming genuinely sincere. "I'm low on the food chain."

She studied him a moment then replaced her gun and extended her hand to him. He stared at her hand a moment with distrust then accepted it. Jackie pulled him to his feet and brushed the dirt from his jacket.

"I'm going to forgive you for attempting to kill me," she informed him. "You were upset about your friend. I get that." Jackie casually leaned against the counter and folded her arms across her chest. His gun and knife remained on the floor not far from them. He could easily go for them. "Now, tell me something I don't know."

He considered the comment and never once looked at his weapons on the floor. Jackie had to admit; she was impressed. He respected her ability to kill him, which meant she probably wouldn't have to kill him after all.

"There is one strange thing I'd overheard," he replied. "It may not be important."

"Try me."

"In addition to the million dollars for each member of your team, there's an additional million if you're brought alive," he informed her. "I thought that was strange." He tilted his head and stared at her. "I have to ask. What's so important about you? We were all sort of curious."

Jackie sank into thought. "Good question." She snapped out of her trance and studied the man. "This is how it's going to go down. You're going to take us to where the Russian is staying, introduce us to your friend, and then you're going to leave town and never come back." Her look was serious and frightening. "It's the only way I can promise I won't kill you because if I see you again, I *will* kill you."

"I'm as good as dead anyway," he informed her. "I don't have a whole lot to lose now that I've crossed Ms. Pendleton. I'm not safe from her anywhere. She'll probably have one of her hired goons kill my girlfriend just to torture me first."

Jackie stared at him a long moment and gave it some thought. She removed a pen and tablet from the nearby drawer then wrote a number on the pad. She tore off the top sheet.

"Have you ever heard of Giovanni?"

He stared at her with surprise and almost choked. "The notorious mobster, Giovanni? Of course, I heard of him. Who hasn't?"

She handed him the piece of paper containing a phone number. "This is the number of his front man. You call him and tell him Whiskey Tango Foxtrot is calling in a favor." She gently cleared her throat. "I heard he has several new job openings at his island resort off the coast of Columbia. As long as you and your girlfriend are working for him, Melissa Pendleton wouldn't dream of touching you." She then tilted her head and considered the comment. "Of course, if you cross him, you'll probably be shark bait instead of maggot bait."

He stared at the phone number then gave her a puzzled look. "Why are you helping me?" the man asked with surprise. "I tried to kill you."

"Believe me," she announced. "If you give me the Russian, we're more than even."

"You want him that badly, huh?"

"You could say that," she muttered. "I have a little score to settle with that one."

He placed the paper in his pocket then looked at her and attempted a tiny smile. "Could you maybe not kill the guy keeping an eye on him?" he asked with a curious look. "He's not a bad guy. Not really."

"Sure," Jackie replied. "I'll make sure Bogart doesn't sneeze on him and accidentally kill him."

Chapter Thirty-four

It was after one o'clock in the morning. The lake was peaceful and calm in the moonlight allowing a panoramic view of several homes lining the secluded section of the lake. A houseboat was tied off to a large, private dock with a few other boats sharing slips on both sides. A vapor light provided dim lighting over the dock and boats but allowed just enough shadow to conceal predators. Zack slipped from the darkness of the houseboat doorway and into the shadows on the boat deck. He remained in the shadows and paused several feet from the railing to scan the dock and the surrounding homes within the woods on the lake.

Although nothing moved, he still didn't appear convinced there wasn't something out there. He crossed the light on the deck, leaped over the deck railing, and softly landed on the dock in the shadows alongside the boat. He again scanned the area but didn't see anything. He turned back toward the boat's permanently secured gangplank. Jackie leaned against the gangplank railing and stared at him without emotion.

"Hey," she casually announced without even so much as a smile.

Zack's expression immediately dropped. He was obviously surprised to see her, but he didn't usually make those feelings known even with facial expressions. He appeared almost frozen as if he didn't know how to react to her presence.

"Are you alone?" he asked and seemed unwilling to take his eyes off her.

"Nope," came a male voice from behind as a dart struck him in the ass.

Zack jumped when he felt the pinch and immediately removed the dart, but it was too late. As he turned, he saw Bogart lowering the dart gun while grinning.

"Hey, Zack," Bogart cheerfully announced while indicating the dart gun. "Look what I found in your car." He watched Zack stumble then collapse to the dock. "Good to see you too, buddy."

Jackie frowned and casually approached her fallen comrade. She eyed Bogart without emotion. "Let's get to work," she announced in a stern, commanding voice.

✝

Zack slowly woke with some disorientation. He immediately realized his wrists and ankles were duct taped to a chair. He jerked in a feeble attempt to pull free then looked across the bland looking room. Jackie casually leaned against a table while staring at him with no expression. Bogart stood alongside the only door while holding an Uzi in his hands. His light-hearted, playful mood was nowhere to be found. He was officially Jackie's muscle and played the role with seriousness. Judging by the sounds outside and the looks of the place, they were in an abandoned bait shop. The windows were boarded, leaving them with plenty of privacy for Jackie to conduct her interrogation.

A devious smile crossed Jackie's face. "Oh, look, Bogart. Our guest of honor is awake."

Bogart raised the Uzi without showing any emotion as he stared at Zack. "Pity," he scoffed then sneered. "I was hoping I'd killed him."

"Do you remember all those stories you used to tell about interrogating prisoners?" Jackie asked Zack while raising a cocky brow. "Stories meant to gross me out?" There was no response. He only stared at her a moment then refused to acknowledge her. "It seems those stories may finally come in handy." She walked toward him in a slow, intimidating manner, although it came across somewhat sexy and caught his attention. She paused before his chair, placed her booted foot on the seat in the free space between his legs, and leaned on her knee. "Simple questions, Zack. Answer them, and you might leave with all your teeth."

He met her gaze and showed no emotion. "Your delivery needs work," he casually remarked. "And you should have Bogart interrogating me. Because this--" He indicated the situation. "This is a bit of a turn-on."

Jackie sneered at his comment and thrust her heel into his crotch. Zack gasped with pain and attempted to endure it. She didn't hit him hard enough to do any damage, but hard enough to get his attention and cause some discomfort.

"That was a warning shot," she snarled and backed away from him. "Now you be sure to let me know whenever I do or say something else that turns you on, so I can correct the situation by tenderizing your balls."

"Sorry, sir," he announced under his breath. "It won't happen again, sir."

She considered the comment. "A bit cocky, but I'll accept it."

Jackie sat on the floor, hugged her knees to her chest, and stared at him a long, silent moment. Zack stared back at her then looked away. He obviously wasn't expecting her to take up residence on the floor like some innocent child waiting for story time. It's possible her actions stirred some past memory.

"Can't look at me?" she remarked. "Is it guilt? Or are you thinking about the two million you'd get for betraying me like you did Kirk?"

Zack twitched but didn't respond or look at her.

She suddenly raised her brows. "Oh, are you a little surprised I know about the additional million on my head if I'm brought in alive?" she asked then smirked adding a throaty chuckle. "Yeah, I tortured that out of some poor bastard before I tore him apart in my father's garage."

Bogart raised a brow but didn't comment.

"You'd be proud of me," she continued while showing little emotion. "I've graduated to your level. You've officially turned me into a merciless killer like yourself." Jackie shrugged. "It's pretty easy to do when everyone you love is either dead or has betrayed you."

"Get rid of the idiot," Zack snarled softly.

"Hey," Bogart snapped, offended by the comment.

Jackie eyed Bogart, made a face, and indicated the door with a nod.

Bogart frowned his displeasure to the situation. "I'll be right outside listening through the door," he grumbled then left.

Jackie stood and approached Zack, eyeing his bound wrists and ankles. She knew better than to trust him, but his bindings seemed secure enough. Jackie crouched down before him and placed her hand on his. Zack immediately tensed from her touch telling her there were still feelings for her. She knew she had him. She kept her index finger close to his wrist and attempted to feel his pulse. It was racing. She just needed to drive it home. She reached up and touched his face with her free hand. He still refused to look at her, but he again twitched.

"The guys took a vote," she gently informed him. "They intend to take you out the first opportunity they get. I don't support their decision, but I won't stop them either. I just wanted a chance to say goodbye. No matter what happens, Zack, I'll always love you." As she straightened, he finally turned his head and looked at her while she remained standing over him. She leaned down and kissed him quickly but warmly on the lips. When she pulled away, he stared at her, obviously not expecting her to kiss him. She leaned closer to his ear and whispered, "Please don't make me be the one who has to kill you."

She pulled back just enough to meet his gaze, wanting to read his eyes. She needed to see if there was anything left of her best friend.

Zack drew a deep breath while staring into her eyes only a few inches from his. His eyes were slightly glossed as if he was close to shedding tears.

"Jackie," he announced gently without taking his eyes off her then hesitated and held his breath.

Although she hid it well, she could feel her heart racing with anticipation to what he was about to say. She just needed to hear some explanation to redeem her faith in him. He needed to tell her that someone else killed Kirk, and he was completely innocent on all counts. It was tough not showing any emotion while awaiting his response.

His look hardened as all emotion left his face. "You probably shouldn't have left Bogart alone outside the door," Zack remarked. "You aren't the only ones being followed."

Jackie felt alarm sweep through her. She took a step back from Zack, removed her gun, and aimed it at the door with concern. "Bogart?"

The door immediately opened, revealing Bogart. For a moment, Jackie was relieved until she saw his hands were in the air. Bogart saw the gun in Jackie's hand and immediately leaped to the floor. Mac aimed her gun at Jackie, although neither woman fired at the other.

"It's nothing personal," Mac announced while keeping her gun trained on Jackie then indicated Zack, who casually watched from his front row seat. "I'm just here for the prick. Don't make this difficult. I don't want to shoot you."

"This isn't exactly the fantasy I had in mind," Zack casually remarked.

Both women glanced at Zack. "Shut up!" they shouted in unison then returned to their face-off.

"All that's missing from this slice of hell is a Russian spy," he muttered then glanced at the door with a curious look as if expecting one to appear mysteriously.

Bogart moved to his feet, putting Mac on high alert. She suddenly kicked the gun from Jackie's hand. When she went for the return kick, Jackie was already spinning into her own kick. Mac took the hard hit and fell backward against the doorframe, losing her gun as well. Surprisingly, Mac darted out the open door rather than accept the challenge and fight her.

"Watch him," Jackie yelled to Bogart as she bolted out the door after Mac.

Bogart retrieved one of the discarded guns and aimed it at Zack while maintaining his distance. He sneered at Zack and shook his head. "You're only alive because she asked me not to kill you," he remarked while placing his finger on the trigger. "If you really love someone, you sometimes need to protect them from themselves. Don't you agree?"

"I think we can both agree that you should point that gun in another direction before you accidentally shoot me," Zack remarked with little emotion. "You've killed more people by accident than on purpose."

"It wouldn't be no accident," Bogart growled then lowered the gun and smirked while cocking his head to the side. "But she needs someone she can trust to replace you in her life, doesn't she? I think I can fill that void. With a little time, I can make her forget you ever existed."

Someone slipped through the doorway behind Bogart. Bogart heard something, but it was already too late. He was struck on the back of the head before he had a chance to turn. He gasped and fell to the floor, dropping the gun.

Zack watched him hit the floor with little reaction. "No offense, Bogart, but your attempt to fill my shoes needs a little work."

†

Jackie chased Mac along the moonlit path in the woods around the lake. As the bait shop and dock disappeared behind them, Mac suddenly slid to a stop and spun into a roundhouse kick for Jackie. Jackie threw herself to the ground and into a forward roll to avoid the flying foot coming at her. She sprang to her feet and immediately blocked the return kick. Jackie heard about Mac's impressive fighting skills. She nearly took down Zack once a while back. Her knowledge of Mac prepared her for a fierce battle with the woman. Despite Mac's fast punches and quick kicks, Jackie was able to predict and deflect them. In Jackie's opinion, Mac's attempt to kick her ass almost seemed personal. She barely knew the woman, but Mac attacked her with an unusual aggression almost as if they were rivals.

Mac came at her with several fast kicks, but rather than deflect them and waste energy, Jackie flipped through the air and out of her path, surprising Mac. As Mac spun to face her, Jackie was already kicking her in the shoulder, sending her backward and into a nearby tree. The hit was moderately hard and slightly stunned the woman.

"It doesn't have to be this way," Jackie informed her and attempted to end the fight before it started.

Mac sneered with hostility. "Oh, shut up!"

She immediately lunged for Jackie with another round of fast kicks and punches. Jackie dived from her path, rolled across the ground, and popped up to her feet. Mac again lunged for her with a series of roundhouse kicks. Jackie ducked one, dropped to the dirt path, and swept her leg out from under her. Mac crashed to the ground but managed to pick herself up, although now slightly out of breath. It was obvious, despite being highly skilled; she hadn't trained in a while.

"Give it up, Mac," Jackie remarked. "We're on the same side here, aren't we? I just want to talk to him. After that, he's all yours."

"I may not want him getting himself killed," Mac replied while attempting to catch her breath then straightened proudly. "But that doesn't mean I want you poisoning his mind and turning him against me."

"Turning him against you?" Jackie suddenly demanded. "How would my talking to him turn him against you?" She hesitated while staring at Mac and came to an instant realization. "Oh, you think if I talk to him, he'll want to return to the team. You're afraid of losing him to me."

Mac fidgeted and became animated and angry. "Forget it," she lashed out. "You couldn't possibly understand."

"Try me."

"Zack and I," Mac cried out then pointed demandingly, "we're alike. We're the tormented souls of this world. He's one of the few people who can possibly understand someone like me. I *need* him; you don't."

Jackie shook her head. "You're selling yourself short, Mac," she remarked. "I know you've made some mistakes, but you can start fresh. You don't need to cling to Zack like a security blanket." She drew a deep breath. "And you're wrong. I need Zack. He's my family. Those guys are all I have left from my childhood. I won't lose them."

Mac relaxed slightly then waved her off. "Forget it," she scoffed. "You still don't get it. Good luck converting him before the rest of your team kills him."

Jackie watched Mac turn and walk away, heading away from the dock and the bait shop. She considered the comment, sighed softly, and then hurried back for the dock.

†

Jackie entered the abandoned bait shop only a few minutes later to find Bogart sitting on the floor while holding his head as he leaned against the table. Jackie looked at the empty chair then glared at Bogart.

"You let him get away?" she demanded with horror in her eyes. "He was tied to a chair. I told you to keep an eye on him. How did he get away?"

"It wasn't my fault," Bogart protested with some irritation. "Someone hit me from behind. I'm fine. Thanks for asking." He then glared at her. "Where's Mac?"

Jackie frowned. "She got away."

"Oh, you let her get away?" he demanded in a mocking tone. "She's like five foot nothing. You can take on ten armed men, but you can't you fight one girl?"

"Very funny," Jackie scoffed then groaned softly. "It's not safe here. We need to go." She helped pull him to his feet. "We only have one more shot at Zack."

He looked at her and appeared concerned. "No, Jackie," he scoffed. "You said we weren't going to do that. Not tomorrow night. We're not going out there."

"Our original plan was to case the mansion until late afternoon," she insisted while studying him. "We'll stick to that plan."

He seemed to consider the comment. "Then we leave," he confirmed.

"Then we leave."

His look was serious as his eyes remained wide and he pointed a warning finger at her. "You promise?"

"Yes, I promise."

Chapter Thirty-five

It was already late afternoon heading into early evening. Jackie sat in a large tree while Bogart stood on the ground outside the brick wall surrounding the back of Melissa Pendleton's isolated country estate. Although quite wealthy in appearance, Sal's estate was grander in every aspect. If she had put the price on their heads, the hefty bounty could quite possibly wipe her out financially. There had to be someone else footing the bill and Melissa was just the front man or front woman, in her case. Several cars had driven onto the estate and parked in front of the elegant mansion. Jackie and Bogart witnessed several cars pull up, although they lost sight of them once they headed toward the front of the mansion.

Several guards roamed the property, including the back of the estate. They were heavily armed with assault weapons containing silencers. Despite what they were hiding, they didn't appear to be expecting trouble, particularly considering the professions of their guests. The backyard to the estate contained a lovely gazebo within a massive garden. There were several trees and shrubs throughout, but there were also large open areas offering no cover for someone attempting to sneak onto the property. While Jackie studied the estate grounds and attempted to see through the back windows of the mansion, Bogart stared up the tree at her while becoming impatient and possibly concerned.

"You promised, Jackie," Bogart scolded. "The guys are probably already here. If they find us--"

"They'll what?" she snapped while looking down at him. "Shoot us? Fire us? What, Bogart?"

"Yell?" Bogart remarked then groaned and cast his back against the wall. "We've been here for hours with no sign of Zack, but you have seen a shitload of guards and over a dozen professional hitmen. Every single one of 'em just dying to get their hands on our asses. They're all looking for us, and we're sitting just a few yards away begging to be shot."

"Case in point," she remarked. "They'd never expect to find us here."

"Case in point," he scoffed. "We're a couple of idiots begging to be shot.

Jackie suddenly tensed. "I see him," she cried out only loud enough for Bogart to hear.

"How convenient," Bogart muttered and smirked. "Now *he* can kill us." Bogart climbed the wall with his rifle and backpack, joining her. As he looked across the massive yard, he saw several guards patrolling the area as well. "Are you sure you want to do this?"

"Do I have a choice?"

"Always plenty of choices in this world, my dear sister," he remarked.

Jackie glared down at him. "Stop that," she scolded. "Hand me my things."

He groaned and handed her the small backpack with the samurai swords sticking out one end. "This wasn't part of the plan," Bogart reminded her. "You weren't supposed to engage the bloodthirsty hitmen."

"You just take your position and cover my ass," she announced and indicated the tree.

"I'm not the world's greatest sniper, Jackie," he informed her. "I shot you once, remember?"

"I'm sure you'll hit your mark and surprise yourself," she replied, although not necessarily believing her own words. "Just get into position."

He groaned then nodded while removing his rifle with night scope from his shoulder. As Bogart took his position on the wall hidden alongside the tree, Jackie dropped down from the tree near him. She wore a black mesh tank top allowing a generous view of her red, satin and lace bra. Rather than her usual stalking pants, she wore spandex shorts, boots up to her knees, and black fishnet stockings to complete her attention-grabbing ensemble. Her double thigh holster revealed a semiautomatic strapped to each leg for that sexy, menacing look, and a shoulder holster containing her twin samurai swords strapped to her back.

Bogart eyed her and shook his head. "Where the hell did you come up with that outfit?" he demanded.

"Othello suggested it."

"Figures," Bogart muttered then eyed her while grinning. "Well, if it's your goal to distract him, I think you'll succeed."

"Use your enemy's weaknesses against them," she informed him then flashed a smile.

They both inserted their ear transmitters before Jackie took off across the top of the wall toward her destination. Zack was too close to the house for her to reach him using the wall alone. She'd have to venture through the yard itself, which contained multiple guards patrolling the area and a small collection of hitmen smoking cigarettes between her and Zack. She needed the element of surprise and as little noise as possible to keep from bringing out the rest of the guards and other hired killers within the mansion. Time was critical since she didn't know how long Zack would remain in the yard. Jackie pulled the wires on two security cameras attached to the wall directed into the yard as she passed. Once she reached a darker section of the estate grounds between her and Zack, she did a forward flip from the wall and landed gracefully on the ground in a crouched position. No one saw her in the darkness.

As a guard approached, he didn't see her until it was too late. She spun into a roundhouse kick and silently took him down. She slipped through the darkness toward a second guard. When he turned, she flipped through the air, caught him around the neck with her legs, and took him to the ground. He managed to gasp, although not loud enough to bring any attention. As she crouched in the darkness, Zack had suddenly straightened and scanned the mansion grounds. For a moment, she feared she'd been detected. He didn't see her, but she somehow knew he was aware of her presence. A moment of panic filled her. She drew a deep breath, pushed it aside, and concentrated on the task at hand. She was running out of time. It wouldn't be long before the team arrived, if they hadn't already, and took their shot at Zack.

There was little place to hide if she wanted to reach Zack. She had to come out of the shadows and go to war with the remaining men. Surprisingly, her biggest fear was Bogart accidentally shooting her. Jackie ran across the grounds toward the armed guards, using the element of surprise. None expected a woman running for them. Before they could even raise their weapons, Jackie spun into a flip and took out the first two. She landed and immediately rolled across the ground as others now fired at her. Nearly silent assault rifle fire struck the ground not far from her as she rolled into a darkened area near the gazebo. The guards fired several muffled shots then stopped and watched. When nothing moved, they converged on the gazebo. Zack watched the situation unfolding while heading toward the commotion. The hired killers drew their weapons and scattered like cockroaches in the light.

As the guards gathered around the gazebo, Jackie somersaulted from the roof, landing behind the men. She spun into high roundhouse kicks and took out the first two guards then flipped through the air to avoid the gunfire from the other guards. They were stunned when she landed in front of them. She kicked the weapon from the first man's hand then drew her samurai swords and went after the next two guards. She knocked the weapons from their hands with her swords then simultaneously lunged forward, running her swords through both men's midsections. Jackie allowed the men to fall to the ground with her swords still intact and dove over the gazebo railing, anticipating the round of gunfire that followed. The remaining three guards fired a barrage of bullets into the gazebo making less noise than if they hadn't had the suppressors on their rifles. After several dozen rounds, they ceased their fire, certain they'd gotten her.

The guards approached the bullet-ridden railing and looked inside the darkened gazebo. Jackie swung down from the ceiling, taking out the first man with her feet. She rolled across the ground and pulled her swords from the two dead men. As she sprang up, she swung her swords for both men, clashing with their weapons, and disarming them. She then twirled the swords and slashed at the remaining two men, cutting them both. A nearly silent shot was fired, narrowly missing her. Jackie rolled across the ground and into the shadows so they wouldn't have a clear shot. As she ran across the grounds avoiding nearly silent gunfire, Zack kept pace, following her from a distance. He knew she was coming for him. He didn't have to go to her.

A rifle fired loudly breaking the silence as the bullet splintered the tree alongside the hitman. He immediately took cover while the remaining hitmen crossed the property, closing in on the location of sniper fire. More shots were fired, forcing them to take cover wherever they could. When the hired killer behind the tree realized the sniper was busy with the other hitmen, he took advantage of the situation and slipped around the tree to shoot Jackie. To his surprise, she was gone!

"Looking for someone?" Jackie asked from behind.

As he spun around, she impaled him through the midsection with her sword and locked eyes with him. "Stay out of my way," she snarled then pulled the sword free and watched him fall to the ground.

Jackie casually stepped over the dead man and saw Zack waiting for her several yards away. As she walked toward him, her eyes locked on him, two of the hired killers stopped in their tracks and considered taking her out. Before they could even aim, they were under Bogart's sniper fire and had to seek cover. Jackie stopped two feet before Zack, took a fighting stance with both swords, one above her head and one in front of her body, and stared at him with cold, hateful eyes. Zack paced in front of her like a caged panther stalking its prey. His eyes swept over her body more than once, taking in her unusual choice of outfit, knowing exactly what she was attempting to do. Every move she made, every stitch of clothes she wore was meant to assault his senses and throw him off his game. By the way he watched her and with how long he took to react, she knew it was working.

To him, she was a stripper, pole dancing in front of him, and he just wanted to sit back and watch a while longer. She didn't move from her attack position, knowing if she showed no reaction or expression it would draw him closer. Soon the temptation would be too great, and he'd want to engage his sexy pole dancer. All her hours of training came down to this single moment. Zack would soon play his hand, and she'd finally know if he was gone forever.

Chapter Thirty-six

Beck crouched in the shadows behind the bushes alongside the house and peered in through the lounge window. The men within the lounge left in a hurry. Beck appeared curious and then touched his hidden ear transmitter.

"Were we made?" Beck asked. "They're running from the lounge with purpose."

"Negative," Monroe responded through his ear transmitter. "Something's happening in the back of the house. I can't see what's going on, but it's caught their attention."

"Probably a major pissing match," Beck responded. "You know how these assassin types are when they get together." He then scoffed under his breath, "Mercenary wannabes."

They could then hear the sniper rifle fire, alerting them of something happening out back.

"Bad news, Beck," came Gil's moderately calm voice over the transmitter.

Beck tensed, shut his eyes a moment, and then touched his ear transmitter. "What bad news?" he asked, although he already seemed to know the answer.

"Our kitten is fighting the tiger," Gil replied.

Beck sneered then cursed under his breath. "If she survives, I'm getting her fixed and declawed." He then touched his ear device and spoke to the others. "Whether we like it or not, she's given us the perfect distraction."

"Are we going in?" Monroe asked over his ear transmitter.

"Yeah, we're going in," he announced. "I want a snatch and grab on the boss lady. We're far enough into the country that it'll take a while for someone to report shots fired to the police. Someone should probably keep an eye on the kitten and offer sniper support."

"Affirmative," Gil responded with little reaction. "She's got a bogey in the trees."

"Bogart," Beck snarled then nodded with conviction. "Him, I'm going to kill." He touched his ear transmitter. "Move in, team." Beck headed for the glass lounge doors and easily picked the lock.

†

Gil and Darth slipped in through the rear kitchen door, only glancing briefly at the commotion in the backyard. Darth seemed eager to join in on the fun, and it took some coaxing to convince him otherwise. Gil shook his head, obviously disappointed with Jackie's decision to go rogue. Darth followed him through the large, empty kitchen and both entered the grand hallway, where they ran into Monroe, who had slipped in through the study door.

"I would have sworn she was here," Monroe informed Gil while looking around. "Maybe she went upstairs at the first sniff of danger."

"Don't underestimate a woman of that caliber," Gil replied. "She could be calling in the reinforcements. It's too quiet down here."

"Yeah, that's because everyone's outside watching 'the psycho Jackie show' out back," Monroe huffed then shook his head with annoyance. "I knew Holden was lying when he said she was sleeping late this morning."

"Darth and I have the backstairs," Gil announced and indicated the kitchen behind him. "You take the main staircase."

Monroe nodded, and they headed in opposite directions.

†

Gil carried his semiautomatic while walking along the back hallway on the second floor with Darth leading the way, sniffing at each door. Gil checked several bedrooms and found them mostly dark and empty. He opened the last door and heard a gun cocking. Darth snarled in response. Gil leaped through the doorway, rolled across the floor, and sat up with his gun aimed at Riley. She held a gun on him as well. Although frightened, she held the gun with conviction and seemed willing to use it.

"I don't know who you are, but get out of my room," she shouted at him.

Gil stared at her a moment while keeping his gun trained on her. He then lowered the gun, immediately relaxed, and carefully straightened so as not to alarm the armed woman. Once his gun lowered, Darth stopped growling.

"You must be Riley," he announced. "Bogart mentioned you."

Riley appeared surprised by his words and lowered her gun while staring at him. "Bogart? You know Bogart?"

He nodded then considered his next comment carefully. "Yeah, he's, uh, well, a colleague."

"Did he send you for me?" she suddenly asked with enthusiasm. "I can be ready in five minutes."

"No, he didn't send us for you," Gil replied seemingly confused by the comment. "We were looking for your aunt. We wanted to ask her a few questions."

She eyed him suspiciously, suddenly not trusting him. "What's the commotion outside?"

"Jackie's pissed," Gil casually replied without showing much reaction. "She tends to throw a mild tantrum. I promise no one is here to hurt you."

"Bogart said if I helped him, he'd send his friends to take me away from this horrible place," she informed him.

"That's why we need to speak to your aunt," he informed her. "We believe she knows the man responsible for putting the hit on us."

"Did he get anything useful off her phone?" Riley asked. "She has everything on her phone."

"No, there wasn't anything specific about who was after us," Gil replied. "Where is your aunt?"

"If there's been a breach on the estate grounds, she probably went to one of her safe houses until she's told everything is clear,"

Riley reported. "It's the Russian, isn't it? She's been keeping tabs on him. She doesn't trust him. He's kind of scary. Trust me, I've seen scary, and he's *scary*."

"Yeah, he's scary," Gil muttered. "Do you know where her safe houses are?"

"There are a few of them," she replied then eyed him with a sly look. "I'm not telling you where they are unless you take me along. I need to get away from here. Bogart promised he'd take me somewhere safe and out of my aunt's reach."

"We can't take you with us," he insisted. "It's too dangerous." He then reconsidered the comment. "Although it's not exactly safe here either. We'll take you to a nice five-star hotel. Once our necks are off the chopping block, you and Bogart can work out something more permanent."

She considered the comment then nodded. "Okay, I'll tell you where the safe houses are on the way to the hotel." Riley then grinned and almost blushed. "Is Bogart with you?"

Gil stared at the love struck look in her eyes and groaned. "I really don't get it," he muttered.

Chapter Thirty-seven

Zack continued to pace in front of Jackie like a stalking predator. He finally stopped while facing her and reached inside his jacket. As he removed his semiautomatic, Jackie twitched. Had he actually been able to resist one, final sparring match between them? Was that how it was going to end? Did he intend to shoot her? Zack casually tossed the gun aside, moved into attack position, and stared back at her. Jackie understood and was willing to play his game one last time. She tossed her samurai swords aside and resumed her attack stance. Zack said something to her in Russian, still playing his Russian act in front of his new 'friends'. He spoke fluent Russian even before his torrid love affair with a female Russian spy, so his new persona wasn't surprising.

Jackie didn't speak Russian, but she had the perfect response to whatever comment he made. In Russian, Jackie proclaimed, "Fuck you!"

Zack chuckled at her ability to curse in ten different languages. "Maybe later," he casually replied in a thick Russian accent then smiled deviously. "Let's see if you survive this first."

Jackie didn't let his comment ruffle her. She maintained her attack position and kept her eyes locked on him. Zack was forced to make the first move. Unlike their usual, friendly sparring matches, Zack came at her with more aggression than usual. Jackie had been so used to his technique and routine; she wasn't prepared for the fast roundhouse kick that came her way. He clipped her on the side. Even though it hurt, he hadn't put a lot of effort into it. If he had, he would have done some damage. She couldn't take that as a sign though. It could quite possibly mean he was just playing with her first. Perhaps he was trying to get into her head as she tried to get into his.

When he came at her with a series of hard, fast kicks, she knew he was serious. She deflected his kicks with her legs and arms, realizing he was already onto the aggressiveness with which their matches usually ended. He was playing for keeps, and she needed to fight him as if he were the enemy. He threw several easy punches, anticipating her ability to block them. Zack was successfully getting into her head now. He was coming on strong then pulling punches, attempting to confuse her. She was already tired of the games and was through letting him lead in their strange, sick dance. It was time to show the old dog a few new tricks.

Jackie flipped through the air, kicking him on her way through, and tossing him off balance. She landed in a crouched position and swept his legs out from beneath him. Zack hit the ground. Before she could spring to her feet, Zack was already back on his and kicking for her. His boot narrowly missed her face. While he went high, she kicked low and nailed him in the gut. He felt the hit, held his abdomen a moment, and then shook it off. Zack spun into a series of kicks, coming at her fast, forcing her to jump back several steps to avoid being kicked. When he spun into a high roundhouse kick, Jackie threw herself to the ground and kicked him in the thigh as he landed.

He didn't let the hit faze him and immediately kicked and punched for her. She successfully blocked the first two kicks and the first punch, but he struck her in the abdomen with the second. Jackie jumped with surprise and looked at him. The hit was barely harder than a light jab. She wasn't sure what he was up to with the aggressive kicks and soft hits. Jackie spun into several fast kicks for him, forcing him to back up with each kick to avoid being hit. On the final kick, he caught her booted ankle and held her in place while she maintained her balance on one foot. He attempted to twist her foot around to pivot her, so she went with it and flipped, kicking him with the leg she'd been standing on. She nailed him in the chest and knocked him to the ground. Unfortunately, she was unable to catch her balance and hit the ground as well. She couldn't deny it hurt, but she wasn't about to let that stop her.

Both returned to their feet and came back at each other with fast, hard kicks and punches. They returned to their more comfortable, typical sparring routine, although it was evident this wasn't playing for fun. Jackie was waiting for Zack to take it to the next level and go for her jugular. Even though it didn't happen, she didn't trust that it wouldn't once she let her guard down. After nearly twenty minutes of familiar fighting, Zack finally made his move. He caught her in a flip and tackled her to the ground, landing on top of her. She attempted to kick him from her position beneath him. He blocked her kick with his hand and grabbed the back of her thigh. Her eyes locked with his. He was feeling her up! Jackie cracked her forehead against his mouth, forcing him to release her. She rolled out from beneath him, sprang to her feet, and kicked him in the side. Zack rolled away from her before she could take another shot at him while he was on the ground then sprang to his feet and again faced her. Their battle continued.

†

Within the mansion, Beck passed the open foyer door and hesitated when he heard a car starting in front of the house. He stepped into the doorway and saw several guards hurry Melissa into the back of a black sedan right before it sped away past the other parked cars. Two cars immediately chased after the sedan. Beck cursed softly and touched his ear transmitter.

"She got away," he reported. "Everyone head to the backyard for kitten extraction."

†

Once the sniper fire ceased in the back yard, several men gathered to watch the fight, respecting that the bounty on Jackie belonged to the man working his ass off fighting her. Most cheered on Zack while a few were actually rooting for Jackie. Maybe they thought if she killed him, they could claim the bounty on her head instead. Or it could have been they just enjoyed watching a hot woman kick the Russian's arrogant ass. As Zack was starting to pant from their epic battle, Jackie knew she had to use the last move she had in her newly acquired arsenal. She needed to get his attention and drive it home hard.

197

She assessed his position then spun around and went into a backward flip meant to deceive him, so he wouldn't know where she intended to land. She barely landed near him before flipping upward onto his body, wrapping around him like a python in *his* signature move. With her legs and arms twisted around various parts of his body, she flipped him backward then twisted him forward, riding his back as he hit the ground with her landing on top of him.

She remained on his back a moment with her arm locked around his neck in the perfect setup to break it and whispered in his ear, "Now I'm you."

Jackie gave his neck a firm squeeze as if she'd break his neck then unlocked her arm and rolled off him, springing back to her feet. Zack panted a moment while moving to his hands and knees and looked at her where she stood over him. Both heard the nearly silent gunshot. Jackie clutched her bleeding leg and went down. Zack recovered from the assault and looked at the group of six hitmen behind him. His eyes locked on the man grinning deviously while holding the recently fired gun.

"Game over," the hitman remarked. "Collect your bounty, Russian."

Zack didn't show any emotion. In a split second, he had his knife from his boot and threw it at the assassin. It struck the well-dressed man in the neck, dropping him to the ground. Zack approached the fallen dead man, snatched his pistol and Uzi from him, and glared with hostility.

"No one interferes in my fights," Zack snarled in his recently acquired Russian accent then walked back to Jackie.

She clutched her bleeding leg and attempted to move back to her feet but couldn't do it. Zack stood over Jackie a moment and watched her attempting to resume their fight, but she had nothing left. A gun was heard cocking behind him.

"Finish her," one of the men announced firmly. "Or we will."

"Fuck that," another man cried out. "She's worth more alive than dead. No one said what condition she had to be in just as long as she has a pulse."

"I say we all take turns with her," one of the men announced while grinning deviously. "Teach the bitch a lesson. If girls want to play with the big boys, they'd better get used to getting fucked by them."

Zack's hand twitched the moment he heard the comment. Sexual assault and crimes against children triggered psychotic behavior in the hardened former SEAL.

"Just finish her off," the first man again ordered with irritation.

Zack aimed the gun in his right hand at Jackie where she half sat clutching her bleeding leg. She pushed her agony aside and stared back at him while straightening proudly.

"Yeah, finish me off, you fucking coward," Jackie snarled. "I'll give the Commander your regards."

The men behind him all laughed at the comment. Zack continued to stare into her eyes as his finger tightened on the trigger. Jackie drew a deep breath and held her head up high. Zack suddenly raised his left hand holding the Uzi and fired in a sweeping motion behind him without even looking. Each of the six men took several shots as the weapon fired in a semi-circle. When the Uzi fire ceased, none was left standing. Zack lowered both guns, shook his head with disgust, and cast the weapons aside. He then looked at Jackie with concern.

"Are you okay?" he gently asked, losing his thick Russian accent.

She was momentarily stunned by his double-cross then nodded while panting. "Just grazed me."

Zack groaned while shaking his head. "I always knew you'd be the death of me," he remarked then extended his hand to her.

Jackie accepted his hand and allowed him to help her to her feet. He immediately pulled her into his arms and held her in a tight embrace. She returned the warm embrace while feeling tears welling in her eyes. Jackie always felt safe in Zack's arms, and she wanted to hold on to the moment as long as she could. She pulled back to meet his gaze, gently touched his face, and then thrust her knee into his groin. Zack clutched himself and dropped to his knees with a groan.

Her look turned hard and cold. "Don't you ever fucking toy with my emotions again," she lashed out with anger.

Zack slowly moved to his feet and held his hand in the air. "I'm sorry, Jackie," he gasped. "Believe me, I'm truly sorry for everything I've done, but we need to go before others organize and shoot us."

"There are no others," she scoffed while glaring at him. "Bogart and Monroe are handling the last of them. According to Beck's message relayed through Bogart, several guards took off when I breached security."

"Did they get Melissa Pendleton?" he suddenly asked with concern.

"No, she took off the moment she sniffed danger."

Zack groaned, retrieved his gun, and pulled her across the yard with him. "We have to stop her."

"We got her men," Jackie protested while stopping to collect her samurai swords. "She's not an immediate threat."

"No," Zack replied and flashed his cell phone, "but this is."

Jackie looked at his cell phone and stared at a picture of Ross tied to a chair. He looked badly beaten and bruised. "Ross," she gasped.

"Yeah, and if she suspects my betrayal has anything to do with Ross or the team, she may put it together and have his captives kill him just to prove her point," Zack informed her. "We need to find him first."

"Why didn't you tell us?"

"We don't have time for story-telling, Jackie," he announced, grabbed her hand, and pulled her toward the house. "Like it or not; you have to trust me."

She cast a look at his hand holding hers then considered the comment while rushing to keep up with him. "I honestly wish I didn't."

Chapter Thirty-eight

Jackie and Zack hurried through the mansion since it was the quickest route to Zack's car parked out front. They crossed the empty kitchen and hurried into the massive hallway with a straight shot to the front foyer door. As they hurried along the hall, both suddenly stopped, alerted to a sound. Jackie and Zack cast their backs against each other with their pistols aimed in opposite directions. Beck appeared in the darkened study doorway with his gun aimed at Zack, but he didn't have a clean shot with Jackie partially blocking him.

"Step away from him, Jackie," Beck ordered in a gruff, low voice.

Jackie stepped in front of Zack; now blocking Beck's shot, and aimed her gun at him, surprising him. "No," she launched back. "There's an explanation for what's happened, and it's worth hearing him out!"

"He's tricking you, Jackie," Beck warned with anger, refusing to lower his gun despite that it was now aimed at her. "The bounty on your head is doubled if they take you alive. That's why he needs you alive!"

"You don't understand," Jackie snapped hotly.

"He killed Kirk! I understand that!"

A gun cocked behind Beck within the darkness of the study, catching his attention.

"A little misunderstanding," a familiar voice announced from behind him.

Beck uncertainly looked over his shoulder then lowered his gun when he saw Kirk standing behind him.

"Now, can we all be friends again?" Kirk asked while raising a cocky brow.

Everyone lowered their weapons. Beck's shoulders sagged with relief. He gave Kirk a big, manly hug, which he actually returned for once. Beck pulled away appearing a little misty eyed then looked around as his commanding attitude returned.

"Who wants to tell me what's going on around here?" Beck finally demanded then looked back at Kirk. "I saw you dead in the field."

"The bastard shot me with a tranquilizer dart," Kirk remarked. "When I woke, he'd taken my clothes and stuffed me in a duffel bag that earlier contained a dead man who looked a lot like me. When Zack finally let me out, I nearly broke his neck. He'd left a Kirk lookalike wearing my clothes, so you'd think he killed me."

"But why?" Beck demanded.

"We don't have time for this," Jackie announced while becoming anxious.

"The house is empty, and it'll be a while before the police are notified about gunshots being fired," Beck replied with annoyance. "I'd say we have plenty of time."

Gil and Darth appeared on the broad staircase with Riley directly behind them. Darth happily greeted Zack. The dog held no grudges.

"Jackie's right," Gil announced as they reached the bottom of the stairs. "This is Riley. She has some interesting information about her aunt that didn't seem important when she met with Bogart the other day on the train."

Zack handed Jackie his cell phone.

"Well this is more important," Jackie announced then flashed Beck the picture of Ross on the cell phone.

Beck's expression immediately dropped. "Son-of-a-bitch!"

"Ross and Lee survived the blast and the building collapse," Zack informed them. "They're being held hostage by the same people who put the bounties on our heads."

"Ross was probably the one giving them certain inside information about us because they have Lee," Jackie informed him. "There's no telling what they've done to either of them the last two weeks."

"If Melissa suspects I've been helping you," Zack announced with concern, "she could be on her way to where they're keeping Ross. For all we know, she may already have given the order to kill him. We need to find her."

"That's where Riley comes in," Gil informed them. "Riley knows where her aunt may have gone, but she wants protection from her. We need to take her along to keep them from killing her."

"Then we should probably go," Beck remarked. "We'll need to collect Monroe and Bogart and get the hell out of here before the police--"

They heard sirens in the distance.

"Time to go," Kirk announced and motioned everyone toward the front door.

"My aunt's cars are in the garage out back. We can take them and leave through the back gate," Riley replied while indicating the hallway toward the kitchen. "The keys are on the wall just inside the garage. I know the security code to get inside."

Beck tapped his ear transmitter as they hurried to the kitchen. "Monroe, do you have Bogart?"

"Copy," came Monroe's reply.

"Meet us by the garage, we have company," Beck informed him.

"Yeah, I hear them," Monroe replied through Beck's ear transmitter. "We're out back securing a few cell phones from Jackie's new dead friends in case there's any new information coming in. On our way to the garage now."

"We'll be there in less than a minute," Beck announced as they headed through the kitchen and for the back door. They hurried outside and toward the garage, avoiding the battlefield strewn with bodies. After seeing the mess she'd left behind, the others cast several concerned looks at Jackie.

She glared her annoyance at them. "What?" she snapped hotly.

None responded and gave her innocent looks. They spotted Monroe and Bogart waiting by the garage doors. Monroe saw them and indicated the electronic lock.

"Minor setback," Monroe announced with noted concern then saw Zack. Without warning, he punched Zack in the face, stunning him but not knocking him down. Zack rubbed his jaw and stared at Monroe with some surprise.

"You shot me, dickhead!" Monroe launched hotly.

"Relax, you big baby," Zack snapped back. "You were wearing a vest."

"Oh, and you knew that?" Monroe demanded.

"You always wear body armor after someone tries to kill you," Zack reported. "I can spot you wearing a vest a mile away by the size of your chest."

"Fight about it later," Beck ordered then eyed the lock. "What's the issue?"

"I can crack it, but it'll take time that we don't have," Monroe remarked.

Riley hurried past Beck and approached the keypad. As she punched in the code, she saw Bogart and displayed her enthusiasm. "Bogart," she cried out happily.

"Hey, Riley," he announced while equally enthusiastic.

"Save the joyful reunion," Kirk snarled at the horny young couple. "We're about to be arrested with a dozen or more bodies surrounding us."

Bogart then noticed Kirk and became enthusiastic. "Kirk, you're alive," he cried out and attempted to hug him.

"Touch me and die," Kirk snarled before he could get too close.

Bogart raised his hands in the air defensively and took a step back. Once the door was unlocked, they hurried into the garage. Riley grabbed two sets of keys for the expensive, new sports cars and handed them to Bogart. Beck snatched them from him without comment.

Bogart suddenly seemed to realize something rather important and turned toward Kirk. "Wait a minute," the country boy suddenly announced with rising irritation. "Were you the one who knocked me out?"

Kirk ignored him as they piled into two separate cars.

"It was you," Bogart gasped as his eyes widened. "You bastard!"

Jackie shoved Bogart into one of the cars then jumped in behind him. Both cars burned out from the garage and took the back way from the mansion grounds to avoid the arriving police.

Chapter Thirty-nine

Within the dimly lit basement was a dark holding cell in the corner. A man's bare feet were wedged within the bars at least two feet from the ground. Soft grunts came from the small prison cell. Ross, wearing only a pair of pants with no shirt or shoes, performed rigorous sit-ups on the hard incline. The bruises on his face were finally fading, indicating his captors were no longer beating him. When he heard the basement door open, he pulled himself up to the bars, removed his feet, and jumped to the floor. He collapsed onto the worn, torn blanket on the concrete floor against the wall and attempted to look relaxed.

"Ross," came a male voice. "It's me."

Ross sprang to his feet and stood before the bars, staring at the guard as he approached.

"Wexler," he announced with mild enthusiasm. "Did you learn anything?"

The Columbian man in his late twenties handed Ross a bottle of water through the bars. Ross immediately accepted it and downed half the bottle then awaited a response.

"She's here," Wexler replied in a moderately thick Columbian accent. "She's in the building somewhere, but I can't get information without slitting my own throat at the same time."

"No, don't do anything to make them suspicious," Ross replied. "I need your help."

"Maybe if I just let you go--?"

"No, that won't work," he insisted. "If they realize I'm missing, they'll kill Lee on the spot. I just wish I knew if she were alright."

"It's a big place," Wexler informed him. "I'll have more time tomorrow morning. There are a few off limit places I haven't looked yet."

"Just be careful," Ross replied with concern. "Don't get yourself killed."

"Not planning on it, I promise," Wexler announced. "They have my mother and sister. If I screw up, they'll kill them." He then appeared curious. "What about your team? Could I contact them somehow?"

"Too dangerous for us both," Ross replied. "With the contract on their heads, they're probably already in deep hiding." He sighed softly, ran his fingers through his mostly gray hair, and allowed his concerns overtake him. "I hope they're okay. If anything happened to them, it's my fault."

"They're in a better position to protect themselves than your girlfriend," Wexler informed him. "I know what you're going through."

"I'm sure, or you wouldn't be helping me," Ross replied with a tiny smile.

"Not that I wouldn't help you," Wexler announced. "I just wouldn't be in this position. I'd have taken my family and ran far away."

"We'll find your family," Ross assured him. "You just keep up appearances and remember the code phrase if my men do happen to show up."

"I'll remember." He straightened and inhaled deeply. "I should go. Is there anything else you need?"

"No, you've done enough," Ross remarked and handed him the empty water bottle. "Thank you."

✝

Lee slept restlessly beneath the covers of the moderately average bed in the bland bedroom. The bedroom door was abruptly pushed open, allowing light to spill into the room, alarming her. Lee jumped up in bed and looked at the doorway. A short, slightly round woman in her fifties and a slender woman in her mid to late twenties hurried into the room. Both women wore their robes covering their sleepwear.

"What's wrong?" Lee asked with concern while holding her chest. "What's happening?"

"We're not sure," Alma, the older woman, announced in a soft voice with a thick Columbian accent and joined her on the bed. She immediately placed her arm around Lee's shoulder. "There's a lot of activity out there. There are never this many guards running around at night."

"I think it's okay," Kelsey informed them from where she stood guard by the bedroom door. Her accent wasn't nearly as thick as her mother's accent. "They're not interested in coming in here." She then looked back at Lee. "You don't think your boyfriend escaped, do you?"

"No," Lee replied. "If he had, they'd probably come for me and use me as bait. At the very least, they'd post a guard inside the room."

"This is wrong," Kelsey remarked, becoming angry. "As long as we have Lee, our chances of escaping increase greatly. Once we get to a populated area, we can call her friends to help us. You said they're big time bad asses."

"We don't even know where to find them," Lee informed her new friend. "If what you heard is true, they're being hunted. If they survived, they're probably in hiding by now. Besides, I can't leave Ross."

"If you really love your boyfriend, you'd escape with us," Kelsey remarked. "They're using you to subdue him, I guarantee it. Without you being held, he might find the strength to get away as well." Kelsey glared at her mother. "Just like we should have done in the first place."

"They have your brother," Alma informed her with concern. "If we leave, they'll kill him."

"What's to stop them from killing any of us?" Kelsey demanded then regained her composure. "I don't want to live like this. Every day we fear for our lives. Eventually, the day is going to come when they don't need her anymore. Then what? Are we going to sit by and watch them kill her? Are we going to stand up and die with her? If we escape, everyone has a slightly better chance of living."

Alma frowned although considering the comment. She proudly raised her head. "Then maybe the two of you should escape," she suggested. "I'll stay behind and bargain for my son's life."

Kelsey shook her head with annoyance. "You can be so damned stubborn."

"At least you know where you get it from," Alma scoffed at her daughter.

The suite door in the living room opened, alarming all three. An armed guard approached the partially open bedroom door. Kelsey backed up to the bed and stood in front of her mother and Lee, who clung to each other with concern. A guard in his early thirties, Jason, stepped into the doorway to the dimly lit bedroom and suspiciously eyed all three.

"Everyone okay in here?" Jason asked.

"Yeah, we're fine, Jason," Kelsey announced and appeared to relax when she saw the familiar guard. "What's with all the commotion?"

"You know I can't tell you that," he replied firmly. "They'll have my head."

Kelsey smiled sweetly, moved closer to the tall, moderately handsome man, and placed her hand on his lower arm. "Who are we going to tell?" she asked while making eyes at him as she caressed his arm.

"I suppose you're right," he replied and took in her beauty with more than a passing interest. "Just some commotion at the big wig's estate tonight." Jason then offered a soft chuckle. "Some woman took out a dozen highly trained professionals with nothing but a pair of samurai swords."

Lee held back her gasp and clutched Alma's arm. Kelsey placed her hand on the guard's shoulder and nuzzled him while raising a skeptical brow.

"I find it slightly disturbing that you think that's humorous," she remarked.

"A woman going ninja on self-proclaimed tough guys?" he teased while grinning. "You have to admit, that's funny stuff. And they're professional hitman, so fuck them."

"Language," Alma scolded.

Jason looked past Kelsey to Alma and offered an embarrassed smile. "Sorry, Alma."

Kelsey linked onto Jason's arm and guided him from the bedroom. "You should probably get back out there before someone misses you."

"Yeah, you're right," he announced. "Just wanted to make sure my favorite girl was safe."

Kelsey playfully placed her hand on his chest and smiled sweetly. "Thanks for the concern." She kissed him quickly on the cheek. "Now get back out there." Kelsey gave him a teasing, lustful smile. "And beware of sexy ninja women."

He gave the comment serious consideration, enjoying the image, and then laughed. "I'll do that."

Jason left the room, locking the door behind him. Alma and Lee stood in the bedroom doorway and stared at the locked door after he'd gone.

Alma frowned her disapproval at her daughter and shook her head. "I wish you wouldn't cozy up to that man," she scolded. "He's liable to come in here and attack you."

"Him?" Kelsey remarked then laughed while waving off her mother. "Jason adores me. He'd probably kill everyone in this place if I offered him a blowjob in return."

"Kelsey!" Alma scolded.

"Desperate times, Mother," she remarked. "You can relax. I'm saving that secret weapon for when the right opportunity comes along." Kelsey flopped onto the nearby sofa and kept an eye on the suite door.

"That opportunity may come along sooner than you think," Lee informed them.

Both women looked at her with some surprise by the comment. Kelsey was a little more curious than her mother was and sat forward on the sofa.

"That ninja woman he spoke about," Lee announced while raising her brows. "I know who he meant."

"Friends?" Kelsey asked with surprise.

Lee nodded while gently rubbing her arms. "If they stormed this 'big wig's' estate, it could mean they know where we are." She shivered slightly. "That's why they're patrolling the area and running around like idiots. They must suspect they're on their way here to rescue Ross and me."

"This could be our opportunity," Kelsey announced with enthusiasm and sprang up from the sofa. "I know our escape route. I've gone that way many times. They won't be worrying about us if your friends show up."

"No, maybe not," Lee remarked. "But they're also going to be patrolling every inch of the building and the grounds. You'll get caught."

"If you're not caught in the crossfire," Alma warned her daughter.

"Think of the bigger picture," Kelsey boldly announced. "If your friends storm the place, these guys will use you and your boyfriend as human shields."

"That crossed my mind too," Lee replied while sighing softly and sank into thought. "We may need to come up with a really good hiding place."

Kelsey suddenly smiled. "I know just the place."

Chapter Forty

The sports cars pulled into a truck stop a little after ten o'clock that night. The guys along with Riley got out of the cars and discussed which of the four locations they felt Melissa Pendleton would flee to after the mansion was breached. All four locations were miles apart. There was some uncertainty and defeat from the team since they knew a lot was riding on finding the right location to search for Melissa and possibly Ross.

"So we have a condemned apartment building, an abandoned mall, a racetrack closed for refurbishment, and an old factory," Beck informed the team. "We already ruled out the smaller businesses still in operation. It'd be difficult to hold people hostage for two weeks with daily traffic."

"All four are big places," Kirk remarked. "We could split our efforts, but it would take all night to search one building with only two-man teams."

"We'd also be left shorthanded when we do find her," Gil informed them. "We have to count on a heavily armed welcome party surrounding the location. Getting in is easy. Getting out could be suicide."

"She's going to have several guards surrounding her," Riley informed them while eyeing the guys. "She wouldn't have left the mansion unaccompanied."

"Then there's this mysterious man who put the bounty on our heads," Monroe reminded them. "If she's going to see him, he's going to have his own militia waiting to shoot our heads off the moment we arrive."

"We only have one shot at finding the right location," Beck remarked.

Jackie then eyed Zack with a serious look. "So tell us, Zack," she announced. "Where would you take someone if you didn't want us to find them?"

Zack considered the question only a moment. "Either the factory or the racetrack," he replied without over thinking the question. "They're in ideal locations away from both homeless people and day traffic." He then considered both options. "If I had to choose one, I'd go with the racetrack. It has hundreds of acres surrounded with a chain-link fence. It's only being refurbished, so all the utilities will still be functioning, and it's far enough away from prying eyes."

There was an unusual silence as the rest of the team exchanged looks.

Beck looked at Zack and nodded his approval of the theory. "The racetrack it is."

"That's a good twenty miles from here," Riley informed them. "There aren't any nearby hotels. If you take time to drop me off, you'll be wasting time."

"You're right," Beck announced and nodded. "We'll leave you here."

"At a truck stop," she cried out then pleaded with her eyes. "Take me with you. I'll be fine waiting with the cars. I even know an excellent spot you can park to keep out of sight with a back way into the place. You need me."

"No, not really," Beck replied.

"She wants to help," Bogart insisted.

"She'll get herself or one of us killed," Kirk launched back then raised his brow at Bogart. "In case you were wondering, that would probably be you."

"We don't have time to argue," Beck announced with a sigh. "We'll take her along and leave her in a safe location with the cars. If there's any sign of trouble, she can take a car and leave."

"Finding extraction vehicles is never an issue," Kirk remarked with little emotion.

Monroe lovingly ran his hand along the expensive sports car and grinned. "Extraction vehicles as nice as these though are hard to come by."

Kirk glared at Monroe as he caressed the sports car. "Do you two need a moment alone?"

Monroe snapped out of his fantasy involving the expensive sports car. "No, I'm good."

"Let's go find Ross," Beck announced.

†

Riley showed them the back entrance to the racetrack, which was mostly used to transport horses to and from the track, avoiding the general population area. It was a little before eleven o'clock that night. Not far from the gate was a section of chain-link fence that had been knocked down by a fallen tree and hadn't been replaced. The rotted tree was in pieces, allowing them easy access through the opening. It would be a long haul to the barn and racetrack building, but they would be able to keep out of sight and maintain the element of surprise most of the way. Riley had been considering her options and wanted to go inside with them at least as far as the horse barn, but they allowed no wiggle room for her new request. She pouted slightly and reluctantly waited with the two sports cars.

The guys took the more scenic route along the trees to conceal their presence. Once they were in sight of the barn, they got a better lay of the land. Zack was given an ear transmitter to keep better tabs on the others as they broke off into pairs. Although the pairing was sometimes altered depending upon the situation, Jackie and Zack were almost always paired together, since they were the only two with identical fighting skills and they seemingly thought alike. They would take the section of building dedicated to the jockeys, which also included the old kitchen and snack bar portion of the racetrack.

Gil and Darth would take the large horse barn, vet's office, and the long building, which was used to hold the horses awaiting their races. Beck and Monroe would immediately head to the basement area once they reached the main building. The basement included the vault, cash office, and security offices. Bogart and Kirk were assigned the betting windows, indoor and outdoor viewing areas, ticket office, and the machinery building. Once they had their assignments, they went their separate ways.

†

213

Despite that the racetrack had been closed for renovations, several strategically placed outside lights remained on every night. The lights were meant to keep the property secure while abandoned and deter vandals or bored teenagers. Outside lights worked to Gil's advantage in certain areas near the large barn, which would be completely dark otherwise. A few of the lights hindered his movement, making it more difficult for him to move around undetected. Fortunately, he didn't see any guards patrolling the barn area. Darth sniffed around the massive, empty barn in the mostly dim lighting. He was finding too many new and exciting smells; leaving Gil with the feeling his partner was spending too much time goofing off.

It was becoming obvious they weren't holding Ross within the large barn. Darth would eventually pick up the scent of someone familiar to him, and there would likely be guards somewhere surrounding the area they were holding Ross. The barn was a waste of time. When Darth had a disagreement with a cat and nearly gave them away, Gil knew it was time to move on before Darth asserted his canine superiority over the cat and started barking. A dog barking on the property would draw attention. Even if they didn't expect intruders, they'd be on alert and attempt to locate the source of the noise.

Heading closer to the main building and away from the massive horse barn, Gil and Darth approached a long building, which contained rows of horse stalls exposed to the outside. It wasn't far from the parade paddock and the track itself. Horses were sometimes kept in the closer stalls prior to races. Once it was their turn to race, the handlers would lead the horses to the parade paddock where those attending the race could have a better look at the horses before they were taken into cubicles within the paddock and saddled. It was a large area to cover, and Darth was enjoying another round of 'name that smell'. Gil was coming up empty and would need to regroup with the others where he'd be of more use. Darth found something of interest, although only of interest to him, and disappeared into the darkness.

Gil was about to call him when he saw a guard patrolling the area near the parade paddock. He didn't appear to be looking for anything or anyone in particular, so he wasn't on high alert. Gil stepped back into the shadows and into one of the stalls to remain out of sight. He poked his head out to check the guard's position when he heard a gun cock from the opposite direction not far from his head. Gil tensed and slowly turned his head to look at the man standing only a foot away with a gun aimed at him. He remained calm and didn't attempt to fight the man.

"Who are you?" the guard demanded.

Gil's look remained unemotional. "You know who I am, and you're late," he announced firmly. "Are we going to do business or just jerk each other off?"

The man stared at him a moment then frowned. "Can't you people find better places to conduct your dirty deals?" the guard demanded. Although he didn't lower his gun, his hand holding it relaxed just enough. He motioned to his partner at the other end of the long building, who now spotted them as well, and then glared at Gil. "Sorry, buddy. You won't be doing any business here tonight. Go somewhere else to do that shit."

As his partner approached, Gil grabbed the first man by the wrist and twisted his arm, forcing him to drop the gun, and then punched him in the face. He didn't go down as he had hoped he would and the man immediately retaliated by punching Gil in the face. He took the hit with surprising refinement. When Gil came back swinging, the guard tackled him to the ground. His partner was nearly upon them and was about to raise his radio to his mouth when Darth tackled him to the ground while snarling and growling. The second guard cried out with surprise and fought against the dog on top of him tearing into his forearm. The man punched Darth in the head, which only enraged him further. He then rammed his knee into Darth's side, forcing him to release his grip from the hard shots. As he attempted to get up, Darth leaped forward and sank his teeth into the man's crotch. The man cried out, catching both Gil and the first guard's attention.

Despite that they had been brawling on the ground, both men looked several feet away and saw Darth clinging to the man's crotch while he screamed, seemingly immobile from the hold. Gil was possibly more surprised than the man he fought. Gil punched the guard on top of him twice in the face, shoved him off, and punched him a third time for good measure. When the man no longer moved, Gil sprang to his feet and looked at his partner with his teeth in the man's crotch.

"Darth," he snarled at the dog in a scolding manner. "Oust!"

Darth released the man and looked at Gil while happily wagging his tail.

Gil shook his head. "No more weekend visits with Aunt Jackie," he remarked. "I don't know what she's teaching you." He wagged his finger at the dog while reprimanding him. "But that is *not* acceptable behavior."

Darth didn't know what his partner and friend was saying, but he gave a playful 'woof' in response and wagged his tail with added vigor. Gil groaned and shook his head.

Chapter Forty-one

Bogart and Kirk had already slipped past the outdoor stadium seating surrounding the track. They thought they'd heard something coming from the parade paddock area, but when no other sounds followed, they continued with their search. The track offered a large, indoor area of stadium seating as well, which extended past the outdoor bleachers, offering an enclosed area to watch the races out of the heat and potential bad weather. They knew Ross wouldn't be tucked away somewhere quite so open, but they could see the luxury boxes at the top of the indoor stadium seating. They were worth investigating.

They checked the main floor and scanned the large area before the betting windows, as well as the secured area behind the closed windows. There was still no sign of Ross or even any guards. Both were starting to wonder if they were searching the wrong business location. Zack was usually great at picking the right location, but he wasn't infallible. They ended their search of the ground level within the betting area then headed up the stairs to the luxury boxes above the stadium seating. There was a private elevator, but even if it worked, they wouldn't risk using it, since their presence would be noticed.

Setup much like private luxury boxes at sporting events, those who could afford private boxes could throw parties and even have the track cater their event. The boxes sat above the indoor stadium, giving an unobstructed view of the track as well as providing small balconies where their party could sit to watch the events outside. Kirk had to pick the locks on each door in order to check all ten luxury boxes. Once they found all ten boxes empty, they headed back into the corridor. The elevator dinged, alerting them to someone's presence. Kirk opened one of the doors and shoved Bogart into the nearest luxury box. They hid within the room on either side of the door and listened to someone walking along the corridor.

Kirk looked at Bogart and darted his eyes toward the door, secretly signaling for him to play decoy. Bogart gave him a look back, declaring 'no way' and gestured with his hands. Kirk gave a more demanding look while raising his brows and shook his fist at Bogart. Bogart vigorously gestured with his hands then gave Kirk the middle finger. Kirk then glared at him with a look threatening to kill.

Within the hallway, a guard carrying an assault rifle headed toward the stairs at the opposite end. The sound of a door opening caught his attention. He turned and saw Bogart standing in the corridor while playing on his cell phone. The guard raised his weapon.

"Hey," the guard cried out. "Hands up!"

Bogart continued to press buttons on his cell phone and indicated with a finger for him to wait a moment without even looking up.

"Are you deaf?" the guard demanded and headed toward him with his weapon aimed.

As the guard got closer, Bogart looked up and grinned while showing him his cell phone. "I caught the little bastard," Bogart announced with enthusiasm. "Have you played this game? It's awesome."

The guard stopped a few feet away and aimed his weapon at Bogart's face.

Bogart's expression dropped. "Oh, you have one of those big guns," he remarked then suddenly grinned. "My friend has one of those too."

Kirk stood behind the guard and poked him in the back with his assault rifle barrel. "You'll want to put that down," he informed the guard. "Nice and easy."

The frightened guard immediately dropped the assault rifle and threw his hands in the air.

Bogart watched the rifle as it clattered to the floor then eyed Kirk standing behind the man. "I can't believe they gave this guy a gun," he remarked.

"Why not?" Kirk casually asked and eyed Bogart. "We gave you one."

"One day I'm going to save your life, and I'm never going to let you live it down," Bogart remarked.

"Yeah, well," Kirk announced with little interest. "Not today." He again poked the guard in the back with the rifle barrel as Bogart collected the fallen weapon. "We're looking for some friends. Have you seen them?"

"Uh, who are your friends?" the guard nervously asked while attempting to get a look at the man behind him.

"You probably know them as prisoners one and two," Kirk remarked sarcastically.

"I don't think we have any prisoners," the guard replied while trembling. "The two Columbian women aren't really happy to be here. They're in the penthouse."

Bogart and Kirk exchanged strange looks at the comment. Bogart shrugged.

"What about a man in his early fifties with gray hair?" Kirk asked. "Are you holding him too?"

"It's my job to keep the homeless guys out of here, not detain them," the guard reported.

"He doesn't know anything," Bogart announced while shaking his head with disappointment. "I doubt the kid even knows how to use the weapon."

Kirk frowned and lowered his assault rifle, allowing the guard to lower his hands as well.

The guard managed a slight, nervous laugh. "You guys had me concerned a moment there," he reported then suddenly pulled a semiautomatic from a hidden shoulder holster.

The moment Bogart saw the gun; he struck the guard in the face with the butt of the assault rifle. The guard struck the wall then fell to the floor. They heard the muffled pop of the gun as it went off beneath him, jolting his body. Both stared at the man on the floor with surprise by what just happened.

"Is he--?" Bogart began then saw the blood rapidly spilling across the floor toward him. He sidestepped the pooling blood then looked at Kirk with horror. "I didn't do that!"

Kirk rolled his eyes and shook his head. "I don't know how you manage to kill so many people by accident."

As Kirk walked away, Bogart stared at the dead guard on the floor, unable to comprehend how it happened. He then hurried after Kirk.

"It wasn't my fault!"

"Yeah, sure," Kirk muttered with disinterest.

†

The track building consisted of the stadium seating, betting windows, and snack areas. Beneath all that, in the basement area, was the security office with holding cells, sometimes referred to as 'the drunk tank', the cash office, and the vault. A separate basement entrance led to the boiler room and other mechanical necessities for the comfort of the track's clientele. Beck and Monroe found the basement entrance to the security office and cautiously took the stairs. Despite the darkness surrounding most of the other areas, the lights were on within the stairwell and the corridor at the bottom. Light shined through the frosted glass on the security office door, indicating someone was possibly home. At the very least, it suggested someone had been within the basement recently.

Their suspicions were enough for both men to draw their weapons from their shoulder holsters, leaving their assault rifles slung over their shoulders. Confined quarters were best left for handheld weapons. They paused outside the security office entrance, each taking a side of the door, and listened a moment. When neither heard anything, they exchanged silent words and nodded. Beck turned the doorknob and discovered it wasn't locked. He slowly pushed the door open, allowing Monroe to peer in from his side of the doorway. A guard was seen sleeping at the desk with his feet propped on top. Monroe gave Beck a look and indicated the guard was asleep. Beck rolled his eyes while shaking his head.

Beck pushed the door open the rest of the way without disturbing the man. Both entered the security office only manned by the sleeping guard. Monroe approached the reclined man and aimed his gun in his face. Beck slammed the door, startling the guard. He jerked in his chair and stared at the barrel of the gun directly between his eyes.

"If you don't scream, we can do this the easy--"

The guard suddenly cried out, as if attempting to yell out a warning to someone who wasn't even there. Monroe punched the man in the face with his left fist, silencing him. He then struck him on the head with the butt of his pistol. The guard immediately dropped to the floor. Beck kept watch through the now partially opened door.

Monroe eyed him and gestured with his weapon. "Why do they always choose the hard way?"

"Did he look bright to you?" Beck demanded.

Monroe shrugged. He found a pair of handcuffs and some duct tape in the desk drawer then bound and gagged the guard, so he wouldn't be able to warn anyone if he woke unexpectedly. Beck locked the security office door from the inside, and both headed for another door leading to the mostly dark drunk tank. They pushed the door open and felt for a light switch. The room brightened considerably. Ross sat up on his blanket on the floor and looked up. When he saw his men, he sprang to his feet as a sly grin crossed his face.

"What the hell took you so long?" he teased.

Beck grabbed the keys from the nearby wall and hurried to Ross's cell. "Oh, the usual," he replied. "Professional hitmen and Zack, the one man show."

"I'll expect details later," Ross replied as Beck unlocked the door. Ross stepped out of the cell and immediately found his shirt and shoes on a nearby chair.

"Smelling a little ripe," Monroe remarked while wrinkling his nose as Ross passed him.

"Well, a building did collapse on me, I was beaten for five days, and I've been washing in a sink for two weeks," he casually replied. "You wouldn't smell so good yourself." He eyed his men as he slipped into his shoes and then his shirt. "We don't have much time. Once they realize I'm out, they'll go for Lee."

"Do you know where they're holding her?" Beck asked as he handed Ross an ear transmitter.

"If I did, I wouldn't have stayed in that dank cell," Ross bluntly informed him while inserting the transmitter in his ear. "I have an ally who's been searching for her, but he's come up empty. She has to be in the owner's penthouse suite. It's the only floor Wexler said he hasn't been able to access. He informed me it's heavily armed."

"We should move the tied guard into your cell," Beck announced. "If they don't look too closely, it may buy us some time."

"I'll alert the others," Monroe announced. "Once they arrive, we can storm the penthouse."

Ross gave Monroe a serious, concerned look. "Is the team still intact?"

"We had a few deaths, but they were eventually resurrected," Monroe informed him. "Holden's on the injured list, so he's sitting this one out."

"I'm afraid I have a lot of apologizing to do," Ross announced to his men while frowning. "They threatened to torture and kill Lee."

"We understand," Beck replied. "Let's just get Lee out of danger. You can buy us a beer later, and we'll call it even."

"After you've had a chance to shower," Monroe muttered.

Chapter Forty-two

The jockey's lounge was almost comfortable enough with which to live. It contained several sofas, recliners, a wet bar, and an excessively large flat screen television mounted on the wall. Undoubtedly, the television only broadcast the live races and replays. The locker room was as nice as any professional sports arena with open box closets rather than actual lockers. The shower room was under construction with most of the original tile already torn up. There was a steam room just off the shower area, but that too was under construction. The dimly lit locker room suddenly brightened as the lights came on. Two guards entered the area, made a brief sweep, and then left, turning off the lights as they closed the door behind them. Zack dropped down from the top of one of the closet style lockers then held his hands up to assist Jackie. She dropped down behind him, avoiding his assistance. He turned and looked at her with disappointment.

"You're going to tear open that patch job I did on your leg," he warned her.

She ignored the comment and walked past him.

He frowned as he watched her pass him. "Now I know how Holden feels when you give him the silent treatment," Zack muttered.

"I'm not giving you the silent treatment," she remarked without looking at him. "I'm resisting the urge to hit you. There's a big difference."

"So you're going to hold it against me forever?"

"I'm not getting into this with you now," she remarked with hostility in her tone as she continued toward the door. "We have a job to do and a friend to save. Get your head in the game or go wait in the car with the other little girls."

Jackie left the locker room leaving Zack stunned by her harsh words.

"I'm not sure if I'm turned on or offended," Zack remarked to himself then shook his head. "This would be a really bad time to tell her I stole her helicopter." He ran his fingers through his short hair then muttered, "And crashed it."

Zack followed Jackie from the jockey's lounge and into the snack bar area, which wasn't far from the betting windows. Zack saw two guards in the distance. He grabbed Jackie around the waist from behind and silently flipped her over the snack bar counter with him. Jackie knew better than to question Zack's snatch and grab. Both crouched behind the counter and listened to the guards in the distance. With an increase in armed guards, they had to be getting closer to where they were holding Ross and Lee. The guards joked with each other as they approached the snack bar. Jackie and Zack attempted to remain still and quiet. Jackie heard something through her ear transmitter. She touched her ear and listened intently. She gave Zack a serious look and mouthed, 'they found Ross'.

The guards got closer to the stand. Zack focused his attention on the sound their boots made as they neared the snack bar. He looked at Jackie, raised his brows, and held up one finger. Jackie nodded and waited. Zack listened to the sounds of their feet and their voices close to the counter. He revealed two fingers. Jackie again waited. Zack listened another moment then pointed his fingers at the counter. Jackie and Zack both leaped over the counter while kicking out. The men were almost exactly on target. They each kicked a guard, knocking them to the floor. Jackie didn't know how Zack was able to calculate a man's exact location just by listening to their footfalls, but she was eager to learn that trick.

The guards attempted to get back up, but Jackie and Zack were swiftly on top of them. Jackie had her man down and out almost instantly. When she looked at Zack, he had his guard by the head. She gave him a warning look. He sneered at her and punched the man in the head, knocking him to the floor.

"We need to tie them up and stash them somewhere out of sight. We have to meet the guys by the main stairs," she informed him with a sense of urgency. "Ross believes they're holding Lee in the owner's penthouse."

Zack removed a roll of duct tape from his thigh pants pocket, pulled off a large piece, and extended it to Jackie. She reluctantly took the tape from him. She was still mad at him, so she couldn't admit that she loved how scary prepared he was for any occasion. Just once, she wanted to empty all his pockets and take inventory of what he had on him.

✝

Melissa paced the temporary security office located inside the penthouse. One of the guards sat before a panel of monitors and scanned different sections of the track building from hidden security cameras. She looked worried while she paced in her expensive dress and designer shoes, tapping her manicured fingernails on her arms folded across her chest.

"What about the other guards?" she demanded.

"At least seven aren't responding to my calls," the guard informed her.

"Why can't you find anyone on the security monitors?" she demanded, growing impatient.

"It's only connected to the track building," the guard reminded her. "We're lucky we have that with the renovations going on."

"I don't like this," she lashed out hotly. "They're here, I know it. Somehow they found us." Melissa sank into thought a moment. Her eyes suddenly narrowed. "Riley," she snarled. "That bitch!"

"The hand radios are sometimes unreliable," the guard informed her. "We should do a physical search of the grounds."

"That's just what they want," she launched back. "Pick the guards off one at a time. We've given them enough advantage already. I knew this was a bad idea." She hesitated then glared at the guard, who remained focused on the monitors. "What's the status on their leader?"

"Tucked away in his cell," the guard replied.

"Have you spoken with his guard?"

"Communication is down within the security office in the basement," the guard remarked.

"Down? What do you mean it's down?" she shouted. "Didn't you think to tell me about this?"

He shifted uncomfortably. "Well, more like the guard is probably asleep and isn't answering his radio," the guard informed her.

The radio on the desk crackled. Melissa grabbed it without hesitation and spoke into it. "This is Melissa," she announced. "What did you find?"

The guard sitting before the monitor appeared uncomfortable and cleared his throat. "If you want to talk, you have to push the talk button," he delicately informed her.

She glared at him with annoyance and slapped the radio against his chest.

The guard fumbled with the hand radio and pushed the talk button. "What's the status of our prisoner?" the guard asked over the radio.

"Negative status," came the response from the other end. "He's gone."

"He got away!" Melissa screeched with anger. "I want them found! Get the girl! If they get anywhere near the penthouse, kill her!"

The guard put out an alert to all the guards. "I need all security to the penthouse," he announced into the hand radio. "We have uninvited guests, and our prisoner has escaped." He received many responses but several guards didn't report.

"How far out are the bounty hunters?" Melissa demanded as her pacing increased.

"Fifteen minutes at most," the guard replied.

"Then we just need to keep the girl secured until they get here and deal with these fuckers," Melissa announced then seemed more confident while straightening proudly. "Locate them! You should be able to find something on the cameras if they're close to the penthouse."

"You don't understand, Ms. Pendleton," the guard announced. "These guys are former Navy SEALs. If they're converging, you won't see them until they're on top of you. They're good at staying invisible."

Both looked at the security monitor and saw Zack standing in front of the camera with a cheap grin on his face. He waved at them, gave them the middle finger, and then shot out the camera. The gunshot was heard on the main level two floors down.

Melissa sneered while staring at the static filled monitor. "That Russian bastard," she scoffed. "I knew there was something not right with him."

The guard was already shouting into the hand radio. "They're in the main building somewhere around the betting windows," the guard announced. "I need every available man on them in the main building."

"Wake the others," Melissa ordered. "Have them guard the penthouse. Shoot to kill."

The guard pushed a button on the console. "I need all security in the barracks to report to the penthouse. Orders shoot to kill."

Melissa attempted a calm appearance and smirked while folding her arms across her chest. "They don't stand a chance against that many men," she announced. "Maybe we won't even have to pay the bounty on their heads if we end this before the bounty hunters arrive."

The guard gave her a strange look, but she didn't notice. Her look was a little too confident at that moment.

†

The suite door within the penthouse living room burst open. Jason and another guard rushed inside the room with their weapons aimed. The living room was empty and moderately dark. Each man went a separate direction and checked both bedrooms. They returned to the living room and exchanged strange looks. The second guard raised his hand radio.

"The girl and her keepers are gone," the guard announced into the hand radio.

"What?" Melissa was heard screeching through the radio, causing both men to grimace.

"Like fingernails on a chalkboard," Jason muttered.

"I want that girl found," Melissa continued her rant over the hand radio. "If those bitches are helping her, shoot them on the spot!"

"Copy that," the second guard announced into his hand radio and nodded Jason toward the door.

Jason frowned and shook his head with disgust. "Kelsey, you stupid girl," he muttered.

✝

Half a dozen guards ran for the main betting area of the building. Ross, Beck, and Monroe watched them pass then slipped into the stairwell leading up to the penthouse. Gil and Darth entered the elevator not far from the stairs. Gil casually pushed the button then clasped his hands in front of him with Darth obediently sitting alongside him as they patiently waited for the doors to close. The guards were already patrolling the penthouse floor when the elevator dinged, alerting them to someone's presence. The four men ran for the elevator and aimed their weapons at the door as it opened. The elevator was empty except Darth, who remained sitting in the center happily panting. The guards exchanged strange looks.

Darth barked once then ran from the elevator. The guards turned and watched the dog run down the corridor. When they looked back at the elevator, Gil stood where Darth once sat and held his assault rifle in his hands. He fired at the group of men, mowing them down with a controlled burst of rifle fire. Gil casually stepped out of the elevator past the dead men. The stairway door opened to reveal Ross, Beck, and Monroe with their weapons raised. They saw the dead guards and approached Gil. Ross motioned for Monroe to go with Gil one direction while they went the opposite direction.

Chapter Forty-three

A dozen men searched the area surrounding the closed betting windows for any sign of intruders, but they were coming up empty. Two headed into the jockey's lounge while two others headed outside toward the track. The remaining eight men stayed within the main area, half patrolling the betting windows and the other half investigating the snack bar area on the opposite end. The guards walked past the betting windows and saw two windows next to each other were now open. They exchanged looks then signaled for the other two guards to circle around to the side door. The first two men aimed their weapons as each approached an open betting window. As they leaned over the counter to look inside, both men were pulled across the counter and through the window, disappearing on the other side. The sound of grunting was heard. Jackie and Zack slid, feet first, out the open windows.

The second pair of guards charged into the secured area behind the betting windows with their weapons aimed only to find the first two guards unconscious on the floor. They looked around the long room. Other than two sets of counters and a dozen rolling chairs, the room was empty. One guard returned to the door while the second approached the open windows. He peered out the first window. Jackie's booted feet struck him in the face as she clung to the bar above her and jumped through the window feet first. The second man spun around, having heard the first guard striking the counter against the wall. Zack appeared in the doorway behind him, caught the guard around the neck, and flipped him through the air to the floor in a newly acquired professional wrestler type move. Zack rolled across the floor and sprang back to his feet. Jackie noted the new move and nodded her approval. Although he barely reacted to her acknowledgment, Zack enjoyed the ego stroke. He held up four fingers and pointed in the direction of the snack bar, indicating the location of the remaining guards. Jackie nodded.

Not far from the snack bar, two guards patrolled the surrounding area. Jackie and Zack were nearly upon them when the two remaining guards stepped out from behind the snack bar and saw them. The original goal was to keep their attacks silent, taking them out a few at a time, so as not to bring an army of guards upon them at once.

"Shit," Jackie groaned while reaching for her semiautomatic in her shoulder holster.

As the men aimed their assault rifles, Zack ran for them, surprising the men and Jackie. Zack slid into home plate, bowling both men over. As they flew to the floor, the two remaining guards aimed their weapons at Zack. Before they could even get him in their sights, Zack sprang to his feet, ran up the wall, and grabbed onto the horizontal support beam. He leaped onto the beam and disappeared into the shadows of the rafters, leaving both men stunned. When they turned, Jackie was already throwing her body into a high flip, kicking one man with her left foot and the second with her right on the way down. The first guard's assault rifle flew across the snack bar and shattered the glass on a framed picture of a racehorse. Jackie grimaced at the nearly deafening sound.

Right on cue, the two guards patrolling the jockey's lounge ran to investigate the crash. Zack dropped from the rafters behind the guards while Jackie rolled across the floor to avoid their rifle fire that immediately followed. Zack tackled the first man to the floor, flipping him several times by his neck, and landed in a crouched position. The second guard had been thrown slightly off balance but recovered, setting his sights on Zack. Jackie ran two quick steps for Zack and used his bent leg to leap into the air. She somersaulted through the air and kicked the guard in the head on her way down. The guard was thrown several feet across the snack bar area and struck the nearby wall with a loud crack. Jackie hit the floor with less precision due to her minor leg injury and ended up on her ass. She grimaced at the pain it caused and noted the blood seeping through the thick gauze pad Zack had secured over her injury on the drive over.

Zack stood over her while grinning and extended his hand to assist her. She accepted his hand and allowed him to pull her to her feet. As his custom and much to her disapproval, he pulled her against him and kissed her quickly on the lips in celebration. When he pulled back, Jackie punched him in the mouth, starting a new custom. Zack jumped back with surprise, not used to it working that way, and held his mouth. He dabbed his bleeding lip then gave her an innocent look.

"Too soon, huh?"

She glared at him then headed across the betting area without a word.

Zack groaned and followed her. "Well, at least you didn't shoot me," he remarked with noted enthusiasm.

"Days not over yet," she called back.

"Kirk was over it in five minutes. That's what's great about guys," he informed her while maintaining his distance. "You women take things too personally."

"So pair up with Kirk," she snarled without looking back at him.

He playfully pouted at the comment. "But I'd rather play with you."

†

Two guards walked past the outside stadium seating and headed toward the track itself. Everything seemed quiet. The dim lighting cast shadows in just about every corner, making detecting anyone difficult. They were about to give up when they heard faint gunshots from inside the building. Both were about to return to the building to investigate when they heard a woman's shrill scream. The guards ran toward the parade paddock with their assault rifles prepared to shoot the first thing that moved. They entered the paddock and looked around only to find it empty. As the first guard turned, the butt of a rifle struck him in the face. He dropped to the ground before Kirk. The second guard spun around, having seen the man next to him fall. Bogart threw a punch for the guard's face. He immediately dodged Bogart's flying fist and punched him in the mouth, startling the conman.

As the guard turned and aimed his assault rifle at Kirk, Kirk kicked it from his hands. Bogart threw another punch at the guard. His attention left Kirk and focused on Bogart. The guard blocked his fist and punched him in the abdomen then across the face, forcing Bogart to stumble backward. Bogart wiped the blood from the corner of his mouth then looked at Kirk, who casually leaned against the fence with his arms folded across his chest.

"You're just going to stand there?" Bogart demanded with astonishment.

"You'll never learn if I keep fighting your battles for you," Kirk remarked.

"Thanks a lot," Bogart snarled.

Kirk casually nodded, indicating the guard. "You'll want to duck."

As Bogart turned, the guard punched him in the face and nearly knocked him to the ground. "Prick," Bogart scoffed at Kirk while catching his balance.

While partially bent over, Bogart charged the guard and tackled him to the ground. Both men wrestled around the sand covered paddock attempting to punch each other with little success. The guard got to his feet first and kicked Bogart in the ribs as he attempted to stand then went for another kick. Bogart caught his foot and twisted it, knocking the man back to the ground. Bogart pulled himself to his feet as the guard sprang back up effortlessly. As the guard straightened and prepared to throw another punch, Bogart snap kicked him in the groin. The man clutched himself and started to drop to his knees. On his way down, Bogart spun into a roundhouse kick and struck the man in the head, driving him the rest of the way to the ground. Bogart stood over the fallen man and stared at him with surprise while panting heavily.

"I'll be damned," Bogart gasped. "That karate crap works." He glanced at Kirk, who appeared surprised to see the man out cold beneath Bogart's feet. Bogart smirked and gave a slight nod. "You may want to duck."

Kirk looked behind him. The guard he'd taken out now stood behind him and punched him in the face. Kirk, barely fazed by the hit, glared at the man. The guard stared with surprise and some concern. Bogart pressed a button on his cell phone and grinned as the app of a woman screaming filled the paddock. Kirk sneered with annoyance and punched the stunned guard in the face.

Chapter Forty-four

In order to avoid the guards patrolling the common areas, Lee, Alma, and Kelsey took the out-of-the way service elevator from the penthouse to the basement. It was a long hike across the basement until they finally reached the laundry room. Kelsey led them across the massive, dimly lit laundry area that appeared to have been abandoned a long time. Lee looked around as they passed large washing machines, presses, and dryers. Everything was coated with thick cobwebs and dust.

"It doesn't look as if anyone's been here in quite a while," Lee remarked while nervously rubbing her chilled arms.

"When they closed the restaurant, they shut down the laundry room," Kelsey informed her then paused before an old maintenance elevator. "No one comes down here. It's easily overlooked." She then indicated the elevator. "This in particular."

Alma appeared equally surprised while staring at the old elevator. "Does it work?"

"Of course it does," Kelsey remarked with a sly grin on her face. "It's how I sneak out of the building when I need to get away from my charmed life. It takes you to the back corridor in the old kitchen, which hasn't been used in years either. It's quite a haul from the penthouse, but this is the only way to avoid the heavily guarded areas. Once we're in the kitchen, we just slip out the back door to the parade paddock, pass the main barn, and head out the back exit. We can hike through the woods and stay hidden for hours. In the morning, we can go to town and get help."

"But Ross--" Lee protested.

"Ross doesn't need you here," Kelsey insisted while casting a sharp look at her. "You're the reason he's going to get killed. If you really love him, you'll leave this place and give him a fighting chance."

They heard someone enter the laundry room. Kelsey shoved her mother and Lee into the old elevator. Jason and the second guard came into view, catching a glimpse of her but not the elevator. She pushed the first-floor button.

"I'll hold them off then meet you in the woods," Kelsey whispered.

"Kelsey," Alma gasped as the doors closed.

Kelsey waited until she was sure the guards saw her then took off across the laundry room, luring them away from the elevator they probably had no idea existed. The second guard cut off her path while Jason circled around from behind. Both aimed their weapons at her, giving her nowhere to run.

"It's just me," she attempted to explain while holding her hands in the air. "I couldn't sleep, so I went for a walk."

"Where are they?" the second guard demanded.

"Who?" she asked.

"Your mother and the girl," he snarled.

"In the suite," she replied innocently. "Where else would they be?"

"Sorry, Kelsey. Wrong answer," the second guard announced with little emotion. "Your services are no longer required."

His finger tightened on the assault rifle trigger. Kelsey let out a slight gasp and shut her eyes as a shot rang out, echoing across the laundry room. She opened her eyes and saw the second guard spitting up blood as he sank to the floor. She looked at Jason where he stood several feet behind her.

Jason lowered his assault rifle and raised a cocky brow. "I don't share that opinion," he casually replied.

Kelsey exhaled as her legs nearly gave out. She smiled at Jason and laughed softly. "I owe you."

"I'll be sure to collect if any of us makes it out of here alive," Jason informed her. "Pendleton called in the 'dogs of war'. Once those guys get here, it's going to be a bloodbath. Is your mother safe?"

"I think so," she replied.

They heard someone entering the laundry room from the main entrance. "They heard the gunfire," he announced with concern. "We can't risk taking your secret way out. I'll get you out another way."

"You knew about the elevator?"

"I've kept tabs on you and your little walks," he replied with a humored smirk. He then indicated an area toward the back. "There's a service door to the boiler room."

✝

Lee attempted to hurry Alma along the darkened, abandoned kitchen, but Alma lagged behind while looking back, waiting for her daughter.

"What about Kelsey?" Alma whispered with concern. "They'll kill her."

"You have to trust her, Alma," Lee announced while attempting to keep the worried woman moving. "If we don't get out of here, they'll kill us for sure. We need to keep moving."

Lee hurried her toward the back door. A guard appeared in the dim lighting between them and the kitchen door with his assault rifle aimed. Lee suddenly stopped and blocked Alma with her body while staring at the guard. Wexler stared at her with surprise and lowered his rifle.

"Lee?" Wexler gasped with surprise.

She stared at the man with a puzzled look, not knowing him, although he seemed to know her. Darth bolted across the kitchen past Alma and Lee and leaped on top of Wexler, knocking him against the door while tearing into his jacket sleeve and some flesh. His assault rifle clattered to the floor as he attempted to remove the dog attacking him.

"Darth, oust!"

Darth released Wexler's arm and snarled at him from less than a foot away. Wexler clutched his injured arm and looked up to see Gil standing in front of Lee. Gil had his gun aimed at Wexler's face and his finger tight on the trigger.

"It's nothing personal," Gil announced, about to shoot the man.

"No!" Alma screamed when she saw the guard's face and realized it was her son.

Wexler stared with panic at the gun then Gil. "Ross Madrid. Alpha Mike Foxtrot," he cried out.

Gil's expression immediately changed as he stared at the frightened man and lowered his gun. "What's your name?"

"Wexler," he gasped. "I'm Wexler."

Gil shrugged with something resembling disinterest. "In that case, you get to live."

Alma ran past Gil and hugged her son. He was surprised to see her and returned the warm embrace. She sobbed while clinging to him.

Gil turned to Lee and gave her a quick, concerned once over. "Are you okay? Did they hurt you?"

She smiled and shook her head. "I'm fine," Lee announced then hugged him. "I'm really glad to see you." She pulled away and stared at him with concern. "They have Ross."

"Technically," Gil remarked, "we have Ross."

"Thank God," she gasped and felt relief for the first time.

Gil touched his ear transmitter. "Ross, we have Lee. She's in good health." He gave her a quick once over. "Even smells good. I guess her accommodations were better than yours. We found your buddy Wexler and a woman I can only guess is his mother."

†

Ross and Beck stopped in the penthouse corridor and listened to Gil through their ear transmitters. Ross shut his eyes a moment and let a breath escape, sighing with relief. Beck shared his relief. Ross's eyes then opened, revealing a psychotic side rarely ever seen.

"Zack," Ross announced through his transmitter as his lips twisted into a snarl. "Time to mark your territory. Level the fucking place."

Beck placed his hands over his eyes, looked away, and groaned softly.

Ross cast a glare at Beck standing alongside him and noted his expression. "Problem?" he demanded with a look that would easily frighten.

"No, Ross," Beck replied with some apprehension then shook his head. "I know what you're feeling. I'd do the same if someone took Pinto."

"Good, glad to hear," Ross remarked then touched his ear transmitter. "Everyone out!"

✝

Jackie listened to Ross's order through her ear transmitter and expressed her shock and disbelief by his words. She looked at the equally surprised Zack standing alongside her. Ross was not one to arbitrarily blow up any installation.

"Has he gone mad?" she proclaimed.

"A little," Zack replied casually. "Don't we all go a little mad once in a while?" He gave her a quick once over and cleverly raised his brows. "I saw your 'woman on the edge' email."

She frowned and attempted to hide her embarrassment. "Not quite the same thing," Jackie informed him then became concerned. "Do you have any idea what this means?"

"Yeah," Zack announced and grinned with enthusiasm. "I get to make a bomb!" His devious smile increased as he stared at her. "And you get to help. This is going to be so much fun. I love couple's therapy!"

Jackie attempted to protest when Zack grabbed her hand and pulled her behind him, nearly taking her off her feet.

✝

Melissa continued to pace the temporary security office while the guard in front of the security monitor attempted to find any movement on the working cameras. When he came up empty, he made several attempts to reach the guards on their hand radios, but no one was responding. His expression reported his worst fears, although Melissa didn't seem to catch on nearly as fast.

"Where are they?" she demanded becoming animated. "Where are the guards?"

The guard shook his head while frowning. "My guess would be they're all gone."

She glared at the man behind the security monitor. "Gone? You think they took out all my guards?"

"Yes, ma'am," he replied casually. "I do."

"Where are my bounty hunters?" she practically cried out nearing hysteria.

The guard flipped through a few camera images and found one of the main entrance. A black SUV crashed through the gates with five others following.

"I'm guessing that's them now," he replied while indicating the first screen.

"It's about time," she snarled then glared at the guard behind the monitor. "Go out there and greet them."

The guard stood from behind the desk, removed his semiautomatic from his shoulder holster, and cocked it. He looked at her and managed a nervous laugh. "You greet them," he announced. "I'm out of here. Have a nice life, Ms. Pendleton."

Melissa stared after him in disbelief as he left her alone in the control room.

✝

Monroe watched the parade of black SUVs race up to the main building as he headed up the steps to the control tower booth. He touched his ear transmitter.

"Boys, the second-string has arrived," Monroe announced then entered the tower booth.

He sat behind the large panel and eyed the dozen or more switches and buttons. He flipped several switches. Lights came on across the entire track, lighting the area. The scoreboard came on as well. He typed on the keyboard then stopped to touch his ear transmitter.

"Talk to me, Zack."

"I need another minute," Zack replied.

"You're getting slow," Monroe remarked while leaning back in his chair. "You used to be able to throw a bomb together in a matter of minutes."

"Jackie's being a whining little bitch," Zack casually replied. "She's sucking all the fun out of conceiving our first love child."

"Yeah, I copy that," Monroe remarked with a soft chuckle at Jackie's expense.

Jackie was heard screaming in the background. "There's no way in hell I'm shaking my ass while you sing, 'I love big bombs'. Deal with it!"

Monroe snickered softly, possibly entertaining the image in his mind. "Waiting for the countdown," he replied.

"On my mark," Zack announced. "Three, two, one. Mark."

Monroe pressed enter on the keyboard. A message flashed on the scoreboard. It simply read, 'bomb go boom countdown' with the time counting down from fifteen minutes. He pressed another button, causing an alarm to wail. Monroe then jumped up from his seat and left the tower booth.

†

Nearly a dozen bounty hunters stormed into the main building with their weapons drawn. It was possible they made a pact to split the bounties in order to work together. As the bounty hunters fanned out into the room, gunshots suddenly rang out. Three lost their weapons while clutching their bleeding wrists and four others took shots to their legs, falling to the floor in agony. The other three looked around while attempting to reach cover. Gunshots exploded on the floor not far from their feet with the ricochet nearly striking them. They immediately dropped their weapons. Whiskey Tango Foxtrot stepped out from their hidden positions with their assault rifles leveled and ready to fire.

Ross shook his head as they approached the surrendering bounty hunters. "Not a single shot fired," he remarked and grimaced. "That's pretty embarrassing, boys."

Melissa appeared from one of the nearby corridors and stopped when she saw the ten bounty hunters at the mercy of the team. She gasped with surprise then turned and ran for a back corridor.

Jackie saw Melissa fleeing. "That's her," she announced and was about to run after her when Zack stopped her. She gave him a bewildered look.

He made a face and cocked his head. "Come on, Jackie," he scoffed. "Like she's getting far in those designer heels."

Jackie considered the comment then nodded. "Yeah, you're right."

Zack offered a sly grin. "Ten bucks says she falls twice before we catch her."

"You're on," Jackie announced and shook his hand.

They headed across the building after Melissa in no particular hurry.

Ross shook his head then indicated the ten bounty hunters. "Let's secure these gentlemen and get out of here before we're all a memory."

†

Wexler stood guard outside the front of the building near the fleet of black SUVs with his assault rifle trained on the main doors. Despite hearing gunfire, his job was to make certain the bounty hunters didn't return to the cars. Alma and Lee checked the vehicles until they found one with keys in the ignition. Darth remained by their side as additional protection, since he would be the first to notice someone approaching. Darth suddenly looked toward the side of the building and snarled, alarming everyone. Wexler aimed his assault rifle in the direction the dog stared. Jason and Kelsey appeared from the shadows and stopped when the saw Wexler holding his rifle on them. Jason aimed his rifle at Wexler. Neither man flinched while holding their weapons on the other.

"Wexler," Kelsey suddenly cried out and ran past Jason to her brother.

Wexler lowered his gun as she ran to him and jumped into his arms. They shared a warm embrace. "Kelsey, I wasn't sure I'd ever see you again. Mother said you were giving them chase in the basement."

"Jason saved me," she informed him then indicated Jason as he approached.

Wexler glanced at Jason and offered a relieved smile. "Thank you, Jason."

Jason joined them with his weapon now lowered although ready if necessary. "I hate to interrupt your reunion, but we need to get out of here," he announced. "Some idiot posted a bomb warning on the scoreboard. We should take the threat seriously."

"Yeah, I know. The bomb is real, I promise. If we're lucky, the idiots who set it should be out any minute," Wexler informed him then indicated the bounty hunters' SUVs. "We need to find another set of keys for our getaway vehicles. If the guys aren't here at the five-minute mark, we're to leave them a running vehicle and get the women out to the main road."

Kelsey joined Alma and Lee in an attempt to find another vehicle with keys left in the ignition. The main building's front doors opened, putting Wexler and Jason on alert as they raised their weapons. Ross and his team, minus Jackie and Zack, left the building with their ten captive bounty hunters. Some looked a little worse for wear than others. Lee saw Ross for the first time and nearly cried out. She ran across the parking lot and threw her arms around him. Her enthusiastic greeting caused him some discomfort, but he endured the pain and held her in his arms. Neither seemed willing to let go. Lee finally pulled away and stared at his battered face.

"Oh, my God," she gasped while gently touching the fading bruises and stared at the cuts on his face. "What did they do to you?"

He looked over her and noted her healthy, unscathed appearance then smiled while snorting a soft, humored laugh. "I'm guessing your stay was a lot better than mine."

She laughed while fighting her tears and caressed his face. Ross kissed her warmly but passionately then immediately pulled away.

"Sorry," he announced almost timidly. "I've smelled better, or so they keep telling me."

"I don't care. I'm just happy you're alive," Lee replied with a tiny laugh while fighting her tears. "I'll give you a nice, hot bubble bath when we get home."

Ross groaned softly and kissed her in response.

Chapter Forty-five

Melissa ran across the grounds as fast as her designer heels would carry her and didn't stop until she reached the large horse barn. She hesitated outside the barn, concerned she'd been followed, and scanned the moderately dark area. When she didn't see anyone, she entered the barn and ran into a bright light shining on her. To her surprise, one of the sports cars was parked in the barn aisle with its headlights on. Melissa slowly approached the car and gave it a strange once over.

"Is that my car?" she remarked softly. She then saw Riley standing alongside the car. Melissa's eyes suddenly widened. "You! I knew you had something to do with this!"

Riley didn't react or comment. Two neatly dressed men stood on either side of the sports car with one standing directly behind Riley.

"Look what we found outside the back entrance," the man standing behind Riley announced while holding a gun on her. "What would you like us to do with her, Ms. Pendleton?"

Melissa sneered her annoyance. "Take the bitch out back and shoot her."

The man behind Riley shoved her toward the nearby door. Something creaked within the barn. Pigeons flew from their elevated perches in the raters and swarmed out the open barn door behind the car. Both armed men and Melissa looked around the dimly lit barn to see what caused the commotion. Riley darted looks around as if anticipating something worse than her current situation. Melissa was in a state near panic, already having a good idea what caused the pigeons to take flight.

"Check the rafters," Melissa cried out.

The second man turned on a light attached to his assault rifle and aimed it toward the ceiling, shining light along the rafters. He caught a glimpse of something dark, but before he could follow it, it was gone. There was a loud grunt followed by a bang. The second guard shined his light across the car. The first guard had struck the side of the sports car and was already sinking to the concrete barn floor. Riley was gone! The second guard, now on edge, again scanned the barn and ceiling with the light on his assault rifle. Jackie somersaulted from the rafters and landed gracefully on the roof of the car with a loud bang. Despite her graceful landing, the drop and her weight severely dented the car roof. The surprised guard aimed his rifle at her. Jackie flipped off the roof and over the guard into the darkness behind him. He attempted to follow her with his assault rifle and light. Instead, he found Zack standing where Jackie should have landed. Zack spun into a roundhouse kick and knocked the rifle from his hand. His return kick sent the man crashing against the passenger side door with a tremendous bang, knocking the wind from him.

Melissa gasped when she saw both men taken out by the Russian. She turned to run and came face-to-face with Jackie, who now stood behind her. Jackie grinned, frightening Melissa. Before Melissa could attempt to dart past her, Jackie flipped through the air, caught Melissa around the neck with her legs, and rode her to the barn floor. The woman screamed the entire way down. Jackie sprang to her feet and yanked the woman up with her. Melissa had been tossed right out of her designer shoes, and her expensive dress was now torn and dirty. Jackie clutched the woman's throat, cutting off her air and causing her to gasp.

"Give us your boss, and you may just live," Jackie informed her.

Melissa wheezed while attempting to loosen Jackie's grip as her hand squeezed her throat. "I don't have a boss," she managed to gasp and stared into Jackie's hateful eyes.

"If you don't have a boss that means it was you who put the hit on my team," Jackie snarled while staring into her eyes. "That also means there's no reason to keep you alive."

"Enough," a man suddenly shouted in anger.

Jackie looked across the barn to the car headlights. Riley was forced into the light by a man standing behind her a gun to her head. Jackie immediately spun behind Melissa, placed her arm around her neck, and stared at the man in the shadows.

"Who are you?" Jackie demanded. "I'll snap her neck; I swear."

"I'm sure you will," came the response.

Jackie watched as Riley moved forward, allowing the man behind her to step into the light. Jackie felt her heart pounding as she stared at former Governor Lyle Kempton holding the gun to Riley's head. She hadn't seen him since she testified against him in court, putting him in jail for multiple murders. She masked her shock and horror with anger.

"I thought you were dead," Jackie scoffed.

"Not for lack of trying from your friend, Zack," Lyle remarked. "I nearly died in prison thanks to some friends of his. Something he didn't seem to realize though. I have friends too. I survived the attack. Some friends of mine faked my death and kept me from returning to prison." He stared at her with a sneer on his face. "And I thought about you and your friends every minute since."

"So you put the bounty on our heads," Jackie remarked. "All of this is because of you?"

"And everything I've been through is because of you," he snarled. "The rest of your team was insignificant. All I really wanted was revenge on you and your friend, Zack. Since he died on Giovanni's island, I had to settle for you."

"That's why you doubled the bounty on me if I were taken alive?"

"Nothing would give me greater pleasure than to torture you slowly before I eventually kill you," he informed her. He seemed to realize something was missing and glanced around. "Where's the Russian?"

"I told you not to take your eyes off him," Melissa growled beneath Jackie's firm grip around her neck.

"I wouldn't worry about the Russian," Jackie announced with a bored sigh. "I'm sure he's behind your boyfriend waiting for some secret signal to take off his head, but I'd really like to finish our conversation first." She was hoping wherever Zack was at the moment, he'd take the hint and not simply kill the man.

Lyle cast a glance behind him but didn't see anyone. The two guards were alert enough to collect their guns and pull themselves to their feet. They saw what was playing out before them and aimed their weapons at Jackie holding Melissa.

Lyle eyed the guards then grinned at Jackie. "I think you're a little outnumbered," he announced with some humor to her situation.

Jackie cast a look at her tactical wristwatch not far from Melissa's neck.

Melissa was becoming annoyed with her predicament and glared at Lyle. "Enough of this! Will someone just shoot the bitch?" she shouted out in anger.

Jackie placed her lips close to Melissa's ear and whispered, "It's not wise to piss me off. I could snap your neck and not lose a second of sleep." She allowed her eyes to stray to Lyle as he held the gun to Riley's head. She watched the Governor's hired goons with their weapons aimed at her and calculated when they'd feel they had a clear shot and start shooting. She again eyed her watch then smiled at Lyle. "Sorry, Governor," she announced. "Your time is up." Her watch counted down to double zero.

✝

The racetrack's main building suddenly exploded into a ball of fire followed by a cloud of smoke and thick debris raining down upon the track and parking lot. The entire area shook for miles. The rest of the team stood behind the bounty hunters' SUVs, which were now moved closer to the racetrack entrance and further away from the building itself. Despite their distance, their vehicles were covered in dirt and debris.

✝

As the ground shook, the barn rattled and seemed to shift. Dirt and debris fell from the ceiling covering those within the aisle. Everyone reacted with surprise except Jackie, who had been anticipating the explosion. While keeping her arm around Melissa's neck, she threw herself into a forward flip, taking the woman with her, rolling her across the ground. Lyle mistakenly released Riley during the explosion. Zack tackled the young woman to the floor, rolling several times with her before springing to his feet near the sports car. Before the first man with the gun even had time to react to the explosion, Zack was spinning into a high roundhouse kick, striking him in the head. He again struck the car with a thud. The second guard snapped back into reality, saw Zack, and aimed his gun at him. Zack was already flipping through the air across the roof of the car and landed on top of the man with the gun, riding him to the ground.

Jackie sprang to her feet and saw Lyle returning to the reality of the situation. He aimed his gun at Jackie, but she was already running for him. He fired at her, missing as she flipped through the air. She kicked him in the head, throwing him against the stall behind him and cracking the wood. The gun flew from his hand and onto the floor a few feet away. Jackie landed from the kick and spun around gracefully facing Lyle. He looked at the gun not far from him and saw her staring directly at him in attack position. His body suddenly tensed. He knew she wanted him to go for the gun. She was waiting for him to give her reason to attack. Melissa saw the confrontation between them and ran from the barn, leaving Lyle to fend for himself.

"I'm not going to do it," Lyle bluntly informed her. "I'm not going for the gun and giving you justification to seek your revenge." He smirked almost smugly. "I'll take my chances in prison."

Zack approached and stood alongside Jackie, allowing Lyle to see him up close for the first time. It took a moment for Lyle to realize the identity of the Russian since he never really got a good look at Zack the only time they'd ever met. Horror suddenly swept over his face.

"You!" he gasped.

"Yes, Governor," Zack announced while grinning. "It would seem we were both resurrected from the dead. Convenient, huh?" He cocked his head and boldly raised his brows. "What makes you think we intend to turn you over to the authorities? If I'd finished the job I started, the last two weeks of hell could have been avoided. I'd be an idiot to give you another opportunity to take out my friends."

"I'll tell you why you're not going to kill me," Lyle gasped then straightened with conviction and indicated Jackie. "Because she won't let you. She's not like you. She won't kill an unarmed man. She needs to be justified, and I won't give her that justification." He grinned. "That's why."

Zack removed his semiautomatic and aimed it at Lyle's face from only two feet away. His look was cold and without emotion. "Take a walk, Jackie."

Jackie remained in attack position and still didn't move. Zack glanced at her and noted her look.

"Jackie," he announced a little louder, jolting her back into reality. He gave her a stern look. "I've got this. Find Melissa before she gets away."

She relaxed her stance and shook her head. "No, Zack," she informed him. "It wouldn't be right. You can't kill him."

Zack groaned with annoyance while Lyle gloated. "We can't let him go back to prison," he insisted. "He'll find another way around the system and come for us again. Holden's partner is dead because of him. Holden nearly died because of him. He ordered the hit on us at Giovanni's island. This is all because of him." Zack suddenly hesitated and sank into thought. "This is all because of me. I went after him, and then he came after the people I cared about." His look then turned serious. "I started this, Jackie. I need to finish it."

Jackie looked at Zack and stared at him with surprise. "You didn't start this." She indicated Lyle with a demanding finger. "*He* started this when he executed a federal agent in front of me and sent his hitmen to silence me." She drew a deep breath and ran trembling fingers through her mussed ponytail. "I've got this," she informed him and extended her hand. "Give me a pair of zip ties. I'll take care of the Governor."

"Jackie--" he protested.

She snapped her fingers and indicated his pocket. "Just give me the zip ties. Melissa's getting away."

Zack frowned and handed her a pair of plastic ties. He headed for the side door, leaving Jackie to tether Lyle's wrists. Jackie fiddled with the plastic ties while staring emotionless at the Governor. As Zack disappeared through the doorway, Jackie's look suddenly turned cold and hateful.

"You ordered a hit on my husband, and you tried to kill my family, you son-of-a-bitch," she snarled with revenge in her eyes. "You've fucked with me for the last time."

"You wouldn't--"

Jackie suddenly spun into a high roundhouse kick and struck Lyle in the face. As he dropped to the ground, she grabbed him by the head and snapped his neck. She let out a slight gasp along with a tiny sob as she released his limp body. Jackie shut her eyes and listened to his body hit the floor with a soft thump. Without looking back, she turned. Zack once again stood several feet from her, having witnessed the entire incident. Jackie trembled slightly and touched her forehead with a shaking hand.

"He, uh, went for the gun."

Zack nodded. "I know."

As Jackie broke down sobbing, he pulled her into his arms and held her against him. She clung to Zack and cried on his shoulder.

✝

Melissa hurried through the torn section in the chain-link fence and saw the unattended sports car. She let out a sigh of relief and hurried to the car, throwing open the door. As luck would have it, the keys were still in the ignition. She was about to slip into the driver's seat when a shadow fell over her from the additional lights at the distant racetrack. She looked alongside her and saw Mac standing by the car door only a foot away.

"Mac?" she gasped with surprise and straightened. "What are you doing here?"

"I saw what happened at the mansion with your guards and the hitmen," Mac remarked and stared at her with a strange look of concern. "Are you okay?"

Melissa managed a smile and an uneasy laugh. "No, not really," she replied and held her head. "I never should have gotten involved with my old boyfriend. You were right. I should have listened to you." She looked around with concern. "It's not safe here."

"He turned out to be a jerk, huh?"

"Sort of," Melissa replied then looked at the distant burning building. The inferno was bound to attract attention, even in the middle of nowhere. "We really need to go." She suddenly hesitated and looked at Mac. "How did you know where to find me? Did you follow me?"

Mac smiled sweetly and shook her head. "No, I didn't follow you," she replied. "I was following *him*."

"Him?" Melissa asked with confusion.

"Yeah, him," she replied with a moderately psychotic grin on her face. "The Russian."

Melissa looked down and saw the gun containing a silencer in Mac's hand. She fired two nearly silent shots into Melissa's abdomen.

248

Melissa clutched her bleeding stomach and stared at Mac with surprise and horror as her legs buckled.

"I didn't save him from your ex-boyfriend just to get him killed again," Mac casually replied then shrugged. "It's nothing personal."

As Melissa hit the ground, Jackie, Zack, and Riley appeared through the chain-link fence. Jackie hesitated when she saw Mac standing over Melissa's body.

Mac eyed Jackie and rolled her eyes. "Figures you'd survive," she muttered.

"Play nice," Zack announced firmly. "We've all had a long night." He touched his ear transmitter. "Ross, we're out. What's your twenty?"

"Heading out the main entrance with Lee, a caravan of bounty hunters, and a few extras," Ross replied through his transmitter. "What's the situation?"

"You can tell our fan club that the bounty's been lifted due to an unexpected death in the family," Zack replied. "We'll meet you at the rendezvous."

Chapter Forty-six

The virtually empty interstate diner was nearly an hour's drive from the disaster left behind at the racetrack. It was a little after three o'clock in the morning by the time the team regrouped. After parting ways with the disenchanted, oddly forgiving bounty hunters at the local hospital, the moderately worn group of fifteen sat at three sets of tables pulled together. They watched the news coverage of an explosion at the closed racetrack. There were claims of several bodies pulled from the rubble in what looked like a drug deal gone terribly wrong.

Beck returned to the group of old and new friends looking exhausted but relieved. "I contacted the safe house," he announced with a sigh. "All parties concerned were happy to hear we're all alive and still in one piece."

Alma and Kelsey returned from the ladies' room and approached the table. Wexler and Jason stood in response to their return.

"We should be going," Wexler announced.

Ross stood as well and extended his hand to the man who'd kept him alive for two weeks. "Thank you for everything, Wexler," he announced. "If you ever need anything--"

He shook Ross's hand. "Back at you, Ross," Wexler replied then grinned. "Thanks for the stolen SUV."

"You're welcome, but ditch it the first chance you get," Ross warned.

Lee hugged both women, expressed her thanks for all they'd done to keep her safe, and then returned to her seat once the four left the diner.

"We should probably get back to the others," Ross remarked. "It's late, and I'm in dire need of a shower."

Everyone nodded in agreement. Ross cast glares around the table.

Monroe shifted in his chair and indicated Mac. "Shouldn't we drop off Zack's girlfriend first?"

"She's not my girlfriend," Zack immediately corrected him, sounding a little gruffer than necessary.

"No, you just owe me about a thousand favors," Mac remarked casually. "You should be happy I stuck around considering how little you trusted me."

"You knew the people after us. You were the one feeding me all the information regarding Ross, Lee, and the hit on the team," Zack reminded her. "I had reason not to trust you."

"So she wasn't actually trying to stop you?" Jackie asked becoming curious then eyed Mac. "You were helping him the entire time?"

"When he needed me," Mac retorted. "Mostly, I was just left in the dark while risking my life."

"You lied about your relationship with Melissa Pendleton," he boldly remarked while glaring at her. "You were sleeping with the enemy--literally."

Mac shook her head while smirking at him. "That's so typical," she snapped. "When a man does what I did, it's called taking one for the team. When a woman does it, she's automatically deceitful and hiding something."

Bogart suddenly became interested in the conversation and eyed Mac while attempting to understand what they were saying. "Wait a minute," he announced while sitting forward. "Who were you sleeping with?"

Riley shifted in her chair alongside Bogart's and gently placed her hand on his lower arm. "I'm pretty sure they're talking about my step-aunt."

Bogart stared at Riley a moment then eyed Mac with a slightly surprised look. "You mean Melissa was sleeping with you and me?"

Mac raised her brow. "Yeah, but in my case, it was because she wanted to," she snapped with irritation. "She was just trying to keep you occupied until her henchmen could take you out in Washington."

"That's cold," Bogart announced then sank back in his chair and shook his head while pouting over his bruised ego. "I really need a steady girlfriend."

Riley smiled sweetly and clung to his arm. He eyed her, noted her look with some surprise, and then grinned in response to her cuddling.

"So this safe house," Ross began and eyed the others. "None of you knew it was one of Zack's secret retreats?"

Everyone but Jackie shook their heads in response.

"When I learned of the hits and discovered Othello snatched Holden from the hospital, I knew the team needed someplace remote and unknown," Zack informed Ross. "I contacted Othello under one of my *other* names and sent him to my retreat."

Beck turned to Jackie and appeared curious. "And you discovered this?"

Jackie nodded without feeling the least bit guilty that she kept the information from him. "I couldn't tell you because you'd probably think it was a setup and force everyone to leave," she replied although it was only a partial truth. She couldn't let Beck suspect she'd intended to go rogue.

"But how did you know?" Monroe asked her with a curious look. "I checked every inch of that place. I didn't find any evidence that Zack had been there. I mean, apart from the ample weapon's room."

"I left her clues," Zack reluctantly replied.

"Why *did* you do that?" Jackie finally asked. "You went to great lengths to make us believe you turned on us, yet you left clues for me that told a different story."

Zack fidgeted but didn't respond.

"He was concerned he'd be killed," Mac informed her with a hint of jealousy in her tone. "He didn't want to die knowing you hated him."

Beck snorted a laugh. "No need to worry about that," he remarked to Zack. "She was an absolute pain in the ass. She refused to believe you'd turned."

"Why not just tell us?" Bogart finally asked the question on their minds. "Did I miss something?"

"They were watching me," Zack replied. "Mac was in their good graces, so I asked her to run interference. I knew they had Ross and Lee and that they'd be distrustful of anyone new." He hesitated a moment. "I also didn't see the point endangering the rest of the team for a situation I'd created. I assumed I could handle it on my own."

"What were you doing at the boneyard?" Monroe asked.

"I thought if I sabotaged the planes, you'd be stranded in the boneyard long enough for me to finish my mission," Zack informed him. "Stranding you there would keep the team out of harm's way."

"So why did you try to abduct me then?" Jackie finally asked.

Mac rolled her eyes and groaned.

Zack cast a disapproving look at her then focused his attention on Jackie. "I realized I couldn't do it on my own, so I needed to recruit you and Kirk onto my 'ghost' team," he replied. "When a Kirk lookalike had an *accident*, I knew I could switch the dead guy for the real Kirk."

Bogart smirked and cocked his head. "And then the 'real Kirk' knocked out the real Bogart."

Kirk groaned with annoyance. "You're like a whining old woman," he snarled. "Get over it."

"Claiming the 'kill' on Kirk also bought me extra points with Melissa," Zack remarked.

"Did she ever pay the million on Kirk's head?" Gil then asked.

Kirk shifted in his chair and avoided looking at the others without comment.

"No," Zack replied without even flinching. "I wasn't expecting to see that money. That would be wrong and immoral."

All eyes were suddenly on Zack and Kirk. Zack looked them dead in the eyes without reaction or emotion. Kirk played with his coffee cup and refused to look at any of them. Ross groaned with disapproval and shook his head.

"I'm curious," Bogart remarked while eyeing Kirk and Zack. "Which one of you is 'wrong' and which was is 'immoral'?"

"I'd rather he left us out of it," Ross remarked.

"Back to my original question," Monroe announced with a serious look on his face while shifting in his chair. "What do we do with Mac?"

She glared at Monroe, clearly annoyed by the question, but didn't comment.

Zack shrugged. "Well, considering all she's done for me and how she risked her life for the team, I'm thinking we get her a suite at a really nice hotel."

Mac glared at Zack as her mouth fell open. Her look turned enraged. "You bastard!"

"Sorry, Mac," he announced while casually sinking back in his seat. "I'm not letting you anywhere near my weapon's stash. I'm not even happy that Holden knows where it is."

Ross slapped his palms on the table, jolting it, and catching everyone's attention. "Then it's settled," he announced. "We'll drop our guests off at the hotel down the road."

Riley appeared almost as disappointed as Mac was. She clung to Bogart's arm and smiled affectionately. "It's late," she informed Bogart. "You could stay at the hotel tonight. I know I'd feel safer having you close by."

Bogart stared at the smile on her face and immediately caught her hint. He gently cleared his throat and eyed the others at the table. "I think I should stay with Riley at the hotel," he announced and casually shrugged. "Make sure she's safe until we're certain no one's after her."

Everyone at the table rolled their eyes and groaned.

Mac frowned and folded her arms across her chest. "That figures."

Kirk snatched the breakfast check as everyone stood to leave. He slapped it into Monroe's hand and followed the others from the diner.

Monroe shook his head. "Why do I always get stuck with the bill?" He then muttered, "Everyone knows Zack's one million richer." Monroe headed for the register while removing money from his pocket.

Jackie was about to follow the others when she witnessed Mac kicking Zack's chair in anger as she passed. Mac didn't say anything, but she was clearly mad at him. Zack remained alone at the table, slouched in his chair, and stared at nothing in particular while playing with a creamer pod. Jackie returned to the table and sat next to him.

"You're really good at pissing off women who can kick your ass, you know that?" she remarked.

"It's my trademark," he muttered without looking at her.

"What's wrong?" Jackie finally asked. "She obviously wants you. What's the problem?"

He didn't respond.

"I know you're not the 'talk about your feelings' type," Jackie announced with a groan, "but you need to make an exception once in a while or you'll go insane."

There was a long silence. Zack remained fixated on the creamer pod. "I don't trust her. Trust is very important to me right now." He was still unable to look at her while maintaining a frown. "Can you ever trust me again after everything I've done? Did I ruin our relationship?"

Jackie affectionately placed her hand on his. He finally glanced up and met her gaze. She smiled warmly and leaned closer to him. "I've been to hell and back for you," she informed him. "It's safe to assume you're stuck with me forever." Jackie gently touched his face then kissed him quickly on the lips. "I love you. Get used to it."

He hid his smile. "I already am."

She stood and extended her hand to him. "Come on, let's go home."

Zack placed his hand in hers without hesitation and joined her.

Chapter Forty-seven

Two days later. The team had returned to the lodge to get back to a somewhat normal life and make necessary repairs while they had the additional manpower. They'd left the place a mess, leaving those who hadn't been there for the final act speechless at the destruction.

Othello stood before the massive hole in the lodge lobby and stared at it while the guys covered it with a large sheet of plastic. "That's one big hole," he reported then resumed sweeping debris from the lobby floor.

Everyone was pitching in to help straighten the place while staying there for a well-deserved rest after their ordeal. It was always nice coming home. Holden's boss, Blake Harris, took care of the mess Jackie left behind at their house and even sent the homicide cleanup crew in so the place would be ready for their return. Gil's ex-wife, Ellie, decided to stay at a hotel near her home in Virginia so she could return to work. Gil and Darth returned to the lodge in Colorado to help with cleanup. Although nothing was said, the last day at the ranger's station was moderately uncomfortable between Gil and Ellie. Once the novelty of sex wore off, their differences surfaced, and it was back to fighting as usual.

Bogart reluctantly left Riley at the hotel in Virginia. After her aunt's body had been discovered, a lawyer representing her aunt's estate contacted Riley. She was about to become a very wealthy young woman, which meant there was an excellent chance she'd never see Bogart again after that. Bogart and Sal sorted through the furniture and moved the salvageable pieces across the room where Pinto and Lee cleaned debris from them. A few pieces could be saved with a little work. The rest was sent out back into the bonfire pit.

Toward the front of the lodge, Jackie, Gil, Kirk, and Zack sorted through the helicopter ruins and salvaged useful parts. Holden was sidelined, forced to sit on the relocated helicopter bench in a supervisory capacity. Although his injuries were mostly healed and the stitches removed, he still wasn't one hundred percent, leaving him on light duty. He was allowed to return to work later next week to a desk job until he was cleared for fieldwork. Darth kept Holden occupied by bringing him sticks. Holden threw the sticks, but a different stick was always returned. On the last throw, Darth dropped a wet stick onto Holden's lap. When he looked down, he saw a man's severely decayed arm. Holden cried out with surprise and tossed it from his lap. Darth barked excitedly and attempted to grab the severed arm, thinking he'd found Holden's new favorite toy. Gil saw the arm Holden was attempting to wrestle away from the dog.

"Holden," Gil scolded. "Don't let him play with decayed body parts. You don't know where that's been."

Holden managed to get the arm away from Darth and placed it in a plastic bag with other 'parts' they'd found in the wreckage. "I realize I shouldn't ask," Holden announced while making a face, "but what happened to the other bodies? Are we burning those in the bonfire pit as well?"

"Don't be ridiculous," Zack casually remarked then tossed Holden a boot with the foot still intact.

Holden caught it, saw the severed foot sticking out, and grimaced while dropping it into the plastic bag.

"All sorts of predators in these woods," Zack informed him while resuming his work. "Something dragged those bodies off in less than forty-eight hours. Judging by the scat I'd found in the lobby, I'm guessing coyote."

"Good thing too," Gil added. "Could you imagine the smell if they hadn't?"

"I don't have to imagine," Jackie huffed while sorting through twisted metal then picked up a hand by its pinky finger and made a face. "It's pretty bad from where I'm standing." She grimaced and tossed the hand toward Holden.

Holden and Darth lunged for the severed hand at the same time. Darth reached it first and took off with it. Holden groaned and limped after the dog.

"Darth!"

Jackie struggled to lift a piece of metal then saw a man's smashed face staring back at her. Unfortunately, she'd found the rest of the pilot. She gently returned the piece of metal to its original position, made a face, and stepped back.

"Zack," she announced while looking at him and smiling almost sweetly. "This panel is too heavy for me to move. Would you get it for me?"

Zack made his way through the debris, paused before her, and handed her what he carried. She accepted what he had in his hand then looked down at the dried, shriveled heart she held. Jackie cried out and tossed it aside. Zack casually lifted the panel and stared at the flattened face beneath it.

"There's something you don't see every day," he remarked then lifted his head. "Holden! Bring a shovel!"

t

Later that evening after dark, the guys sat around the massive bonfire while sharing a bottle of expensive brandy. It was possibly going to be another one of *those* nights. Jackie sat on Holden's lap while they laughed and had a good time with the others, who were mostly drunk. Lee and Ross were extra lovey with the added alcohol. After everything they'd been through the past two weeks, no one was surprised by their overly affectionate nature. Now that they were drunk, the guys would soon need to chase them to their room before their behavior became obscene. At least at the lodge, they spent most of their day in their room making up for lost time while sparing everyone else their overly affectionate homecoming. Jackie finally realized Zack hadn't returned after being MIA at least an hour. She whispered something to Holden. He smiled and nodded.

As Jackie walked away, she heard Kirk shouting something about getting the hose and turning it on Ross. Although it sounded like a joke, Ross had done the same thing to a few of the guys in the past for the same sort of behavior. Jackie headed further away from the lodge and toward the tree with Zack's headstone beneath it. Zack sat on the ground with his back against his headstone. She somehow knew she'd find him there. Jackie approached and sat alongside him. She was aware he was intoxicated, even though he was good at hiding it. She leaned her head against the headstone and looked at the tree and the night sky.

"Do you like the spot we'd picked out?" Jackie asked while grinning.

He looked around and nodded his approval. "A lot nicer than my plot in Virginia."

"I picked that plot," Jackie informed him, moderately insulted by the comment. "You're two rows from the Commander."

"Yeah, but the one in Virginia has such a boring headstone," he remarked with a groan. "Seriously? Couldn't you have chiseled something witty on it? Like, 'here lies Zack's toe; may he rest in pieces'."

"That was the Commander's call," she informed him without regret. "Take it up with him during your next near death experience."

Zack inhaled deeply and allowed his head to rest against the headstone behind him alongside her. "You're right about my inability to share my feelings," he announced, although he refused to look at her. "Alcohol does help me overcome that though. Since my last brush with death, I've been wrestling some particularly nasty demons."

Jackie had to hold back her interest in fear of reverting him to silence, but she was overjoyed he was finally willing to open up to her.

"When you were little, your father and I thought it was adorable how you wanted to be so much like us," he remarked while grinning. "We taught you how to fight, shoot, and take control of your own destiny." His grin slowly faded into a frown. "Lately, I've been wondering if that was a mistake. That night you tied me to a chair, every horrible thought I'd ever had about your upbringing surfaced."

She groaned softly and turned on her hip to face him. Jackie took his hand in hers and affectionately caressed it while staring into his eyes. "I am so sorry for what I did to you in the bait shop," she announced feeling guilt-ridden over it, chilled by her own actions. "I was out of my mind."

"That?" he suddenly questioned then laughed softly and patted her hand. "Oh, Jackie dear. I'm such a sick bastard; I'm counting that as foreplay."

Jackie cringed and pulled her hand from his. "Let's just stick to the horrible feelings you'd mentioned."

"I was sort of enjoying the new direction this conversation was taking," he remarked then sighed. "But, okay. For a moment when I looked at you, I saw no emotion. I saw a glimpse of me in you, and I didn't like it." He held his breath while staring into her eyes. "Despite all the years of training and grooming, I don't want you to become me."

She again took his hand and offered a warm smile. "I'll make you a deal," Jackie announced, catching his attention. "I'll only take on your more charming qualities if you try to take on a few of my better ones."

He chuckled in his throat. "Deal." Zack turned on his hip to face her, squeezed her hand, and stared deep into her eyes. "There's something important I have to ask you, and I want an honest answer."

Jackie noted the enthusiasm in his eyes and enjoyed seeing him so excited for an actual open conversation. "Of course, anything."

"If Mac hadn't interrupted, what did you have planned for the rest of the interrogation?" he asked. His look turned serious. "The more details; the better."

Jackie pulled her hand away from his and frowned. "You need professional help."

He shook his head, faced forward, and allowed his back to strike the headstone. "Typical woman," Zack scoffed while folding his arms across his chest in a mild tantrum. "They want you to open up and then get offended when you do."

Jackie couldn't help but laugh. She clung to his arm and rested her head on his shoulder. Her smile faded as she drifted into thought with a curious look. She wasn't sure why she sank to his level at that moment, but her ego wouldn't let it go.

"Did I actually stand a chance at getting a confession out of you?" she asked.

He chuckled softly, placed his arm around her, and pulled her tight against his side. "Eventually, yes," he replied.

She lifted her head despite his firm hold on her and smiled with delight. "Really?"

"Yes, given the proper dedication on your behalf," he casually replied then considered his answer. "Although I must warn you, that's one game I can play for hours." He cast a serious look at her and raised his brows in challenge. "Duct tape's in my left leg pocket if you're game."

Jackie gave a stern glare and was about to scold him when they heard a scream from the lodge. Both looked to the distant patio in time to see Ross and Lee running for the door, soaking wet, while Kirk and Monroe chased them with the garden hose. Jackie nuzzled Zack's shoulder and sighed softly.

"Yep, I'm home."

The End

Other books by Holly Copella!
Reviews left on Amazon are appreciated!

"The Battle for Andrea Marie"

A cruise ship attack turns six survivors into overnight celebrities after they take credit for the heroic act of a stowaway who died saving them.

The cruise is just what Jess needed--a bit of harmless fun far from her daily grind. But what begins as a relaxing vacation turns into a desperate fight for her life when terrorists take over the ship and start piling up bodies. Teaming up with a mysterious stowaway, Jess attempts to send out a distress call but knows they cannot wait for help to come. If she or the few remaining passengers have any hope for survival, Jess must act now. The papers dub it "The Battle for *Andrea Marie*," but to Jess it is the moment she fought side-by-side with her enigmatic Romeo, saving the ship--and losing him. She thinks the story ends there, but really, the nightmare is just beginning...

"Insanely Deadly"

When the dead return to life, it's up to an admiral's daughter and a mildly insane, former war hero to save their small town.

Jetta Cross, a Navy Admiral's daughter, is tasked with keeping her father's comrade, a former war hero turned town crazy, grounded in the real world. Capt. John Hunter is still fighting the war in his head, where imaginary dead people are part of his world. When a viral outbreak brings about a zombie uprising, Hunter is left to his own devices. He must resume his role as a one-man commando unit in order to destroy the ravenous undead. With Hunter still fighting his own inner demons as well as the undead, the townspeople fear their zombie neighbors may not be the only threat. Stranded at the island's luxurious resort with a handful of workers, Jetta is forced to live up to her father's reputation and take charge of the deteriorating situation at the hotel. She must wage her own war against the infected before the government declares her hometown a total loss.

Holly Copella

"Deadly Institution"

A town recluse suspected of killing his wife teams up with a young woman in order to stop a killer.

After being accused of murdering his wife, Konrad Asher turns his back on the town that once adored him. Ten years later, he still holds his grudge and the title of the most feared man in town. With the reopening of the burned mental institution, where his wife had died, former employees are now murdered one-by-one, throwing suspicion back on Asher. A young local reporter, Jacey, is forced to reveal her long-time friendship with the infamous recluse in order to clear his name not only in the recent murders but to exonerate him in the death of his wife as well. Will Jacey's relationship with Asher invite the killer closer to her? Or is the killer already in her life?

"Screenplays: The Island Collection"
"Jungle Princess", "A.L.F. Resort", "Brighton Island"

Discover how romance and fun in the sun can be downright *chilling*!

"Jungle Princess" is a romantic/thriller that leaves a teenage girl stranded on an island with two male shipmates and a creature of "unknown" origin. She soon discovers the island is home to an abandoned prison with several prisoners roaming free. What really killed over one hundred prisoners? And is it still out there--?

"A.L.F. Resort" is a romantic/thriller set on an island resort with Artificial Life Forms as the main draw. At this resort, all your fantasies come true...until a malfunction removes safety inhibitors on the A.L.F.'s. Zombies, biker gangs, and mobsters run amuck, turning fantasies into nightmares. A young reporter gets more of a story than she anticipates, but will she survive long enough to write the story?

"Brighton Island" is a romantic/thriller set on a private island. When the owner's niece brings her psychic friend to the mansion, his presence awakens the spirits' tortured souls. As the psychic attempts to solve the old murders, the niece is confronted with the possibility that she's next to join the mansion ghosts. Stranded on the island with a crazed killer, her uncle wages his own war to save them. Will his "shock and awe" tactics actually save them or get them killed?

"Death Displacement"

A grief-stricken man travels back in time to seek revenge on the woman who murdered his girlfriend but inadvertently falls in love with her.

Kane is about to marry the woman he loves. His life is perfect. A few weeks before the wedding, a vindictive woman from his girlfriend's past mysteriously arrives and kills her. He learns of a traumatic accident that happened five years earlier, which triggers Riley's hatred for his girlfriend. Distraught over his girlfriend's death, Kane uses an antique time machine to travel into the past in order to find and destroy the woman responsible. When he runs into Riley's younger self, he realizes she's not the monster she later becomes, and he can't bring himself to destroy her. With a little help from his oddball friend from the past, they formulate a plan to prevent the accident that sends Riley down her destructive path. Kane's plan backfires when he falls for the younger Riley. His new tortured existence is further complicated when future Riley, his girlfriend's killer, shows up with her own devious agenda that doesn't include him. Will he be able to stop the time ripple, which ultimately ends with his girlfriend's death? Or will future Riley take him out of the timeline forever--

"Dead Village"

After strange happenings isolate a small resort town from the rest of the world, nearly one hundred residents seek refuge at the closed hotel. Only eight survive the night. And that's just the beginning...

One day after the entire population of Fox Ridge Village disappears, a car wreck forces several unsuspecting crash victims to seek help at the closed summer hotel. Within the hotel, they discover the grisly aftermath of a brutal slaughter. Crash victims Vander and Devon, a reluctant clairvoyant, team up to solve the riddle of the "haunted hotel" and the mass hysteria plaguing the remaining survivors. By the time they discover the hotel's secret, they're already drawn into the hysteria. As the body count continues to climb, it's a race to isolate the source and bring everyone back to reality before they kill one another. Will Devon be able to communicate with the traumatized spirits before their fate becomes her own?

"Misfits, Inc."

A seemingly ordinary, young woman meets four misfits who claim she has given them supernatural powers.

While on a business trip to a remote island paradise, a bored secretary, Hailey, has her world turned upside down when her path collides with a psychic freak, Skyler. He attempts to convince her that they had met in his dreams, and she had chosen him as one of her four mystic warriors. After Skyler foresees a woman's death, they discover an unidentified creature has killed one of the guests. They are joined by a lounge pianist and a rich playboy, who also claim they had met her in their dreams. If Skyler's prophecies are genuine, the evil entity controlling the ravenous creatures needs to destroy Hailey to ensure its survival. Reluctantly accepting her fate, Hailey has to locate the last and most powerful of her chosen warriors, The Guardian. Their fate is in doubt when The Guardian turns out to be a self-absorbed, former cat burglar with a bad attitude. Can Hailey turn her company of misfits into an elite team of mystic warriors? Or will The Guardian's secret agenda destroy them all?

"Basement Dwellers"

A viral outbreak at a hospital leaves a mortician, sheriff, and coroner fighting for their lives against a horde of undead and the CDC.

After a massive car wreck leaves several survivors in critical condition at the local hospital, a surgeon uses experimental drugs on his critical patients and accidentally causes a zombie outbreak. When local mortician, Lexx, receives an infected corpse as her client, she becomes stranded in the hospital basement during CDC quarantine along with the local sheriff and the coroner. The infamous surgeon struggles to find a cure for his infectious blunder by using the other survivors as test subjects. Meanwhile, Lexx and the sheriff attempt to locate his missing sister, who's stranded somewhere in the battle zone that once was the emergency room. It's a race against time and the ravenous undead. Can they survive the undead before CDC sanitizes the hospital of all infection?

"Witness Protection"
Also available in audiobook!

After witnessing an execution, a resourceful young woman attempts to disappear while being pursued by a hitman and a handsome federal agent.

A helicopter pilot, Jackie Remus, reluctantly agrees to go on a date with one of her clients, but her date is unexpectedly cut short when she witnesses a man being murdered. After narrowly escaping with her life, she is placed into protective custody. When the safe house is breached, Jackie makes a daring escape from both the hired killers and the handsome FBI agent, who wants to return her to protective custody. With a little help from her sly and crafty friend, Monroe, Jackie is convinced she can disappear until the trial. While on her journey to meet with her friend, she solicits help from a few shady but lovable characters along the way. Although she manages to stay one-step ahead of the hired killers, the federal agent remains in hot pursuit. Will Jackie reach Monroe before she's captured by the FBI and returned to protective custody? Or will the hired killers silence her first?

"Town Darling"

After surviving a brutal attack that claims the lives of those she loves, a young woman seeks revenge on a corrupt town.

Going back home is never easy, but for Casey, it means returning to her corrupt hometown where she barely survived a brutal attack. Accompanied by two family friends, she seeks justice for the night that destroyed her life. Her physical scars are nothing compared to her emotional ones, forcing the local sheriff to believe that the town darling is back for revenge. As the conspiracy for her revenge appears to be leading up to the coveted town fair, the sheriff is determined to stop her from fulfilling her vengeful scheme...but guilt over his role on that fateful night continues to haunt him. Will his desperate need for Casey's forgiveness be his undoing? Or will Casey's desire for revenge destroy them both?

"Unconditional"

A young woman puts her life on hold to care for an unstable, highly skilled combat soldier, who believes someone is trying to kill him.

A botched military coup leaves a team of elite fighters injured with one clinging to life in a coma. When Harlan wakes from his coma, he's left with no memory of his past life. His commander's daughter, Indy, takes it upon herself to care for the fallen war hero. She's challenged with more than just his physical care as she combats with not only his memory loss but also his newly found desire for her. His infatuation with her becomes the least of her worries when he sinks back into his role of a combat soldier. Believing his life is in danger, his fighting skills surface, turning him into an unpredictable and dangerous man. Will his memory return to him before Indy is forced to commit him? Or will he finally find his nemesis, "the coyote", and possibly claim the life of an innocent person?

"Witness Protection 2"
The Return of Whiskey Tango Foxtrot

Believing she holds the clue to millions in missing laundered money, a young woman is placed into the protective care of a former Navy SEAL team.

Feeling sorry for her recently separated co-worker, Leeann invites Wiley to join her and her friends on their night out. Little does she know that finding her co-worker murdered is just the beginning of her nightmare. Leeann unknowingly holds the key to fifty million dollars in potentially laundered mob money. With hired killers pursuing her, the FBI places her into a different kind of protective custody. Former Navy SEAL team Whiskey Tango Foxtrot reunites to keep Leeann alive at their secret hideaway. What should be an easy assignment takes an unscheduled turn when secrets, lies, and betrayal threaten to derail their mission. Is the team prepared for a war on their own doorstep? Will Leeann's misguided trust endanger the lives of those sent to protect her?

"Deadly Institution 2"

When blackmail turns into murder, a young woman finds herself caught in the killer's crosshairs.

The small town of Stony Ridge is no stranger to scandal and persecution of the innocent. When a brutal killing shakes the town's prestigious country club, Jacey McMurray seeks help from a self-proclaimed vigilante, Konrad Asher. As her professional and personal worlds collide, Jacey fears the stress of the country club killings have finally taken their toll on Asher. Can a stressed out vigilante stop the killer before he strikes again?

"Awaken the Dead"

A grieving innkeeper struggles to keep her haunted hotel out of foreclosure.

After losing her parents in a suspicious boating accident, Harley Brandon is determined to keep the family hotel out of foreclosure. Unfortunately, the hotel ghosts have other plans. Built with tainted money, the century old Horizon Hotel thrives on a tradition of murder, scandal, and suicide. As the paranormal activity increases to alarming levels, Harley discovers the truth about the hotel and its residents. Can Harley save her friends from the hotel's frightening hidden secrets?

"The Pen Pal"

In order to save her friend, she must enter the mind of a serial killer.

When her best friend is abducted, no one believes Jolynn saw it in a psychic vision. With nowhere to turn, Jolynn reluctantly joins Agent Harris Slade and his team on their hunt for a sadistic serial killer known only as "The Pen Pal". Finally confronted with the killer, Jolynn realizes she must enter the mind of the psychopath in order to stop the brutal killings. But when her vision reveals a particularly disturbing death, can Jolynn sacrifice her lover for her friend?

"Already Dead"
Supernatural Collection

From the already dead to the undead. Three supernatural tales of "things that go bump in the night".

"Bloodletting" - A vampire themed resort allows guests to *participate* in their Bloodletting Ritual to celebrate the island's legendary vampires.

"Reaper of Souls" - A young woman must outwit an evil sorcerer in order to save her brother or become one of his minions forever.

"Already Dead" - When Flight 220 crashes, ten passengers make it to an isolated island, but only one man lives to tell the lie.

"Witness Protection 3"
Alpha Mike Foxtrot

A helicopter pilot risks her life to help a team of retired Navy SEALs rescue two girls from a killer.

When former Navy SEAL team Whiskey Tango Foxtrot asks for a simple favor, Jackie reluctantly offers her air-taxi services. What could go wrong? What begins as a search and rescue for two girls turns into a fight for survival against a heavily armed drug cartel. Wanted by the law with the cartel in hot pursuit and their home base breached, the team is forced to call in a favor from a questionable ally. Unfortunately, their new safe house isn't what it seems. Without knowing who the real enemy is, can Jackie and the team save their young witnesses from the hands of a killer?

"Witness Protection 4"
O-Dark-Hundred

A simple assignment turns deadly when a retired Navy SEAL team uncovers a plot to kill a notorious mob boss.

When Whiskey Tango Foxtrot embarks on a simple stalking case, they're not prepared for a trip to a private island paradise owned by an infamous mobster. With one of their own suffering from traumatic head injuries, the team is left scrambling to decide what is real or imagined. The situation escalates even further when they uncover an assassination plot where everyone is a suspect. Now targets themselves, can the team survive their trip to paradise?

Coming Soon!
"Once Upon a Disaster"

And

"Cemetery Stalkers"
Horror Collection

ABOUT THE AUTHOR

Holly Copella has been writing since the age of twelve when her frustration at a book's poor plot drove her to author her own story. Over the last decade, she's written a number of screenplays, some of which she's now adapting into novels. Her fascination with zombies and other darker material lends an edge to her writing, which tends to lean toward horror. As a fan of Agatha Christie, she appreciates the craft of a good plot and the importance of creating significant characters.

Hailing from Pennsylvania, Copella lives in the Endless Mountains on a farm with her rescue horses and other animals. In addition to writing and reading fiction, she enjoys riding horses and traveling to Las Vegas and Disney World.

www.ingramcontent.com/pod-product-compliance
Lightning Source LLC
Chambersburg PA
CBHW061131200626
46817CB00016B/830